Grounds for Remorse

Books by Misty Simon

Grounds for Remorse

Cremains of the Day

Published by Kensington Publishing Corporation

Grounds for Remorse

Misty Simon

KENSINGTON BOOKS
KENSINGTON PUBLISHING CORP.
http://www.kensingtonbooks.com

KENSINGTON BOOKS are published by

Kensington Publishing Corp.
119 West 40th Street
New York, NY 10018

All Kensington titles, imprints, and distributed lines are available at special quantity discounts for bulk purchases for sales promotion, premiums, fund-raising, educational, or institutional use.

Special book excerpts or customized printings can also be created to fit specific needs. For details, write or phone the office of the Kensington Sales Manager: Attn.: Sales Department. Kensington Publishing Corp., 119 West 40th Street, New York, NY 10018. Phone: 1-800-221-2647.

Kensington and the K logo Reg. U.S. Pat. & TM Off.

First Printing: June 2018
ISBN-13: 978-1-4967-1223-3
ISBN-10: 1-4967-1223-4

eISBN-13: 978-1-4967-1224-0
eISBN-10: 1-4967-1224-2

10 9 8 7 6 5 4 3 2 1

Printed in the United States of America

Chapter One

I did not trust the man sitting at Table Four. I wanted to, I really did, especially since he was my best friend Gina Laudermilch's new boyfriend. Despite the want, though, I just couldn't bring myself to do it. There was something shifty about him. He was too perfect. The hair, the clothes, the manners. The way he brought her a rose for every date, and added an extra one each time, special multicolored ones that Monty the florist only created upon request. My checkbook knew for a fact that they cost the moon and stars.

Gina had asked me to fill in at her coffee shop, Bean There, Done That, while she got ready for the date. I did my best since this was not my normal job, but I definitely kept my eye on the guy.

This was date four. Sure enough, he had four rainbow-colored roses, the colors bleeding like a watercolor canvas, in his manicured hands. For a guy who ran a company that upgraded houses—from new roofs to redesigning the interior and outside makeovers—I was surprised and suspicious about the fact that his hands looked so smooth.

And as perfect as he was, I still couldn't figure out why he'd posted himself on the Internet dating site Gina swore by. Why would he need to? Especially with the way every female, single or not, stared at him as if he were a fallen angel. His name was Craig Johnson, and there was something off about him. I would hold my opinions in check, though, until I could figure out what it was.

Tallie Graver, best friend extraordinaire and superb at keeping my mouth shut in the interest of peace. That was me.

The downtown coffee shop teamed with patrons. The donuts flew while Gina's mom, Mama Shirley, poured the coffee. I might be a whiz with the vacuum cleaner, but I didn't have the panache to pour coffee like Mama. She could start with the carafe at the cup and raise the coffeepot up in a very impressive stream of liquid goodness without spilling a drop. Me, not so much. I tended to slosh it over the side, and most customers wanted their coffee in their cup, not in their laps.

That left me in charge of wiping off the counters and collecting dishes until Gina made an appearance.

Gina, who was five minutes late in coming down. But Craig still smiled at everyone as if it didn't bother him at all. Which left me continuing to keep an eagle eye on this cyberspace Lothario. I wasn't sure how I felt about this whole Internet dating thing and had never tried it myself. Now that I had Max Bennett, the Taxinator, as I affectionately called him, I hoped to not be looking again anytime soon.

While this guy looked nice enough on paper, I couldn't shake my gut feeling. And ever since I'd left my ex-husband, and had been right to do so, I tried to trust my guts.

But I knew how much this meant to Gina. And no matter how I felt, I intended to let it unfold as it would. Of course, if he was a troll, then all bets were off, but I didn't know anything about his character yet.

Laura, the new girl Gina had hired for the afternoon rush, whisked across the floor of the Bean, pouring coffee and scooting cups onto the tables along with pastries and sandwiches and muffins. As she delivered a cup of steaming coffee to Craig, he gave her a twinkling smile. She said something to him that I couldn't hear over the din in the busy café, then pointed behind her. With an even brighter smile, he lifted a hand and waved to the person who'd sent the coffee his way.

It wasn't easy, but I leaned over the counter to get a look at whom he was waving at. I only succeeded in almost falling head over heels onto the floor. That, and hurting my sternum. And then I had to straighten back up because a woman came to the counter asking for a pastry.

As soon as Laura came back behind the counter, I was going to snag her and grill her. I had a feeling that Craig the Magnificent would not have waved and smiled the way he had if a guy friend had sent him a cup of coffee. . . .

Time to get Gina down here before he did something that would make me jump over the counter instead of just leaning over it. After taking out my phone, I texted her to let her know the Lothario was here and she should get her ass downstairs, pronto.

She texted back with one of those overly long strings of emoticons involving all kinds of hearts and little yellow faces blowing kisses, clapping hands, and a cupid. God, I hoped this guy was not going to end up being a loser.

I was half tempted to walk over to his table just to block him from any other admiring female eyes when Gina burst through the swinging door at the back, cutting off that thought. She practically floated to the table with a beaming smile on her face. Her black hair was perfectly coiffed, red lipstick shone on her lips, and she was dressed in her best outfit.

My hope that this guy was not a jerk, and that my intuition was off, rose exponentially. She was invested, and as her best friend, I was then invested, too.

Scooting his chair back, he stood, taking her in from head to toe in a way that spoke volumes. She was lovely, and he'd better appreciate that, along with her good heart and her generous ways. Or I'd tackle him to the ground myself.

After walking around the table to kiss her on the cheek, he moved her chair out and motioned her into it. Only then did he hand her the roses. Nicely done, in my opinion.

I deliberately let my bad feelings dissipate as I headed back to Mama Shirley and her stellar coffee-pouring skills.

"Think this one's a keeper?" I grabbed the rag on the end of the counter and pretended to clean a spot that was already shiny. This was Gina's fourth guy in as many months. The rest had been wrong for her in one way or another. I had my doubts that this one was any better.

He was a smooth talker, though. I was close enough to hear what Gina and Craig cooed at each other. Some of his lines were definitely swoon-worthy, I'd give him that. I wouldn't have fallen for them, of course, but he did have good delivery and perfect timing. I'd give him that, too.

"I don't know." Mama Shirley interrupted my critique of Craig's game. She scrunched up her face and my stomach clenched.

"Should I have told her to stay upstairs?" I whispered.

"I don't know that, either. I can't quite get a bead on this one, and I'm usually pretty good with that kind of thing. Something might be off, or I might just not be ready to lose my baby to a man."

"Well, it's early days, right?" I leaned back against the counter so Gina couldn't see my face. "I'm just not sure, though."

Mama looked at me out of the corner of her eye and barely moved her mouth when she said, "Time will tell."

"Fair enough." I tossed the rag into the sink and reached for the nearest napkin dispenser when the front door crashed open.

"You bitch!"

I spun around to find out who was making such an entrance and whom she was directing it at.

A flurry of brown hair and flying elbows came across the polished wood floor as the woman went after Gina, tipping her chair back and going for the eyes. In a flash, I was behind my best friend and saved her from falling over completely and crashing to the floor. But it took precious seconds, and I wasn't able to stop whoever this was from grabbing Gina by her perfectly coiffed hair.

Mama Shirley was faster than she'd probably ever been. Rolling pin in hand and the hounds of fury in her eyes, she wedged herself between the woman and Gina, practically sitting in Gina's lap. Mama brandished her rolling pin at the woman and yelled what sounded like a war cry.

My ears hurt and I winced. Gina came by her volume honestly.

"You'd better back off," I chimed in, trying to get the woman's hand to loosen in Gina's hair.

"I will bean you so hard, you're gonna see stars," Mama Shirley added.

That was apparently enough to get the woman to let go. She took a few steps back, her double Ds heaving and her nostrils flaring.

Who *was* this person?

"You keep your filthy hands off my husband." She pointed her finger at Gina from about three feet away, which had Mama Shirley raising the rolling pin.

She stood down again, backing away to rest a hand on Craig's shoulder. "Come home with Michelle. I need you, my sweet, sweet husband," she crooned to the man who sat stupefied in the chair across from Gina. Or maybe not so stupefied. On closer inspection, his ears were burning bright red but his face was far more sheepish than it was horrified—or even confused as to who this demon woman was.

I cast a quick glance at his hands as they lay flat on the table, but there was no ring. Not even an indentation where one should have been.

He was married? Married and his wife had come to

pick him up like an errant child who'd wandered out of the yard?

This was not going to be pretty.

"You're married?" Gina said, her voice low, which was always a precursor to it going up not only in octaves but in decibels, too. When she jerked to her feet, her chair shot out behind her, bumping the person at Table Three. "Married! You ass! I would never have even clicked on your message if I had known you were married. You cheating son of a bitch!"

Decibels at max pitch, an octave that dogs could probably hear across town. I had to get her calmed down before she truly went ballistic.

"Now, Gina . . ."

"Don't even, Tallie." She looked over her shoulder at me. "Don't even tell me to calm down. No one has ever calmed down just by being told to do so, and it's not going to happen now." She whipped back around to the man. "Get out of my shop now, and take your *wife* with you."

"Gina, let's be reasonable." He actually tried to talk with her. The man must have had a death wish.

Her hands clenched at her sides, and her own modest Bs heaved with her every breath. "Get. Out. Now. I swear I will kill you for doing this to me if I ever see you again. Maiming you would not be enough to satisfy me. I will poison your drink, boil you in a vat of coffee, shove hot pokers in your eyes. My imagination knows no limits. Do not ever come near me again."

He seemed to finally understand that this was not a situation he should be calmly sitting in. He rose gracefully from his chair, his wife clinging to his arm like she was afraid he might step toward Gina. I really hoped he didn't make that fatal mistake or he might get his eyes scratched out. And as much as I wished harm on him for hurting my friend, it wouldn't be good for business or for Gina.

He did stretch his hand out to her as if she might brush fingertips with him. Honest to God, was this guy an idiot or what?

But then the wife pulled him away and they left Bean There, Done That in a hurry. He cast one last look back over his shoulder, making Gina hiss like a cornered snake.

"Calm down, girl." Mama Shirley smacked her daughter in the arm. "This is not the place or the time. Don't make yourself a spectacle."

Gina took a deep breath, then blew it out hard enough to ruffle the bangs she'd meticulously styled for what was supposed to be a big date with a fabulous guy and ended up being a tragedy.

"Right," she said. "Time later for being pissed. Now I have to serve coffee." She turned to me, her eyes slightly watery, and I knew I was not going to leave her alone this evening. Max was coming into town, but he could hang out by himself or with my brother for a few hours while I let my best friend vent.

"Are you going to be okay?" I asked.

She shot me a look with raised eyebrows and haughty lips pursed.

I was not going to be deterred. "I'm serious. Are you going to be okay?"

"Yes, I'll be fine. I have things to do, and I don't need you for the afternoon now that this . . ." She trailed off and my heart clenched for her. She always was the fun one, the one who didn't take life seriously.

But lately that had switched as she'd told me she'd started feeling like she was missing out on life. Hence the Internet dating. She had gone on to several dating sites in hopes of finding Mr. Right. All she had managed to do was dig up every single Mr. Wrong.

"Call me later, if you need me." I put my arm around her shoulders and hugged her to me. Even if she didn't call, I'd be there.

"I will. Thanks, Tallie." She stepped back and smiled, a crumpled one with her lips quivering, but it was still a smile. "He's scum, and I hope I never see him again. I'd better never see him again or I will come up with the most heinous way to end his miserable, cheating, asinine life."

Well, then.

Hours later, I watched from my third-story apartment across the street from the Bean for Gina to turn the sign to CLOSED. Max had called to say he was held up in traffic, so as soon as she flipped the sign, I texted Gina that I was coming over.

Opening the exterior door on the side of the Bean that led to the stairs straight up to her apartment, I braced myself for what I would find. Gina was resilient, but at the beginning it could be a train wreck. After walking up the staircase, I knocked on the door on the landing. She yanked it open and I couldn't miss the way her eyes were red and her hair in a messy bun on top of her head. Her nose was red, too, and it was as if several boxes of tissues had exploded over the room in an avalanche of epic proportions.

This might take a little longer than I had originally thought.

While she went to put on a pot of tea, I sent a quick text to Max letting him know where I was and to come up as soon as he got into town.

I didn't know if having him here would help or hinder, but it might be good for Gina to see that not all men were jerks.

The kettle whistled in Gina's large kitchen and nearly drowned out the sound of her first sob. Jumping up from the couch, I ran for her. I found her with her head bowed and her shoulders hunched, leaning into the breakfast bar my brother had put up here for her a few years ago. Gina had the top two floors as her living space, so it looked more like a house on top of a shop than a simple apartment like mine, above the funeral parlor across the street.

I pulled her to me by putting an arm around her shoulders. "Was he really that good that it's worth this kind of crying?" I asked.

She shook her head, then sniffed. "No, it's just that I really thought I had found a good one. And he turned out to be even worse than that guy who said he was an engineer when really he was out of a job altogether and simply engineering ways to not have to go to work ever again."

Holding her hands in mine, I chuckled softly. "I remember that one. He was convinced you made enough money that he could be a kept man and move out of his mother's basement. I wasn't surprised when he didn't make it to date number two."

She sniffed. "And there was the one who swore he was in the market for a real relationship and tired of all the games." She stepped away to pour the hot water into a ceramic pot covered in hand-painted ivy. After filtering it through a tea ball filled with fragrant loose-leaf tea, she set it aside to allow it to steep. I loved my lattes and my mochas, but there was something incredibly soothing about a well-made cup of tea. I normally just heated water in the microwave and plunked a tea bag in the cup. Gina made it an art.

"I remember him, too," I said after I pulled my nose out of the steam rising from the pot. Earl Grey, one of my favorites.

"He didn't amount to anything since he wouldn't stop pawing me and got pissed when I told him to keep his hands to himself." Taking the pot to the square table in the middle of the kitchen, Gina set it on a trivet, then dug in the cabinet for something. Out she came with butter cookies, my favorite kind, after my mother's snickerdoodles, of course. I loved to dip these in my tea.

"Then there was the one who left you with the tab and made you drive him to his friend's so he could play pool because you were too boring."

She snorted. "All because I wasn't willing to battle him in some game on his phone."

"And why did you continue to use the same site? It sounds like there weren't many good ones on there." I placed my hands around the teapot, loving the warmth of it and anticipating the slight zing Earl Grey with sugar and lots of cream would bring to my tongue.

"Because all the other ones weren't that great and Melanie swore by it. It's how she met Brett. I want a

Brett." The plate of cookies appeared on the table, perfectly arranged and scrumptious looking.

I dug in to the cookies and glanced at the microwave clock to see if the steeping process might be done.

"You can pour." Gina pulled two delicate teacups from the cupboard above the stove and placed them in front of me.

"I just don't know if you're going to find a Brett on this site. Why not try the old-fashioned way?"

"Go to a bar? Blind dates? No, thanks. Can I have Max?"

That made me bobble the teapot and almost put my tea in my own lap.

Gina laughed. "I'm kidding. But it would be nice." She sighed. "Does he have any friends?"

The outside doorbell at the bottom of the stairs saved me. The last thing I wanted to admit was that I hadn't really met any of Max's friends. And I was pretty sure she didn't want to date the only friend of his I did know—my brother.

"I'm not expecting anyone," she said, staring at the interior door to her right like a creeper was directly on the other side. Not that they could be since Gina had her house locked up tight and whoever it was had only rung the doorbell downstairs. You couldn't get up here unless Gina opened the downstairs door for you.

I guess there could have been an unwanted someone downstairs. I wouldn't have put it past Craig to try again even after the way Gina had cut him down in mid-puppy-dog-eyed stare, but I had doubts. Max had texted about twenty minutes ago to let me know he was stopping at my apartment across the road and then heading over to Gina's. I had a feeling that it was my man who was expected, not the unwanted man Gina didn't want to see.

I texted Max to see if it was indeed him.

His quick text back with a big YES was all I needed. "It's just Max. Is it okay if I go let him up?"

"Yeah, whatever. I guess you'll be leaving then. I'm sure you'd rather spend time with your boyfriend than your mopey friend." She sank back against the couch.

"Never. If you want him to go away, I'll send him back to the apartment. I can catch up with him later."

Gina rolled her head toward me with watery eyes. "Really?"

I gulped. I really did want to see my boyfriend, whom I hadn't been with in almost three weeks, but Gina was important. Max would understand. "Really."

"No." She sat up straighter and arranged her hair a little better. "Tell him to come up. Maybe we can order some dinner and play games."

"Sounds good." Letting myself out the door to the small landing at the top of the stairs, I shut the door behind me and calculated how long I would have to greet Max properly before Gina came looking for us. I figured one long hello kiss would not be out of order. Hopping down the stairs, I spotted Max through the glass insert in the middle of the door to the outside. His dark hair was shiny in the old-fashioned streetlamp the borough had recently installed to give the town that Old World feel they said brought in more tourists.

I yanked open the door and went to pounce on

him but saw he was carrying flowers a split second before I would have leapt. "Oh! Are those for me or are you masquerading as a delivery boy again?" We had met years and years ago in elementary school when he had hung out with my brother, but he'd been out of my life for years after that when he went to live with his grandmother. It wasn't until he'd come up from Washington DC to look into my late ex-husband's dirty money schemes that I'd met him again. He'd been staying under the radar by pretending to be a delivery guy for Monty the florist, but eventually I had remembered him, and his cover was blown.

Now I smiled at him with my arms outstretched. But he wasn't looking at me. Instead, he looked at the flowers clutched in his hand while using the other hand to rub his chin.

"Was the question really that perplexing?" I joked. "If they're for Gina instead, to make her feel better, then that's even sweeter, and I will instantly forgive you for not bringing me flowers."

Finally, he looked up at me and wiggled his jaw back and forth with his fingers.

"These were just delivered to my jaw. The guy came around the corner, saw me, threw the flowers with the vase at me, and then ran off, booking around the corner."

"What?" Running myself, I got to the corner and peeked around the front of the Bean, but I saw no one even walking on the street, much less running.

Returning to Max, I stroked his face. "Are you okay? I'm so sorry. Did you recognize the guy?"

"I will be, and no, I didn't recognize him."

I took the card out of the flowers as I relieved him of his floral burden. He smiled his thanks, then grimaced.

"Hurts?"

"Yeah. I'm strong but my jaw is not made of steel. That vase is heavy."

Petting his jaw, I tried to make it better, or at least not worse. "I want to get you ice right away but can you hold on for just a second more? I want to know whom these are from before I decide if I want to give them to Gina or not."

"It's fine. The sting is going away. I think it surprised me more than anything. The guy was a little thick around the middle and had blond hair, but other than that I didn't get much more of an impression."

"Hopefully he signed them so we can call it in." I turned the card over in my hands, hoping against hope that they were from a special someone that was going to get his ass kicked for coming around where he was not wanted.

"What are we going to call in? A drive-by flowering?"

Leave it to Max to try to make a joke out of it. "Maybe." I handed the flowers back to him to break the seal on the small envelope.

"What is taking so long? I gave you enough time to get in a good kiss before I came looking for you."

As Gina stepped out onto the stoop with me, I whipped the card behind my back. Max was not as fast with his vase of flowers.

"Oh, Max, how sweet. Did you bring those for Tallie or for me?"

Poor Max—he looked at me with pleading eyes, and I figured lying to Gina would not make the situation better no matter whom the flowers were for. She'd had enough lying for the day.

"Some guy just threw them at him." I waved the card at her. "I was going to find out who they were from before we brought them up or threw them out, depending on whether I thought it would be worse to give them to you or not."

"I'm a big girl, Tallie. I can decide for myself." She held her hand out, palm open flat. "Hand the card over. I can handle this."

I had a hard time actually letting go of the card when I held it out over her outstretched palm. She took the decision out of my hand, literally, when she snagged the card and turned away from Max and me.

I heard the growl and stopped her from ripping the card into shreds just in time.

"Don't do that. Whoever it is, they threw the vase at Max and hit him in the face. That's evidence."

"I want to burn it. Burn it all. Flowers, vase, card. That dirty bastard."

"Craig?"

"Yes. What is he thinking? I guess I wasn't direct enough when I told him I'd boil him in a vat of coffee if I ever saw or heard from him again."

Max laughed. "I bet that was worth the price of admission."

Gina sniffed and put her nose in the air. "I thought it was pretty magnificent myself, but I guess it didn't make the impression on him that I meant it to if he had the gall to come here with these flowers."

A group of people walked toward us on the sidewalk. "Let's take this inside." I shooed them both in front of me. "No need to bring anyone else in on it before you figure out what you'd like to do. And Max needs ice for his jaw."

Her face went from anger to concern in a heart-beat. "Oh God, Max, I'm so sorry. Get upstairs. It's open. I'll be up in a second."

I waved Max on, but stayed outside with Gina. I was not about to leave her. Mama Shirley was not the only one who could be brutal if she wanted to be, and I was sure that leaving Gina on her own right now would only lead to one of those moments where I'd have to bail her out of something or other.

Placing my arm around her shoulders, I brought her in for yet another hug. "This is hard, I know."

"You're wrong." She shrugged out from under my arm. "It's not hard. It's irritating and aggravating, but it's not hard. I'm tempted to call his wife and tell her what he did. Fighting that temptation, because I don't want to deal with her or him, is the hard part."

"Would it gain you anything?"

"Satisfaction?" She laughed, but it wasn't full of mirth. "No, it won't get me anything, and I don't want to deal with that woman any more than I want to deal with her husband. When you came downstairs it finally hit me that I've seen her before. She went to high school with us, but was in a much different group. And she used to come in for coffee until I en-couraged her to go somewhere else because she was always measuring my floors and trying to tell me that she could make the place shine if only I'd sell it to her."

"Wow, that's a double whammy. Bitchy wife and philandering husband. What a pair."

"No kidding." Blowing out a breath, she wrapped her arms around her torso. "I'm good now. Let's get up there, make sure Max has his ice, order some pizza, and dig out a bottle of wine. I think I want to be sloshed tonight and then sleep like the dead instead of making someone dead. You're right, it wouldn't be worth it. Satisfying in the moment, maybe, but in the end, he's not worth doing jail time for. And she's not even worth thinking about. I hope they suffer together."

"That's my Gina."

"Yep, that's me." She hugged me and then kept her arm around my waist while we trooped through the side door and up the stairs. She was going to be okay. I'd make sure of it.

And if I ever saw Craig again, I'd take a piece out of him, not just for hurting my friend but for hitting my boyfriend. He'd better not show his face around here again if he knew what was good for him.

Chapter Two

We played games, drank wine, ate enough pizza to make me have serious concern that I might burst, and then I tucked Gina into bed. All in all, I felt it was a good end to a crappy day.

"You don't think Gina's in any danger, do you?" I asked Max as we made our way across the street to my family's funeral home. I lived on the third floor in an apartment. I couldn't have asked for quieter neighbors.

"From the guy who threw the flowers?" Max tucked my hand into the crook of his arm, and I melted just a little bit more. All those years ago when I followed him and my brother around like the pesky little sister I was, I would have never guessed this was where I'd end up.

"Yes." The gentle summer breeze that blew across the sidewalk brought with it the smell of fresh-cut grass and mellow sunshine. Nine at night and the horizon had just darkened. I loved summer, and I was happy Max was here for a ten-day vacation. Gina would get over this latest loser in the long stream of losers and find her own happy again. Maybe Max did have a friend I could introduce her to. It was worth asking.

But not now.

He squeezed my hand. "I don't think she's in danger. From what you told me, Craig seems like the type to sneak around, but he got scared earlier and he ran. Maybe he thought I was dating Gina now. Maybe he'll stay away."

"It's funny you say that. She asked if she could have you." I used my key to open the back door of the parlor so we could walk straight up the private stairs. If I could avoid my mother, I would be happy. She'd been asking for weeks when Max was moving up here and if he was going to live in my apartment with me. The answers were that I had no idea, since we hadn't even talked about him moving up here from Washington DC, and as much as I adored him, my apartment was sometimes even too tiny for me and my cat Mr. Fleefers.

As soon as we entered and I locked the door behind me, Max enveloped me in his arms, and we finally got to that proper greeting. His kiss was sweet and intoxicating and, unfortunately, interrupted by my mother.

"There they are! Look at you two lovebirds."

I groaned and leaned my head against Max's chest before stepping back. We hadn't even talked about love yet. I was certainly not going to let my mother be the one who introduced the topic.

"We're heading up, Mom. Are you going home soon?"

"Yes, of course I am, you silly goose. Daddy asked me

to come out and grab a few things from the storeroom while he showered. I'm heading back to the house now."

Daddy. I held in a groan. I hadn't called Bud Graver "Daddy" in almost twenty years. I hadn't yet figured out why she still called him that.

She looked us up and down and I stepped back while clearing my throat. Heaven knows why. I was a grown woman. But she was my mom.

Wrapping the plastic bag around her wrist, she cocked her hip and seemed to be settling in for a talk. Anything but that.

"So, what are you going to do this week? You know your brother Jeremy's on vacation. Tell me you're at least taking the week off from cleaning, Tallie. I know Daddy needs you here, but people can clean their own houses for one week."

"I was thinking I might just help Tallie clean, Mrs. Graver. How hard could it be?"

Mom and I looked at each other and burst out laughing.

"Yeah, I think you might want to find something else to do. But thanks for offering." I leaned over and kissed him on the cheek.

"I told you he was a keeper. Get him to move up here, honey, before he gets away," my mom tried to whisper out of the corner of her mouth. Of course, it came out a whole lot louder and, with Max standing close, there was no way he had missed it.

Love. Moving. Keepers. I think she'd covered all the awkward conversations now. Time to get her moving along.

"Maybe we could come over for dinner one night this week," I said, throwing myself onto the altar like a sacrifice to not start conversations I wasn't yet ready to have.

"Oh, that would be so much fun. I'll call you about it."

"Sounds good. We'll see you later then."

"Bye, Mrs. Graver." Max kissed the back of her hand. "Have a great night."

She blushed like a schoolgirl. Max had some of his own suave moves. "Oh, isn't that sweet? You two are shuffling me along so you can be alone together. I think that's wonderful, and I'm going home to tell your dad right now. He'll be happy to know that you're here, Max. He always did like you. Don't hurt my baby, and he'll keep on liking you, too." She reached up to pat his cheek but chose the one where the flowers had hit earlier.

Fortunately she didn't even notice when he flinched, just hitched up her grocery bag of items and trotted out the door I had just locked.

"Sorry about that." And I really was, for all of it. The patting had looked like it hurt no matter how soft her hands were.

He worked his jaw from right to left as he had earlier. "No worries. Your mom's a lot stronger than she looks."

"No doubt. Do you need me to kiss it and make it better?"

The gleaming eyes told me to make a run for it right before he grabbed me. We raced up the stairs, where he caught me right outside the door to my apartment. I'd missed him. And I looked forward to having him here this week. And if talk did turn to love or moving, I hoped I would be ready with the right words. I hadn't done such a great job in the relationship department a handful of years ago. This one was far too important already to mess it up.

I jolted awake and nearly knocked Max off the bed when the siren at the firehouse next door blared in the middle of the night. I had trained myself to sleep through it when I'd first moved over the funeral home my parents and brother owned. It also helped that my father had installed soundproofing up here at my request.

Tonight, though, I'd had a hard time falling asleep and had wandered to the window a few times to soak up the moonlight and watch the few cars driving on Main Street. I had been restless even with Max's arms wrapped around me in the Murphy bed that I'd lowered from the wall.

So, it was no surprise that I heard it and shot straight up in bed. As softly as possible I removed myself from under Max's arm and went to the front windows of my apartment, where I'd be able to see the direction the fire truck headed. The lights could be mesmerizing as they strobed across the brick buildings of Main Street in our small town. Pennsylvania liked its sirens and its volunteer firemen.

But though the siren blared and the lights flashed, they didn't get far. In fact, they pulled across the street and stopped outside Gina's.

What on earth?

"Max. Max!" I shook him, then ran to my closet for a hoodie to throw over my pajamas. No time to waste on a bra, and the hoodie would cover up any sagging. Plus, the dead of summer could still get a little chilly outside in the middle of the night.

He sat up, his hair going in all directions. "What's going on?"

"The fire truck is in front of Gina's house. I have to go over there."

Points for him that he was out of bed and stepping into his jeans before I'd finished my second sentence. "See if you can get a hold of her. She might not be able to answer, but maybe she can. Just check." He went to the window as he pulled a shirt on over his head. "I don't see flames. But an ambulance just pulled up."

"Oh no. That could mean anything." They came out for all reasons, generally anything that involved a call to the emergency line at the police station. What had happened? Was Gina hurt? Had I left her alone and Craig had come for her? My stomach tried to claw its way up my throat.

Stepping into shoes, I hit my Gina speed dial as I flew down the two sets of stairs to the main floor. Max was right on my heels. By the fourth ring, Gina still hadn't answered, but then it didn't matter because I saw her standing on the sidewalk with her arms wrapped around herself and a blanket over her shoulders.

At least she was alive. While I'd booked it down the stairs, horrible visions had flashed through my head of Craig getting in her house and killing her in her sleep. Seeing her standing there alleviated that fear at least, but it didn't indicate what had happened.

I didn't even look for traffic as I ran across the street and jerked to a halt in front of her. I opened my arms and she stepped forward. But Chief Burton put an arm out between us, keeping her from hugging me. The man was the bane of my existence.

He still held a grudge over the stuck-up, snobby bitch I had been for the past five years. I'd thought helping him with a double murder a few months ago might have softened him up, but that didn't seem to be happening with the way his eyes were flinty and his stance forbidding.

"What are you doing?" I demanded.

"This is a crime scene, Tallie."

"A what? What happened?" Quickly taking in the scene, I saw no blood and no broken windows. Nothing out of the ordinary, except my friend standing on the street with a blanket around her shoulders.

"Go home. We're taking care of it. I need you to step back. We don't want to contaminate anything until we have all the evidence we need."

"Gina?" I met her eyes. Max stepped up next to me and put a hand on my outstretched arm.

"Don't leave me, Tallie. Please." Her voice quavered with distress and I wanted to punch Burton in his shiny badge.

Instead, I glared at him and almost said the scathing words that were positively boiling on my tongue. But I did not want to make anyone even madder. I settled for taking a step back. "I'm not leaving. I won't touch anything, but I'm not leaving."

Burton sighed, pinching the bridge of his nose. Not my problem.

"Do you want me to call your mom, Gina?" I asked.

"God, no, please."

"Can you tell me what happened? Why are the police and the fire department and the ambulance here?"

Burton stepped between us again. "You can stay, but I'll be asking the questions. Right now, this is a need-to-know basis and you are not someone who needs to know anything." Burton stood with his back to Gina, fully blocking her from my sight. Kicking him would be a very bad idea, I told myself several times, while I fought down the urge to do just that.

I tried a different tactic with the silvered-haired man who was the strong arm of the law around these parts. "Can you tell me what happened then? I live in the neighborhood and would like to know what has happened to bring everyone out before dawn."

He frowned at me, his bushy gray eyebrows pulling down to form a V. "There's been a death and that's all you need to know."

A death? I reeled back into Max's arms, my brain now going to the threats Gina had made earlier toward Craig. No way would she have done that. I knew it in my heart. Plus, I didn't even know who was dead. I wouldn't jump to any conclusions until I had more facts.

And then the gurney rolled past me and Max. A hand flopped out from under the sheet, the manicured fingernails masculine and way too clean. It was Craig. To say this was not good was a gross understatement.

I stayed with Gina until they loaded her into the back of a cruiser. They didn't let me say anything to her, and I followed their rules because I knew that once my cousin, a cop, was involved I could get access. I would demand it, even call his mother to yell at him if he didn't do what I asked him to do.

Once they drove away with her, I ran back across the street and up the stairs to put on a bra and some more decent clothes. I was going to that police station and demanding to talk to her, even if she had to make her one phone call to my cell phone while I stood in the station's waiting room.

By the time I threw open the door to the two-story brick building a block and a half away, I could see that my job to get Gina was going to be even easier. Mama Shirley was already there raising a ruckus.

"You get my girl out of that cell right now or bad things will happen to you. Mark my words."

"Are you threatening me?" Burton asked.

She bristled, her chest inflating until she resembled a linebacker. "It's not a threat, you buffoon, it's a warning of what's to come. Now, go get my girl."

Fortunately, there was no rolling pin in sight, and since she was dressed in a housecoat with the edges of her nightgown hanging right below and her slippers on, I had a feeling she had no weapon on her. I left her with Max and turned around to make a phone call to my Uncle Sherman. There had to be something he could do, or maybe as the fire chief he knew what was going on.

As soon as the ringing stopped, I jumped in. "Sherman, I know it's early, and I'm sorry."

He sighed. "No worries. I'm up anyway and know what you're calling about. I don't know anything, Tallie. Burton told me nothing and he's keeping close-lipped about this one, the bastard." Frustration bristled over the line. "Don't know why, but it might have something to do with the trouble you got into a few months ago when that socialite and your ex-husband were killed."

Exasperation soared through me at the statement. I'd had nothing to do with that, only in figuring out who had done the foul deeds. "Neither of which were my fault."

"Well, Tallie, I know that and you know that, but he was not happy you got so involved."

"But he can't keep you out of the loop," I demanded as I leaned against the wall, keeping an eye on where everyone was and half an ear cocked for what was being said in the room. Nothing much more than a stare-down between Shirley and Burton.

"Sure he can, if it's not a fire. I don't need to know, apparently. That's exactly what I was told."

"Me too."

His sigh blustered through the phone line. "Not surprising. I think we're going to have to wait to hear more."

"Mama Shirley is not going to be happy with that."

"Mama Shirley can give them hell all she wants, but if I were you I'd stay out of this one as much as you can. Wait for Burton to announce the info, or get it from Gina once they release her. All I know is there was a dead body at the bottom of her stairs, and she was standing over it when she called the emergency line."

Since no one would let me see Gina until after she was processed, no matter how much I begged and yelled and pleaded, I left Max at the station to see if he could schmooze anyone. I ran back to the apartment and picked up a few things for Gina that I hoped would fit her and then went back to the police station. They couldn't keep her if they didn't charge her, and I was pretty sure they weren't going to charge her. How could they? There had to be another explanation for how Craig had ended up at the bottom of her stairs dead. And I wasn't leaving until I had my best friend. Chief of Police James Burton could try to remove me all he wanted, but I wasn't budging.

I had just returned to the station with a bag of clothes in hand when Craig's wife came storming in, demanding blood.

Poor Suzy at the front desk could only stare at her with her mouth hanging open as the woman screeched every profanity I knew plus some I tucked away for future use. Several I'd never heard strung together quite like that before.

My cousin, Matt, came out from the back with a lazy walk, and looked the woman over before slapping his hand on the counter with a crack.

"How can we help you, miss?" he said in a deceptively calm tone following that loud bang.

"It's Mrs. Mrs. Johnson, widow to the recently deceased Craig Johnson who was killed before his time." "Haughty" and "dramatic" were the only two words I could think of to describe her.

"What can we do for you, Mrs. Johnson?" Matt asked politely, yet with a slight edge. "We were out at your place and let you know we were doing everything we can to find out what happened in that stairwell. We'll let you know as soon as we have any new information."

She narrowed her eyes at him and clenched her hand into a fist on the counter. I wouldn't have been surprised if she'd slammed it down to mimic Matt. But she seemed to pull herself together. "I'd like to file a complaint against the woman who killed my husband."

I shrank into the corner of the waiting room,

hoping she wouldn't see me, or if she did that she wouldn't remember me from the Bean yesterday. I wanted to hear this complaint so I could defend Gina against it.

"We're not even at the 'allegedly killed' position yet and we can't assume anything at this point," Matt explained, far more patiently than I would have been able to manage. "The woman you're referring to swears that she was sound asleep and only found your husband at the bottom of her stairs with his neck twisted at an odd angle when she was going to open her shop."

That was more than I had before, thankfully. Matt gave me a thumbs-up behind his back. Uncle Sherman might want me out of this, and I highly doubted Burton would take kindly to me solving another death in our town, but Matt seemed to be on board with giving me information. At least the police weren't automatically charging Gina and refusing to look at anyone else. I'd be thankful for that as I continued to wait for this woman to get to the point of her visit.

Mrs. Johnson's hand went to her throat as she fell back a step. "You've just described exactly how she killed him. By pushing him down the stairs and then pretending that she had no knowledge. And my complaint will add to the evidence." Her voice rang with conviction. "I want you to take my statement. Now."

I was on board with taking the statement now, as long as it was out here.

Burton chose that moment to appear in the reception area. He gave me a hard look before turning to Matt. "Take the woman's statement in your office. We'll want as much information as possible. Ask if she has anything else we could work with, too, while you're at it." He turned to Mrs. Johnson. "We're sorry for your loss, Michelle, and we'll be working diligently to make sure the right person is charged, if this was indeed a crime. Please rest assured his death will be ruled as the evidence proves out."

A slick way to say that they might not even believe it was murder. The man could have fallen down the stairs all on his own.

Though how he had gotten in the stairwell in the first place, when I knew for a fact I had locked the door behind me when Max and I had left, I had no idea. I kept that question to myself because it might lead them to look harder at Gina, and I wanted time to talk to her before they grabbed the magnifying glass.

We all watched Matt lead Michelle behind the counter. I was relieved when they went out of sight without her ever looking at me.

That relief died quickly when Burton turned in my direction.

"Tallie." Burton stood with his arms crossed, his face a hard study in disapproval.

I shook my paper bag of clothes at him. "Just here to deliver some clothes if Gina needs something more than a prison outfit. I'm assuming you took her clothes for evidence."

"You'd be assuming wrong, and you better not have gone into her house to get clothes."

"What kind of fool do you take me for?" I asked, then clamped my mouth shut. I shouldn't invite that conversation. "Anyhoo, I just wanted to see if Gina was ready to go yet, and if I can take her to my house."

His face did not lose any of its harshness. Tough

crowd here. Yes, I had helped him solve the two murders that had occurred nine months ago, and yes, I had been a pain in his ass when I was married to my departed ex-husband, but I was just Tallie now. Not Tallulah Phillips, the entitled wife of the jerk, Walden Phillips the Third, whom I still thought of as Waldo, even if he wasn't alive to be annoyed anymore. Just Tallie Graver, divorced, cleaning woman, part-time funeral helper, and best friend to the woman who should not be sitting in a jail cell because of some guy who could not take the hint that she wanted nothing to do with him.

We hadn't reported the run-by flowering and now I wondered if we should have, to add to the evidence. I'd talk it over with Max once we were alone. Speaking of Max, he was pretty quiet next to me. I turned to find him with his hand over his eyes and shaking his head.

"How involved do you plan on getting in this thing?" Burton asked, his voice low and his brow even lower. "I'd like to brace myself for more of your accidental findings."

"No involvement." I raised my free hand as if in surrender. "I just want to take my friend home. I'll let you and the illustrious police force do all the policing." I crossed my heart with my index finger and held up what I thought I remembered as the Girl Scout pledge sign.

All it got me was another full thirty seconds of Burton staring at me.

"I promise?"

"Yeah, it's that questioning sound at the end that

makes me nervous and I'm not a nervous kind of guy, Tallie."

I cleared my throat. "It wasn't a questioning sound. I was trying for reassuring."

"Well, you didn't do a very good job at it." He put his hands on his hips and widened his stance. "I'll let her go with you under the condition that you stay out of this thing. You can take Shirley home, too, since she's back there, along with her daughter, but in a different room. I've found I don't have the stomach or the time to deal with charging her with threatening a police officer with a rolling pin."

Good Lord, and it wasn't even nine o'clock in the morning yet. And where had she hidden the rolling pin in her nightgown? I'd missed a lot while running to my house for clothes. I'd have to get the lowdown from Max when we were alone.

"I'll take them both with me and make sure they stay out of trouble," I promised, hoping it wasn't a lie in the making.

His brow did not unfurrow. In fact, it seemed to sink even lower over his eyes. "I'm more concerned about *you* staying out of trouble, young lady."

I almost snorted. I was in my late twenties. He didn't have to call me young and I wasn't even sure I could be deemed a lady. Female, woman, warrior, yes. Lady? Not so much. "I'll do my best." That, at least, was a better promise than the others I'd made.

He pointed his finger at me. "Your best had better be good enough."

I almost came back with something pithy, but screaming erupted in the back along with a series of grunts. I stood with my mouth open and my eyes wide as Gina screamed her way down the hallway, Michelle right at her back and Mama Shirley following close behind doing her own war cry. Matt must have been the one grunting, because he stumbled down the hallway clutching his stomach and hunched over.

Chaos reigned as Gina hid behind me, Michelle tried to go through me instead of around me, and Mama Shirley caught Craig's widow by the hair.

"Not this time, you wretch!" Mama Shirley yelled. Matt was still trying to catch up with the trio when Burton stepped in, giving a shrill whistle.

Everyone stopped as if someone had hit the pause button on a remote. It was a strange tableau. Mama Shirley had a hank of Michelle's hair in her grip and had bent the woman backward. Max had stepped up and shoved himself between me and the woman. Even Matt had stopped with one hand on the wall and the other still clamped on his stomach. Someone, and I was betting on Michelle, must have socked him hard for him to still be nursing it.

"This will stop right this instant," Burton yelled. "Everyone back away from everyone else and then don't move another muscle while I sort things out. If you touch each other at all I will have you all in cells before the minute hand makes it one more time around the clock, and I am not kidding."

I stayed where I was since I was sandwiched between Gina and Max. Gina took a step back, Max took one to the side, which put me face to snarl with Michelle. She tried to step opposite Max, but Mama Shirley hadn't let her hair go yet.

"Shirley." Burton stared her down.

"You said not to move."

He grunted, which is never a good sound from him.

She got the hint without having to be told a second time. Letting go, she stepped back and crossed her arms, giving the glaring Mrs. Johnson the evil eye. "I've got my eye on you, and I'll have my rolling pin back soon, so don't step out of line again."

"Shirley." This time Burton sighed her name as if the whole weight of the world had just crashed down on his shoulders.

"It's truth talk."

"And I'm not going to give you the rolling pin back until you're across the street and far away from this woman."

Now it was Shirley's turn to grunt. "She stays away from me and mine and we won't have an issue." Gina's mom shrugged, but when Burton turned to Gina, Shirley did that gesture that told Mrs. Johnson that she was watching her and mouthed the word "Beware."

I had a feeling this was about to turn into an all-out war if I didn't get Gina and her mom out of here fast.

"I'll take them now, Chief Burton. I'll make sure they get where they're supposed to be." I did not mention that the place was going to be my apartment or at least the parlor in the funeral home. We had no wakes scheduled today, so the bottom floors were empty. My brother had a few days off, which meant he wouldn't be bustling around. My dad might be there, but he'd be on the second floor doing paperwork.

"Keep an eye on them," Burton said to Max. Not me, never me, but Max. Oh well, it wasn't the worst thing that could have happened.

Max and Burton shook hands as Max escorted us out, leaving Mrs. Johnson standing with Matt's hand on her shoulder. I had a feeling she wasn't going to get off without some kind of reprimand for her behavior. I'd be happy with jail time.

Chapter Three

Cookies were in order after we walked the two blocks back to my parents' business. As businesses went, it wasn't the most glamorous, or even the most profitable, but it was beautiful in a slightly gothic way.

I took the lead and had everyone follow me through the tunnel next to the massive three-story building to come in the side door of Graver's Funeral Home. My shoes sank into the plush carpet as I waited for everyone to pass me and go into the yellow parlor. There were plenty of chairs in there and the sunny color might alleviate some of the anger and bad vibes coming off the two women I'd brought with me.

"Can I get either of you something?"

"A new life?" Gina asked, a tear leaking out of her eye.

"It's going to be okay." Max crouched in front of her, patting her knee.

Standing next to him, I put my hand on her shoulder and Mama Shirley put her hand on the other shoulder.

"We've got you, honey. Nothing's going to touch

my baby." Mama patted her shoulder and rose from
her chair. "We need to get the Bean There, Done
That open. Business as usual so people don't assume
your guilt. Have you gotten clearance from the cops?"

Mama was all business, as if nothing had happened, but Gina still looked shaken. She'd come
across a dead body. I knew how that felt after finding
my former employer and then my ex-husband dead,
separate times but the same feeling, sick to the stomach, jittery, shocked. Gina hadn't even had time to
process anything as she'd been taken right into custody, then assaulted on her way out of the holding
cells at the police station. She might need a couple of
minutes.

"Can Max help you do that while I let Gina have a
little breather? He's very good at making coffee." I
stole a glance at Max. He shook his head, but I steam-
rolled on. "He can get people started with coffee and
whatnot while you get the baking going. I'm sure we
could run to the store and grab some muffins if you
need them to get started."

Mama shook her head so hard her bleach-blond
curls went flying around. "This is Gina's store and in
Gina's store we don't do store-bought. Gina always
has some frozen in the big freezer downstairs. I'll
thaw them and others can wait if they want something
more. Or I could make real breakfast this morning.
Does that stove still work in the back, Gina?"

"Yes, but . . ."

"Don't start with me, young lady. People are going
to be in there to get the gossip. I'll give it to them in
the form I want them to have it while flipping pancakes at the same time. More sturdy breakfast items

mean more time spent at the table. People will wait for a seat or share tables with strangers if they have to."

With that she walked out. When Max didn't follow her, she came back into the room. "Come along, Max, you're about to learn how to make pancakes the old-fashioned way."

He gave me one helpless look, but I shrugged at him. I couldn't do anything more than that. Gina had started shaking, and I was trying to keep her still until her mother left so that the other woman wouldn't stay instead of doing something constructive.

Finally, he trailed along behind Mama Shirley, and I sat down in her vacated chair. "You can let go now."

I scooted my chair closer as Gina broke into sobs, her shoulders shaking and her eyes streaming with a flood of tears.

"What can I do to help?"

"I was in jail. In jail! I never wanted to be in jail."

"It's over, sweetie. Now we move on."

She shook her head. "I thought I could maybe love him, and then I hated him, but I never wanted him to die. I just wanted him to go away. How did he get in my stairwell in the first place?" She lifted her gaze to my face. "You locked the door behind yourself when you and Max left, right?"

"I thought about that, and yes, I'm sure I locked it. Maybe Craig was good at picking locks. We don't know much about him that's true if you think about it."

She fisted her hair in her hands. "I don't want to think about it. God, what a mess."

The front door opened and closed. Did Max forget something? Was Mama Shirley's mother's intuition buzzing, so she came back because she felt that Gina was in distress?

Nope, it was just my oldest brother, who was supposed to be on vacation. He slipped through the parlor door as if he didn't want anyone to know he was there. Turning toward the door, he closed it quietly.

"Jeremy?"

He jumped about a foot and banged his shoulder against the door he'd just closed.

"For God's sake, Tallie. What are you doing down here?"

"Uh, I was about to ask you the same thing. I thought you were going away on vacation."

Gina shot up from her chair, smoothing her hair and her shirt at the same time. Skirting around the chair, she held the back so hard her knuckles turned white.

"Gina." Jeremy gave a small nod.

"Jeremy."

I looked back and forth between them. They'd never exactly been friends, but these weren't even greetings. Their names sounded more like first volleys in a war I wasn't aware had been started.

"Tallie," I said, trying to dissipate the tension until I could get Gina alone and ask what in the world was going on.

They both stared at me as if I'd grown a second head. Maybe I had because I felt like I was in some odd dimension where my brother and my best friend had engaged in something that made them pretend they were strangers. If what was running through my mind was true, I was going to have a very stern talk with both of them. Separately, of course.

"You didn't answer my question," Jeremy pointed out.

"You didn't answer mine, either," I shot back. "And don't pull that oldest child crap and say I have to listen to you because you're older. That point became obsolete years ago. Now, why are you here when you're supposed to be on vacation?"

"I had a few loose ends to tie up. I was just doing that." The table to his left apparently needed straightening because he turned and stacked brochures for our services here at Graver's Funeral Home, then moved along to the wall and made sure all the many memorial plaques were hanging just so. When he moved to the various objects you could have your loved one's ashes put into, I shared a look with Gina. Something in her eyes and the way she fidgeted with the seam at the top of her chair told me she was about to bolt. What the heck was going on?

"I'd better go," Gina said, a little breathlessly in my opinion.

"You have nowhere else to go but up to my apartment. Your place is still under investigation."

Jeremy suddenly did not find the urns and necklaces fashioned from ashes quite as fascinating.

"What happened?" He focused on Gina when he asked the question.

I waited a few moments to see if she'd answer, but she stared at the carpet as if she hadn't heard.

"Um, there was a death at the Bean. I guess you didn't hear?"

His hand stretched out toward Gina, but he dropped it without making contact. Straightening his tie, he cleared his throat and narrowed his eyes at me when I opened my mouth. I closed it again.

"I'm sorry to hear that, Gina. If there's anything we at Graver's can do, please don't hesitate to let us know." He looked at his watch as if it held all the answers to all the mysteries of the world. "I should go. Good luck."

And he was out the door, much more quickly and much louder than when he had entered.

"Good luck? Really?" Gina blew out a breath and shook her head. "Good luck. I think that about sums up my whole last twenty-four hours."

Max came in where Jeremy had just left. "What was he doing here?" he said, hooking his thumb back over his shoulder. "I thought he said he was going on vacation."

Gina turned away as I shrugged. "He said he had things to wrap up but not what they were."

"Well, I tried to flag him down, and it was like he was lost in another world."

I shook my head. "I don't know. I do know that he's acting weird, though, and I also know I don't have time to worry about why." I sat down on a sofa in the casual conversation area of the parlor and dragged Gina down with me.

"I should go," she said, resisting my hand on her arm.

"And I'll say it again—where are you going to go? To your mom's? She's having her own issues and you don't want to be there right now. Plus, she's running the Bean. You can't go to your house, and the Bean is doing fine, isn't it, Max?"

His nod was decisive and quick, thank goodness. "The Bean is fine. I was just coming over to let you know that your mom is whipping up pancakes, scones, and cinnamon rolls like they're going out of style, but people are grabbing them up. The line is seriously out the door. We were able to get a hold of Laura, but she's running late."

Gina's head snapped up, the light coming back into her eyes. "I really should go. I have to help, Tallie. I can't leave people in line." She made to get up again. I held on tighter.

"They'll be fine. And a line means people talking, and people talking could bring out info that we need if we're going to make sure the right person gets caught. If it was murder."

Gina gasped and Max groaned.

"You said you weren't going to get involved in this one. I heard you tell Burton," Gina said, accusation tightening her voice.

"I lied." And that was the last word on that. "Now, let's go over the facts while Max returns to dish duty, and then we'll see what we know, and what we still need to know."

"I don't know if that's a good idea." Doubt marred my boyfriend's brow.

I didn't have time for doubt. I was going to save my best friend if it was the last thing I did. "I do, and that's the end of that. The police didn't exactly come off all shiny and experienced when Darla and Waldo were killed. I'm not going to let them pin anything on Gina if I can help it. I know she didn't do this, and the rest of the town will know it, too, once I'm done." I hugged him for good measure. "Now scoot."

After shooing Max away with another quick kiss and a promise that we'd see each other later, I pulled Gina into the little kitchen in the back of the funeral home. No use sitting out in the parlor if it would draw more people in. I needed information, not visitors.

I made myself a cup of tea and then made a cup of coffee for Gina out of the single-serving machine. No, it wasn't her usual, but the way her face was wan and drawn, it was just going to have to do. I couldn't take the time to run across the street to get her a real cup of the good stuff.

"Are you okay?" I asked, mixing creamer in with my tea until it was blond.

Her shoulders drooped. "I don't know, to be honest. I feel like I'm all over the place inside. I'm sad but I'm also angry and shocked and distraught and pissed and so many other things." She turned weary eyes on me. "And I'm so thankful that I have you."

"Now, don't start crying." I grabbed tissues just in case because it looked like my warning was not going to be heeded.

"I can't help it." As she took the tissues out of my hand, she sniffled. "I mean, one minute I think I might finally have found someone nice to spend some time with and the next I find out that he's married, then not even twelve hours later he's dead at the bottom of my stairs. I feel like someone put me on a roller coaster and won't stop the ride even though I'm going to barf."

"Please don't barf." I nudged the trash can toward her with my foot. Just in case, anyway. "It's going to be okay. I promise. And while I wanted to see you happy, I just kept feeling like something was off with Craig, anyway. He seemed too perfect. Even Max isn't that good."

That got a watery chuckle out of her, which was better than the full-out crying I could see verging in her eyes.

She sniffed again and dabbed the tissue at her nose.

"I know. I just really wanted it to work, and not only did it not work, but then I have to go stumbling over him in my own hallway. There was no chance he was sleeping, either. His eyes were wide open and staring at me, but his head was at a weird angle like one of those creatures in the horror movies you liked to watch when we were younger."

"Creepy." But since she seemed willing to talk about it, I got a pack of stickies from the drawer next to the silverware and started jotting things down.

"Are we really going to do this?" She eyed my makeshift notepad.

"Yes, we are, because if we don't, I can't guarantee that Burton or anyone else will. I know he tries, but without my help last time I'd still be running from some deranged killer and none the wiser about all that money Waldo had stashed away." All the money that had gone to taxes and cleaning up debt Waldo had left floating when he'd died in his own house. I'd done what I could to pay people off and leave at least a little for my own nest egg, since the debts to some of the bigger corporations weren't mine. But the little people that he'd screwed out of their life savings? I'd made that right as best I could. It had left me precious little to save for my own dreams, but at least I'd been able to do something right, after my disaster of a marriage.

"I don't think Burton really believes I did it."

"That's something, but it's no guarantee. Remember, you told everyone in the Bean yesterday that if you saw him again you'd kill him, poison him, or boil him in coffee, which amounts to the same thing. I'm sure that's going to get back to Burton's ears, and he's going to have some more questions for you."

"Oh my God. I totally forgot about that." Her fingers drummed on the dining room table my mother had bought at a yard sale years ago and had refinished. "Should I go talk to him about that now before he hears it from someone else?"

I found no inspiration in the lacquered cupboards lining the wall. I really wished I could. Of course I wanted to clear Gina's name, but I had also been looking forward to Max's vacation and spending time with the man I hoped would be more than my boyfriend. Maybe. Someday. "No, I think we need to make our own list and then go in with a plan. I'm sure with Mrs. Johnson already having been there that she did not skimp on telling him exactly what she heard and how much she hates you." I tapped my pen on the small stack of square paper. "Why does she hate you? I mean, obviously, she might have thought you were trying to steal her man, but it seemed to go deeper than that. Ideas?"

"I've been wracking my brain, but I can't come up with anything. I vaguely remember her from high school, but we never really had anything to do with each other. And as far as the coffee shop, I did ask her to leave, but I would think that shouldn't have made her hate me like this. I just didn't want to fend off her offers to buy my shop every day. Maybe she's pointing all her hatred on the one she knows he was cheating with? She didn't seem surprised to find him in there, and the tone of her voice was soothing to him but accusatory to me. Do you think he'd been cheating for years, and she always just turned a blind eye?"

Why was it always with the cheating? Why couldn't people stick to their vows? If I ever married again, and that might be a big "if," it was going to be to someone who actually liked me, not just loved me or said they did.

I scribbled some doodles on my top stickie. "It's possible that she finally has a face to go at with the hate, but it still feels like there's something more." I contemplated that for a moment and still came up with nothing new. "What do you really know about Craig? Not that stuff from his dating profile. The real life stuff." It was a valid question, but my stomach got queasy when Gina's mouth fell into a frown and her bottom lip quivered.

Shrugging, she wrapped her arms around herself. "Nothing, I guess. I know he owns that home upgrade company. He took me by the office once, but other than that, I suppose everything else was a lie." The chair scooted back as she jumped up. "Using the bathroom, be right back."

She wasn't successful at holding back her sobs before she slammed the door behind her. I left her alone this time because maybe she needed this release before she could move on. They hadn't been together long, but Gina had told me they'd talked for weeks before they'd met for the first time face to face. The anger was soon going to come roaring out full force, if I knew my friend. And I did.

I was ready for it. It was what would ultimately prod her to want to find out who did this. Whoever it was hadn't just killed Craig, they'd also dragged Gina into it by trying to place the blame on her and killing him in her house. When she thought of that she was going to be pissed. Being pissed would make her want to get justice, and for that I was her girl.

In the meantime, I was about to dig into the life and times of Craig Johnson and find out exactly what he'd had going on in the real life he hadn't shared with Gina.

I was right in the middle of checking out the tenth site where Craig listed a profile when Gina emerged from the bathroom. Her nose was red, along with her eyes, but her shoulders were set and her mouth was a straight, flat line. There was my fighter. She would want to work. Believe me, I had plenty for her to do.

"Better?" I asked, knowing she wouldn't want to be petted or coddled.

"Yep, thanks." She came up behind me, and I made no move to shut the lid on my laptop. She wouldn't have been happy with me if I'd tried to shield her.

"How many?" she asked.

"Too many." When she took the seat next to me, I turned the laptop toward her and moved the mouse. "You weren't the first, and you might not be the only one at this particular time."

The growl beside me sounded like a feral cat, but I let it pass.

"He was a jerk. A real ass, but I still didn't want him dead."

"I know that, and you know that, but his wife is gunning for you, people overheard you saying you'd boil him in coffee, and the police might not have any other viable suspects. We need to give them some." After handing the laptop over to her, I took out a notepad and a pen. A real notepad this time—the time for stickies was over.

"Tell me everything you know." I held my pen at the ready like a reporter waiting for the juiciest story ever. Or even better, like a detective getting the intel to then pursue the suspect. I was really getting into this sleuthing thing. I didn't know if that was a good or bad thing, but now it was necessary, so the reasons didn't matter, only results.

Gina raised her gaze to the ceiling and steepled her fingers under her chin. "His name is Craig Johnson, and he's a philanderer. Or at least he was." She blew out a breath, looking at me again. "He owned a company that could refurbish houses or upgrade systems and said that he had a partner."

"Excellent, a partner." I scribbled it onto my notepad. "Name?"

"Steve? Drake? Manny?"

"Are you just pulling names out of the air? None of those sound like each other."

"No, those were guys I thought about clicking on instead of Craig." She laughed derisively. "I should have chosen anyone but the golden boy."

I reached across to give her hand a squeeze.

"No, I've got this." She typed furiously into the laptop. When she was done, she smiled and turned the computer around so I could see the screen. "Johnson and Fuller Construction. Drake Fuller. And I did almost click on him."

So both men were out looking for playmates. Was Drake married, too? He had to have known Craig was messing around if Craig had taken Gina to the office. Or maybe Craig had only taken her because he'd known the office would be empty. My pencil tapped in a staccato beat on the pad in front of me.

"Perhaps we should go talk to this Drake about an addition onto my apartment. Or maybe opening up the third floor to use more of the space so I don't have to be cramped in just the one room with a Murphy bed."

Gina's eye sparkled for a moment, then dimmed.

"Don't you think he'll be grieving? Or that the death of one of the owners would cause the office to be closed?"

Either of those were possibilities, but I was not going to let a "maybe" deter me. "Seems to me that there's a chance that it could be open and now would be a good time to hit him with a few questions. Let's call."

Shredding a tissue in her hands, Gina shrugged. "I don't know, Tallie. What if he is there and he thinks I did it? I don't want anyone else going down to the police station and making this harder than it already is."

I understood her concerns, but this was important. Too important to dillydally or worry about what others thought. "Don't get cold feet now. We have to start somewhere."

"I just want it to all go away." She settled back into her chair, the smile long gone and the fire in her eyes banked.

Squatting in front of her, I placed my hands on her knees. "I get it. I do," I said when she huffed out a breath. "You think I wanted to try to find out who killed Darla and then get caught up in the thing with Waldo?" I rose to my feet and answered before she could. "No, I didn't, but it was important, and this is important, too. It could be that he just broke into your house and then fell down the stairs. There could be truth to that. But unless we explore the options, we won't know the players. And if we don't know the players, then we won't know what to watch out for."

"You're right. I know you are, but I'm so tired and it hasn't even been twelve hours."

"You can take a nap on the couch up in the apartment if you want. I'll call Drake and go by myself.

That way you don't have to worry about being seen or questioned by him."

The more I thought about it, the better the idea sounded. I could cover far more ground by myself, and Gina needed to run through the rest of her emotions. It hurt me to see her hurting, and I was going to do something to fix this. After all the years that I had separated myself from her, here was my chance to redeem myself.

After escorting Gina upstairs and locking the door behind her, I trotted down the stairs and almost ran smack into my older brother.

"What are you doing here again?" I asked, holding onto the wall behind me to keep from toppling over.

"I, um, wanted to see if there was anything I could do for your friend."

"She's been your friend, too, for years. Why are you acting like you've never seen her before?"

"If she didn't tell you, I'm not going to either." And he walked away, shutting himself into the kitchen. I heard the lock click, but I still banged on the door.

"You can't say something like that and then shut me out."

"Yes, I can," he said, clear as day through the sturdy door.

I could go around back and unlock the other entrance with my key, but a call was coming through on my phone. I'd left a voicemail for Drake Fuller on my way down the stairs. It appeared he was calling me back.

I would deal with my brother and Gina later.

Whatever they had going on was probably none of

my business—or they'd tell me that anyway, but that didn't mean I'd pay attention.

The office of Johnson and Fuller was about twenty minutes away, which in central Pennsylvania meant I drove through seven towns to get there. It was a pretty drive with the sun shining and flowers in bloom. People were out in their front yards mowing the grass and putting down mulch. Little of it registered, though, because I was trying to come up with the best way to approach the remaining partner at the home renovation firm with questions he might not want to answer. In fact, I needed to ask Drake Fuller about his partner and if he knew that the guy was a cheater. And if there was anything else he cheated at.

Could a dissatisfied customer of his firm have followed him to Gina's and just happened to be at the right place at the right time to take revenge for a shoddy job on a building? I wasn't ruling anything out at this point.

After I parked in front of the building, I stepped back to take in the storefront. They'd taken the street view and dressed it up like a house exterior. Light blue with white trim and black shutters, it invited you in to a home and the dreams of one of your own. They'd done a good job. It looked inviting and homey. I wondered how Craig's death was going to affect their business and who got Craig's portion when it was all said and done.

Opening the front door, I wasn't greeted by a happy receptionist but a bawling woman who was throwing paper towels over her shoulder onto the floor. How many women were crying in a twenty-mile radius due to the death of this guy?

To be fair, though, she could just be crying over the loss of a wonderful boss and man, but I didn't think so.

"I can come back," I said, having no intention of doing any such thing but thinking it was probably best to lead off with that.

"Oh!" Her head popped up, a brassy yellow and orange that was teased within an inch of its life. She dabbed the paper towel under her eyes, though it didn't touch the streaks of mascara running down her face. I would not stare, I told myself, as I did just that.

Scooting her chair closer to the desk, she folded her hands on the smooth surface and seemed to be trying to compose herself. A few sniffs and another eye swipe, this time with her finger, which came back black, and she stared at me.

"I don't think we're open. We've just had a terrible loss, so you might want to come back another time."

"Now, Noreen, there's no need to turn away a customer. We must all soldier on even with our recent loss." The man was tall with a flowing mane of silvering hair and a nicely pressed shirt. With his sleeves turned up at his wrists, he looked approachable and hard working. With his chiseled good looks, he appeared trustworthy and honest. But there was something about his eyes and tone that made me hesitate. Then again, maybe I was just looking for suspects everywhere and trusted no one unless I'd known them for at least twenty years.

"I'm so sorry. When we spoke earlier I didn't realize

you'd lost someone in the firm," I lied. Hopefully he wouldn't know any different or my cover would be blown—like Max's was nine months ago when he tried to pass himself off as a flower delivery guy.

"That's okay. It's a shock, of course, but the firm is still standing, and we still have to do business. Drake Fuller," he said with his hand outstretched.

"Tallie Graver," I returned, waiting to see if he recognized my name.

The answer to that was no. The smile didn't change and the handshake was over after a brief moment.

"Why don't you come on back? Noreen can get you a cup of coffee."

"Oh, that's okay, no coffee necessary." I followed along behind him, but still heard the wailing that resumed after he shut the door to his office.

Plush carpet muffled my footsteps and warm mahogany wood decorated the office from the desk to the framed art on the walls.

Settling himself in behind his desk, he mirrored Noreen's pose from earlier with his hands folded on the blotter. Was that something they did on purpose? Like did they learn it when they walked into the building?

"Now, my apologies for the tears out there. My partner, Craig Johnson, was killed this morning and Noreen is taking it hard. He was a good boss to her. A good partner to me. This will take some time to get over. In the meantime, I can't let the company fall apart. I wouldn't want to leave the widow with nothing."

"Of course." Interesting that he would mention the widow. What did she have to do with it? I made a mental note to ask Max if he could search records for tax returns and profit reports when I got back home.

"So you said this was a smaller project?"

I fought the urge to clasp my own hands in my lap. Keeping them wrapped around my purse was my best option.

"Yes, nothing too big. The house I live in has a third-floor apartment that I'd like to consider expanding to cover most of the third floor. It would mean knocking down some walls, installing others, and making the previous attic into a living space."

"I see." He settled back into his chair, and though he might have seen what I was asking for, he did not look impressed with the prospects. Too small of a job? I could have faked something bigger, but I was already going to be in enough trouble if he saw through my ruse that I wasn't willing to throw a fake house in there, too.

"The attic is four thousand square feet," I offered.

That brought him forward. I wasn't sure if I liked this guy, but I couldn't tell yet if it was a genuine unease, or if I was simply projecting and wanting him to be the one who'd hurt Craig to get Gina off the hook.

"That's impressive. Might I ask where you have an attic that's four thousand square feet?"

"I live on the third floor of Graver's Funeral Home."

"Ah, the name. I should have put the two together." Taking a sheet of paper from under the blotter and a fancy-looking pen out of a silver cup, he began making big loops that I couldn't understand from my point of view.

When he turned the letterhead around, I almost wished I had left before finding anything out.

Why don't you worry about your friend the home wrecker and killer instead of snooping where you don't belong?

Chapter Four

I sat frozen in my oversized chair, not sure what to do. Was he just telling me to mind my own business or was the note more sinister than that? Fortunately, I didn't have to get up the nerve to ask him. I would never be so thankful to be interrupted, as Noreen came running into the office with a clipboard.

"Drake, this just came in and they want a signature from Craig or they won't release it."

As much as I wanted to know what kind of delivery would make a specific signature absolutely necessary, I also wanted to get out of there before Drake had a chance to follow up on that note.

I did, however, snatch up the note he'd made the mistake of writing on his own stationery.

Booking it out of his office, I waved to Noreen as if I didn't have a care in the world.

Of course, inside I was shaking like one of those hula girls people still liked to put on their dashes. I made it to the car and turned the key in the ignition hard enough to almost snap the metal. As I raced down the street I considered handing the note over to Burton but, really, this was not a threat. Not yet at least. I might eventually get into trouble for snooping when I had specifically been told not to, but I was keeping it just in case the murderer ended up being Drake.

I stopped in at the Bean for a few minutes, hoping to extend the nap Gina was supposed to be taking. The place was jumping. Max hadn't lied when he said there was a line. Not that I had truly doubted him, but I thought he had been trying to make Gina feel better about the situation.

And speaking of Gina, I would not have to wake her up from any kind of nap since she was pouring coffee like a pro and yakking at all the regulars sitting at the counter.

So much for trying to keep her out of the public eye until we could figure out what had happened.

Within seconds I had a hot mocha latte in my hand and was being escorted into the back of the Bean with no explanation. Gina tugged me along even though I wanted to see what was going on out front and hear if anyone was talking. Although, this did give me the chance to scold her for not staying put like I'd asked her to.

"Tallie, you won't believe the word that's going around." Gina plunked herself into a chair while motioning me to take the other one.

"What word?" I sipped and enjoyed, putting thoughts of Drake Fuller out of my head to concentrate on Gina's news.

"Burton's coming for me."

That enjoyment went right out of my head and nearly out of my mouth as I sputtered, "But he said that he didn't believe you did it and was looking into all the other possibilities."

"Apparently, the wife was more convincing than we had assumed she'd be and has some kind of evidence that makes Burton think he needs to bring me in for more questioning."

"What could she possibly have?"

Gina raised eyes swimming in tears to me. "I have no idea. I went out on a couple of dates, exchanged some e-mails and texts with the guy. Nothing more. I've been going over and over in my head what she might have, and I'm coming up blank."

I did not like seeing Gina so defeated. While I knew that I should stay out of this and let the professionals handle the murder investigation—or rather what had been thought of as a suspicious death—if Burton was coming for my best friend, he'd have to go through me first. I was going to figure this out one way or another.

"I wish she didn't know what I looked like." I took another sip of my latte. "Then I could go in and see what I could find."

The watery eyes turned hopeful. "Are you sure she registered you on her radar? The first time she was in your vicinity she was trying to pull out all my hair and the second time she was screaming her head off. Maybe she has no idea you even exist."

That was certainly possible and not easily dismissed. "It does help that I'm often invisible to people. And what's the worst that could happen? She could say no to talking to me at all, and I would just figure out a way around her. That Drake guy is a dead end at this point anyway, so I need something to go with next." I almost mentioned the note in my pocket, but didn't want to add to Gina's feelings of hopelessness by letting her know that someone else thought she had killed Craig.

"Do you know anyone who knows her who could recommend you as a cleaning lady so it doesn't look like you're just calling her out of the blue?" she asked.

I ran through all the people I knew, from both my married days as well as my current life, but came up empty. "I'll put out some feelers. From the looks of the Johnson and Fuller office they must have some money, and I still have a few people I might be able to call on. Plus, Letty's out of town for the week with her mom, so all the jobs are mine, anyway."

Nervousness vibrated off my friend as she wrung her hands in her lap. "Are you going to have time to help me? I don't want you to lose money, but I also don't want you spreading yourself too thin."

Reaching forward, I gripped her clasped hands. "I would turn the world upside down for you, Gina. No worries. Though I think we might need to have a conversation about you and my brother here soon."

Her eyes widened in a way that told me far more than she probably wanted me to know. Just great.

"I need to get back out there, Tallie. I'll see you later and bring any gossip I have with me. Are you free after six?"

I mentally checked my miniscule calendar. As far as I knew I had nothing on it. "Your house or . . ." I trailed off. "Are you allowed back in yet?"

"No, not yet. And I might be staying the night in jail anyway. I'm not going to lay myself at the police's door, but if Burton comes before I close who knows what will happen? Barring that, my mom has demanded I stay at her house tonight."

"Jail might be preferable," I said to lighten the mood.

She giggled. "You know my mom has the ears of a bat when she wants to. You might not want to say that too loud or you'll go back on the bad-girl list."

"That's the truth. I still haven't completely gotten off it from when we were teenagers."

Laughing, she rose from her chair and then the laughter stopped abruptly. "No, and Craig would have been on it too if he was still alive." She bit her lip. "You don't think . . ." She halted and bit her lip harder.

"You're going to draw blood. Stop it."

"I just wonder."

"What?"

"I did not harm that boy," Mama Shirley said from the doorway.

Oh man, how long had she been standing there?

"Of course not, Mom." Gina lowered her gaze and gripped her hands together until her knuckles turned white.

Mama Shirley came further into the room. Using the flat of her hand, she lifted Gina's chin. "It's not that I wasn't angry enough. I considered sitting outside your house in my car last night just to keep an eye on the place after I heard about the drive-by flowering from Lois at the diner. She heard it from her niece who saw it happen. But I did none of that. You're a grown woman and can take care of yourself. I know this and you know this. I'm trying to put it in practice, but I can't make promises, at least not beyond the one where I tell you for sure that I did not hurt that boy."

"I didn't think you would have done it on purpose. I just . . ." Gina gave a frustrated groan.

"I'm the only other person with a key to your house portion of the building door. I thought about that, too."

Well. I hadn't thought of that. I was going to have to put that on my list of things I needed to know. I wasn't even sure if the door had been jimmied or if there was no sign of forced entry. And without Uncle Sherman getting any info and no time so far to grill my cousin, I might have to just go check things out myself. Carefully, of course, since I didn't want to get in trouble for interfering.

"No one really thinks you did anything, Mama Shirley," I was quick to say. "I just want to make sure that you didn't see anything when you did sit outside Gina's house until midnight, though." I narrowed my eyes at her, daring her to lie. Going up against Mama was not my norm, but I had just realized whose car I'd seen last night sitting on the street.

I hadn't thought about it at the moment, other than briefly, since Max had called me back to bed, but Mama's words had triggered the memory for me.

She pressed her lips together and crossed her arms over her impressive bosom.

Mine wasn't as impressive but I mimicked her stance. I didn't call this formidable woman on the carpet lightly, but if she'd seen anything, I needed to know.

She broke first, surprising me. I really had thought we'd still be in our standoff for ten minutes at least.

Sighing, she tightened her arms across her chest. "No, dammit, I didn't see anything. There was a car that went by three times, but I didn't pull up to the curb until you left Gina's. I only left at midnight because nothing had happened, and I was falling asleep." She flipped her hand in the air. "I didn't want to get dragged into the police station for loitering or sleeping in my car. That Burton seems to need more revenue lately. He even pulled me over last week for a ticket going five miles over the speed limit. He's always waited until ten and then just given me a warning, but this time it was a real ticket, and he tried to ticket me for my music being too loud. Who doesn't love a good polka? You tell me that."

I was not touching that under penalty of death. Mama Shirley loved polka almost as much as she loved bingo and the stories she still taped during the day on a VCR.

"So you saw nothing except a car pull around a few times. Did it park at some point or did it appear lost?"

She shrugged, seeming to pull in on herself even more. "I don't know. It was the third time that I really noticed it, but when I saw it was a lady, I didn't look again. I was only on the hunt for that Craig nimrod."

I believed her, though I wish she had seen more. "Okay, any chance you saw what kind of car it was?" Because if it was the wife, then I might be able to cast more doubt on her to block her warpath regarding Gina.

"I wish I did, but I don't remember anything other than it had big tires for such a small car. Other than that, it was just a car. I only know the older ones, not these new-fangled things with their fancy heated seats and consoles that glow in the car like a sun. I only trust my Chevy."

The car that had made it through six decades. Okay, then, that was not going to help. Big tires could mean anything—an SUV, a Jeep, one of those cars that people seemed to think needed big tires when it clearly didn't. "Well, if you happen to see it again and it triggers something for you, would you mind taking a harder look?"

"Pshh. I wouldn't know it if it tried to run me over." She turned to her daughter. "Now that we have all that out of the way, you need to get back to the front. People need their coffee, and they need to see you going about your daily business. That Burton won't be able to take you out of here without an uproar by the citizens of this town."

Somehow, I didn't think that would stop him, but I kept my mouth shut. At this point I had things to look into and a job to hopefully score.

Back at my apartment across the street, I stuffed a cookie in my mouth. I'd stolen them out of the cookie jar my mom kept in the kitchen on the first floor. No one was here today since we surprisingly didn't have any bodies in the building getting ready to be buried. I knew that both worried and overjoyed my dad. As much as he made his living off the dead, he still didn't like to see people die. The natural ones, the old-age ones where the person's time was up after a long life, he was happy to make their passing as easy as possible for the remaining family. The young ones broke his heart, but he did his best job with those.

He was the epitome of professionalism and compassion. His three *I*'s of this business were tacked up on the wall for everyone on staff at Graver's to memorize. INDULGE, INTER, INSPIRE. Indulge the family. Inter the fallen. Inspire the living to continue to live, and hopefully to use us again when it was their time.

Right now, I just wanted to be inspired with a new lead about who might have killed this man and left him in Gina's stairwell. And how anyone had gotten in there without a key.

I truly believed that Mama Shirley wasn't my culprit. It didn't surprise me in the least that she'd sat out in her car to watch Gina's house, but she wasn't a killer. As much as she always seemed to be prepared to bean someone with her rolling pin, she would never go that far.

That left me with Drake, who thought Gina had done it, and maybe the widow. But why would Michelle kill her husband when she seemed to overlook his every transgression? Why this time?

The door to my apartment opened and closed, and I turned to find Max leaning back against the wall with his head resting against my wallpaper.

"Long day, dear?" I asked with a chuckle.

"Good Lord, I don't know how she does that every day. I never thought I'd be so happy to be let go from a job."

"You're the one who offered."

He stepped toward me. "Actually, if I remember correctly, you offered me. And I only went because I thought it would be easy to handle. A few customers, some coffee, a little conversation. But that wasn't it at all. I'm bushed."

"Poor baby. Good thing I turned you down to help with my cleaning jobs."

"Yeah, I think my desk and I will be new best friends when I get back to it in ten days."

I told myself ten days was far away. That I wouldn't

miss him too much when he went back to his regular life. I didn't listen very well as my heart clenched at the thought of watching him leave again. "In the meantime, do we have anything planned? Gina wanted to get together to go over some things she heard today, and I should try to call this widow to see if I can clean her house for her."

Max took another step toward me and swooped me into his arms to kiss me.

I was in a mid-breathless gasp when my phone rang in my pocket. I didn't want to answer it, but with Gina in peril, I knew I had to. I could have been her one phone call if Burton had actually thrown her in our tiny jail. Backing out of Max's arms, I answered the phone but kept his hand in mine.

"Hello?"

"Tallie Graver?"

"Yes, this is Tallie." I had no idea whom I was talking to and the number had come up on the phone with no name attached, so it wasn't one I already had in my contact list.

"My name is Michelle Johnson and you came highly recommended by Mrs. Jacobson for a job I need you to do."

I almost squealed in glee, not just because someone had recommended me, but because Craig's wife had called me. I'd have to send Mrs. Jacobson some flowers from Monty or give her a discount off her next cleaning.

Now I didn't have to track Michelle down. It did cross my mind that once she saw me for whatever this job was that she would be reminded I was friends with her arch nemesis and the woman she thought had killed her husband. But I was willing to chance it. I could always put my curly hair up in a bun and wear no makeup. I'd been told by my mom that the difference in appearance was striking enough that I should never do it again.

"Yes, Mrs. Johnson. What can I do for you?"

"My house needs an overhaul. I have things that need to be cleaned and if you have any capabilities of having furniture moved, I would be willing to raise your regular fee."

Things moved? Already? Her husband's body wasn't even in the funeral home yet. In fact, I believed he was still at the county morgue and probably not even fully cold. And she already wanted furniture moved? But I wasn't looking this huge blessing in the mouth.

"Yes, I have people on staff that I can get to help with a project like that. When would you like this done?"

"Tomorrow." The word was sharp, but then she softened her tone. "I'm sorry. It's been a trying day. If possible I'd like it done tomorrow, but will completely understand if you already have other houses scheduled."

Again, I went to my mental calendar. I had three houses due to be cleaned tomorrow, two of them Letty's that I'd agreed to take over since she was on vacation. But I might be able to put one of them off to the next day and just clean like a fiend to get everything in. I was not passing up the chance to clean this woman's house and move whatever she thought she needed moved.

"Tomorrow will be fine. Eight?"

"Let's make it ten, if that's okay. I have a headache

right now and need to rest, but I'll be ready for you at ten."

I took down her address and we said good-bye. After doing a little dance around the room, I was stopped by Max's hand on my arm.

"Who was that?"

"Mrs. Michelle Johnson, recent widow and needer of cleaning services and, apparently, furniture removal." The glee in my voice should have been contagious. Instead Max frowned at me.

"You're not really going to get involved in this, are you?"

I stared at him as if he'd grown a whole new set of eyebrows. "Of course I am. Gina is my best friend and I am not going to let the police hang her for something she didn't do."

"Tallie, I'm sure you can trust that they'll do a good job. If they really thought Gina was guilty they would have picked her up today, not let her run the coffee shop and serve people while roaming free."

"How little you know. The police are perfectly capable of doing that. And I'm not trusting Burton with this one. He didn't exactly find the killer last time, did he?"

Max didn't say anything at first, just stared me down with his lips pressed together.

"The answer is no, as you are well aware. And that just goes to prove that he might not be able to find the killer this time either." Did I really have to spell it out for him? He'd been right there with me.

"If there even is a killer." The skepticism in his voice cut me to the quick. "This Craig guy might have just fallen down the stairs on his own and died of a broken neck."

"He might have," I conceded. "But that doesn't mean I'm just going to wait for them to figure it out."

Pulling me in close again, he rested his chin on the top of my head. "I wish you would."

Fat chance. "Unfortunately, that is one wish I can't grant. Others, yes. This one, no."

He sighed, but I had to give him points for not trying to talk me out of it anymore. Waldo would have ignored me and expected me to be the docile little thing I had always been since he footed all the bills. It was true that at times I had caused mischief, which was just one of the reasons Chief of Police Burton didn't trust me. I had always toed the line, though I wasn't doing that anymore because this was the new Tallie. I was happy that Max did not try to make me stop just because he said so.

"I have a feeling we're in for a long night and an even longer day tomorrow. Where do we start?" he asked with a sigh.

"Thank you." I grabbed him around the middle in a big hug. "First, I was wondering if there was any way you might be able to get a look at the books for the remodeling firm Craig co-owned with Drake." It might have been a long shot, but I felt I should at least ask. I tipped my head up as he looked down into my eyes.

"That's one wish I'm going to have to deny you."

I hated to have my words thrown back at me, but it made sense.

"Unless the widow brings them to me for analysis, as she should be the new part owner and might be interested in knowing what she's walking into."

Bingo! "I'll add it to my list of things to talk about while I'm vacuuming and moving furniture." I squeezed him, loving the feel of his lean body up against mine. "You'll help with the moving, won't you? I know you're on vacation, but it would really help me and I kind of promised her I had a team that's more than just me and Letty. And Letty's on vacation, so really it's just me."

His forehead cleared and he smiled. "We could drag Jeremy into it, too, since he seems to be wandering around a little lost on his vacation. We were going to go hit some balls at the batting cages, but if I have to help move, then he can, too."

"Fantastic idea. I'll see about a truck from Uncle Sherman and our new moving company will be in business."

"Why do I get the feeling I've just signed up for far more than I'm ready to handle?"

I patted his smooth cheek. "You'll be fine. I'm sure it's not that much stuff, and it could be fun if you look at it correctly. Building those manly muscles, helping out a distraught widow, digging into clues to solve a murder mystery. Tell me you've had a better vacation."

"We could be in the Bahamas." He kissed my nose. "Let me know when and where tomorrow. I'm going to go talk with your brother while you handle Gina. She just walked across the street from the Bean."

He and I trooped down the stairs and I met Gina at the back door while seeing Max off.

"Rough day?" I asked. Her eyes were pinched and her face drawn.

"Just a little." She sank into a chair at the table in the small kitchen downstairs. "Do you mind if we just hang down here for a little bit? I don't feel like climbing all those stairs right now."

"Sure. I think I have some cookies." I went to the

cabinet to see if that was actually true. I'd been raiding the stash pretty frequently lately.

Gina stopped me midgrab. "I'd rather have some real dinner. I've been living on caffeine and cinnamon rolls all day. My stomach hurts."

Facing her, I tried to come up with an alternative to our usual pizza and wine. "Greek?"

A smile lit her face. It wasn't a big smile, or her full-force happiness, but it was something. "Yes, please."

I made the call to a little family-owned restaurant down the road that had the most divine food, then let Max know it would be ready in thirty minutes. After agreeing to pick it up, he said he'd be bringing Jeremy with him. Apparently, my brother was not going along with my plan to help clean out the widow's house and needed some more convincing.

I decided I should have that conversation with Gina before my brother came through the door with the food she so desperately wanted.

"So, Jeremy is going to be here along with your food." I didn't have long to wait for her reaction.

"I can just get something at my mom's." She rose from her chair, full of energy this time, and started pacing the small room done in rose and evergreen. Nervous energy?

"Sit down. We have to come up with a plan. I got a call from the widow today. She wants me to clean out her house. I need Jeremy's help, so I'm going to have to convince him. I might bring in Dylan, too." My younger brother was handy with tools and landscaping. Mrs. Michelle Johnson might need his services, too. And it would be better to have more hands for moving depending on what she wanted to get rid of.

"She called you?" Fidgeting with the hem of her shirt, she avoided my gaze.

"Yes, and this will be the perfect way to get access to her house." Enough of that; now it was time for the interrogation. "So, what happened with my brother? I asked him, and he said if you hadn't told me yet that he wasn't going to be the one to spill."

I watched her walk around the small kitchen like a caged animal, but I wasn't letting her off the hook. If this was going to be awkward I wanted to know now, so that I could start working on how to make it less awkward.

"It's nothing," she said, totally unconvincingly.

"It has to be something, or you would have told me by now. I've heard about all kinds of things over the years that were 'nothing'—from one-time dates to the ones you walked out on before they even started. I've heard about second and third dates and those you ended up with longer than you had intended. So, if whatever happened with Jeremy was really nothing, you would have mentioned it and we would have had a good laugh. This is more." I was convinced of it. She sighed, her signal that the words were going to come fast and furious. I wasn't disappointed.

"It was one night. We ended up at a bar together after one of my more disastrous dates. He told me he'd been waiting for someone to show up. We got to talking and drinking and then he came up to my apartment. I stopped it before it went any further than a few kisses, but ever since then we've avoided each other. I'd like to keep it that way." She sat down in the chair, obviously spent from the waterfall of words. "Does he know I'm going to be here? Because if he doesn't I don't want to be a surprise."

"Bafflement" was a small word for what I was feeling. This couldn't be the whole story. "A few kisses? You and he have been avoiding each other after a few kisses? You and Matt kissed years ago, and that never seemed to bother either one of you. What's the big deal?" Although in my head I was trying really hard not to imagine my best friend kissing my brother. Not that they weren't both adults, and I loved both of them. But if something went wrong between them, I wouldn't know whom to console and whom to smack in the back of the head.

Her shoulders jerked up and down in a shrug that looked forced. "I don't know why it's different, but it was, and I don't want to talk about it anymore. Okay?" She put her head down on the table and blew out another breath.

I knew when to back off, and with this information I could now watch them together and assess. It did explain the way Jeremy had reached out toward Gina in the funeral parlor earlier today and then dropped his hand as if he knew his touch wouldn't be wanted.

But why wouldn't she want him? Yes, my brother could be a little unbending sometimes, and Gina was more of a free spirit, but that didn't mean they couldn't be perfect for each other. The more I thought about it the more I liked the idea. My mom could start bugging Gina and Jeremy about children instead of me and Max, especially since I wasn't even sure if Max and I were going to be together forever or if the long distance of our relationship would eventually wear thin.

That was a thought for another time, though.

"Okay, we don't have to talk about it anymore, but just know that if you really did want to be with my brother I'd be okay with that. I wouldn't want to hear any details, of course, but I'm okay with the whole idea." Or at least I could be if it came to it and if it made them both happy. Oh, and if no one did anything stupid so that I had to choose whom to support.

Another sigh was my only answer after my announcement. Fine then, we'd just see what happened.

"I can call and let him know you're here if that will make you feel better."

"No, you're right. We're adults and it's fine. It's just Greek food with friends. I'm sure it will be just fine."

That was the second time she'd used "fine" in one breath. Hopefully I hadn't miscalculated how easy this should be. Outright awkwardness between the two of them would put a damper on my anticipation of great food and conversation involving murder, moving, and how to get the widow to want to confide in me and hand over the books to Max. But I'd been up against worse before and I was not one to back down.

Chapter Five

The smell of spices and fried cheese filled my apartment as we all settled in for good food, and hopefully, good planning. I had limited space in my part of the third floor for entertaining, but Jeremy and Gina still managed to not be within ten feet of each other. Jeremy had taken the chair under the front window and Gina had chosen to sit at the table with Max and me. Lordy, I had hoped for better than that, but I'd just deal with it.

"So, Jeremy, I need you to help me with a job tomorrow." I dug into the chicken, perfectly seared on its skewer, wrapped in flatbread.

"Yes, Max mentioned something about that. I'm still on vacation. And if we get the job for the recently deceased, I can't make any promises."

Out of sight of my older brother, I rolled my eyes at Max. "You're not doing anything, and you know with a murder they're going to keep the body longer. Don't try to back out with that pitiful excuse. Plus, it would really help Gina, and we should all want to help Gina."

Gina, who kicked me under the table, obviously felt that I was laying it on too thick.

I skipped right over that one and went on. "The widow wants the house cleaned and things removed. We can do this. As an added bonus, it will give you the perfect opportunity to offer your services, brother mine."

He pinched the bridge of his nose, which was a gesture I was very used to seeing since he often thought I had ridiculous ideas. If only he knew how it never worked.

"I can clear it with Dad to make sure he wouldn't mind, if you're worried about taking on outside work." I smiled sweetly and batted my eyelashes at him.

As he continued to glare at me, it was obvious my sweet smile did nothing for him. It didn't have to as long as he went along with my plan.

"Good Lord, Tallie. Enough. Yes, I'll help. Don't involve our father. I can make my own decisions. I would be happy to help with your project, especially since it will give me a chance to keep you in line."

That was a point for him, I couldn't deny it. Max muffled his smile by taking a bite out of his gyro. I looked to Gina for support, but she was softly smiling, too. Fine then, but I was going to be the one in charge, and Jeremy might not take kindly to that.

"Then we'll meet here tomorrow at nine to get everything in order. I'll talk to Dylan."

"It's a sound plan," Max said. I squeezed his hand to thank him for his support.

Now for the info-gathering portion of the evening. "Has anyone heard anything more around town about enemies or reasons someone might have wanted Craig gone?"

"The Bean was buzzing with the details of what happened but no one seemed to have any new info. The rumor of my imminent arrest seems to be just that. I didn't hear anything else significant." Gina poked at her food.

"I haven't heard anything," Jeremy offered.

"I did hear something at a table in the back, but I don't know if it means anything." Max drummed his fingers on the table. "If Mildred from the bead shop is to be trusted, she thinks that the house-upgrading company might be in some serious trouble now that one of the owners has died. The gossip is that they might have more debt than assets, since Craig was trying to expand operations, but they didn't have the capital to do that just yet."

"Something to consider." I used the notepad at my elbow to jot down the note.

"There wasn't much else," Gina said. "He doesn't live in town. You know how small towns around here can be. You can cross over into another town without even knowing it, but if you're not a part of that community, you might not know anyone who lives there."

True enough. When the victims were a socialite and my ex-husband, who both lived here, it was easier for me to glean information. But no one knew anything about Craig. His company had a Web site that I'd checked out without much success. There wasn't much there beyond the basics, not even bios for the two owners. And I didn't know anyone else who knew him, so I had no one to get the gossip from.

"We'll figure this out," I promised Gina. "It might not be easy, but I'm in for the long haul. We'll find out what actually happened. Hopefully before you have to spend a night in jail."

Jeremy stiffened in his chair. "Why would she spend a night in jail?"

"*She* is sitting right here, Jeremy Graver, and they might put me in jail because apparently Chief Burton thinks I might have pushed Craig down the stairs and killed him myself."

He stiffened further, and I was afraid he was approaching rigor mortis. "That's ridiculous. You're the gentlest person I've ever known. You would never hurt another person intentionally."

"Does that mean you think I might hurt someone unintentionally?" She swiveled around in her chair to look straight at him for the first time since we'd all walked up the two flights of stairs to my apartment.

An awkward silence followed Gina's question while Jeremy shoved a big bite of his salad into his mouth and took far too long to chew the leafy greens with balsamic vinaigrette.

"Off topic," I said, to break the tension I could have cut with my favorite squeegee.

They could work that out later, once we got Gina off the hook for a murder that I knew in my heart she had nothing to do with. But we'd have to find out who had committed the crime before Burton felt like he had to appear to be making progress by arresting someone, anyone, and settled on Gina.

There was something to be said for being able to call in your family to help. I hadn't yet told them I wasn't going to pay them, but pizza from Sal's would take away the sting, hopefully.

Uncle Sherman was the first to show up, at eight-thirty, with his big truck and a frown that told me I'd better behave myself. He might not be a big fan of the chief of police, but he was even less of a fan of me messing with police investigations that he thought had nothing to do with me. Part of me wanted to defend myself before he even opened his mouth. I wouldn't be involved now if it weren't for Gina's neck on the line. But the other part of me shushed that first part. If I didn't speak it, then he couldn't rebut it.

I simply smiled at him and told him everyone else would be along shortly.

Gina took a few minutes to come across the street with cups of coffee and breakfast items.

"Thanks, but we're going to have to eat these here before we go to Michelle's or she's not going to be happy seeing your logo." I accepted my cup and drank. Perfect temperature, perfect sugar, perfect taste to start my morning off right.

"Got it." Gina laid out the rest of the food. "I wish I could come with you, but if you think she'd be upset just seeing the logo of the place she hates, she'd be furious to see my face. So, instead, I'm going to close for today at ten. Laura called in sick and I just don't have the mental stamina to serve people today. I'll try to do some more research for you. I'm also going to pull together the e-mails and texts I exchanged with Craig to see if there's anything she could think she has on me. I might not have remembered something significant in my excitement over what I thought was a shiny new Mr. Right."

And there was my girl, thinking and researching. We'd get through this as long as Burton remained at a distance. I was a little surprised that he hadn't arrested her yet since it had seemed like a sure thing yesterday from the talk in the coffeehouse. At this point, though, I certainly wasn't going to alert him to the fact that he was slacking when it involved my best friend.

"I think that's a good idea," I said. "Where's Mama Shirley going to be?" It was important to know where all my players were in case something happened.

"She's at home with the ladies from the knitting club. They have some sort of all-day event to make hats for cancer patients."

"First, that is awesome, and second, that is a good thing because I don't want her anywhere near us, either, and I don't want her interfering. Have you talked to Laura?"

"No, not yet," Gina replied. "I called her cell but she didn't answer. So I called the house where she rents a room from Mrs. Farrell, on Marble Street. Apparently the poor thing has been down for the count with some kind of headache and hasn't come out of her room for hours."

"We'll try again later, or buzz by the house after we get the cleaning done." I did want to talk to Laura. She had delivered that cup of coffee to Craig from another patron. Had that been the thing that poisoned him? I put it on my mental list of things to ask.

Jeremy pulled up in his sedan. When he emerged from the shiny black car, he and Gina nodded to each other. It was an improvement over the awkwardness of yesterday, but better left alone at this point. I had things to do and people to do them with.

* * *

Once we pulled up to the average-sized, two-story house on Front Street, I really wasn't sure if everyone I had with me was going to fit in the place. Perhaps I had overestimated the number of things the widow wanted moved.

I trotted up to the door anyway, because I'd made a promise, and if people had to come and go as necessary, we'd make it work. Michelle, in full-on black, answered the door and then dramatically leaned against it. All that was missing was the back of her hand on her forehead, which she promptly did.

I rearranged my thinking. With the call yesterday, I thought perhaps she had moved from sadness to anger and that's why she had wanted everything moved out. That maybe she had finally figured out that Craig and his womanizing ways were not worth her tears.

But this was not the same woman I had talked to on the phone. This one looked like she was going for a movie part.

"Thank you so much for coming out, Tallie. I can't begin to tell you how grueling this has been." She took my hand in both of hers and squeezed it, then tucked it against her cheek.

It took everything I had to not pull away. Either she was pretending I hadn't seen her at her worst, or she really had no idea who I was. I was going with the last one since she tugged me into the house and immediately began talking about everything.

"So I'm thinking about changing all this. The couches look like some leftover frat house throwaways and the decor is very man cave, in my opinion.

I want airy and open and light pastels. I'm thinking that I should get it all done now so that I can be ready for my new life. I've been stuck in a rut for what feels like forever. Now I can finally breathe fresh air, and I'm thinking it's time to shui my feng." She laughed and hugged me.

Not a trace of sadness or the madness from yesterday when she was demanding Gina's head on a platter.

"We can help as much as you need," I assured her.

"Wonderful." She pulled me close again even as I was trying to escape. "And I have my eye on this perfect little shop across the river. It has a ridiculous name but the best coffee in the whole area. I'm thinking the owner might be running into some trouble, so I should be able to pick it up at a steal. I'll talk her into giving me her suppliers' names. I can rename the place, and it will soar as it never has before under her inept management!"

Jeremy came up behind me at that. It wasn't easy, but I restrained him without making it look like I was doing so. Obviously, she was talking about Gina's shop. For what? Did she really believe Gina had killed Craig, or did she just see an incredible opportunity to blame Gina, and so be able to get her hands on the shop she coveted? She used to measure for furniture whenever she came in for a cup of coffee.

Thank God, I had made Gina stay away. I would have to make it a point to tell anyone who had heard this conversation not to mention it to her, as it might send her over the edge. All it did for me was to more firmly entrench me in the need to absolutely, without a doubt, prove who had killed Craig before they got away with it.

This, of course, gave me a new angle and moved Michelle from possible suspect to most likely suspect on my list. If she'd found her husband at the Bean, then what would have stopped her from following him when he went to sneak into Gina's house?

Michelle continued to talk and I listened—even though her voice was grating on my nerves—just so I wouldn't miss anything. There was really nothing to miss. She talked about more colors, and more furniture, and gave me the places where she was shopping, and the things she'd like to pick up, and what pictures she wanted hanging on the walls.

All pretty standard stuff, although I would have to admit that she had an eye for details and simple touches that could make the place shine. Why hadn't she done this when Craig was alive? Had he kept her from sharing her vision? Or had he just never listened, preferring to have things his way? And why would a man who redesigned homes for a living make his home so blah?

I checked out her digs and found it to be modest. Although on second thought, it wasn't nearly as small on the inside as it appeared to be on the outside. This was doable. And I was very happy we had brought Uncle Sherman's truck. A couple of trips to the dump, maybe a few more to the consignment shop, and we'd be done. I could knock out the cleaning of this place in two hours tops while the guys did the hauling and the running. I wished Letty was here to help, but her mom was sick, and I understood the need to be near family.

I still had hope that while I cleaned I could get this lady talking about something besides the new duvet she'd like on her bed and whether or not she should get a pillow-top mattress since she'd never been allowed to have one.

I waited for her to take a breath when talking about the organic food she was going to buy to start trying out recipes before she took over the coffee-house she'd been dreaming of for years.

Finally, she drew in a breath, and I jumped into the miniscule space before she got rolling again. "I'm going to get the guys started if you can point us in the right direction, and then I'll be back to clean."

"Of course. I'm not paying them to stand around and talk to me, am I?"

That's exactly what I wanted her to do, so I forced myself to pat her arm. "It's all part of the job, and I have a wonderful crew today. Talk all you need to. I just want to make sure we're rolling along while we chat."

"Okay, empty the living room except for the elec-tronics and then we'll move to the dining room."

I directed Jeremy, Dylan, Uncle Sherman, and Max to do just that, then followed along behind Michelle as she moved into the next room. It was filled to the brim with furniture lining every wall. I didn't even know where to start looking first. A server sat next to a china hutch, which sat next to a side-board flanked by two needlepoint chairs. A café table resided in the corner, all white wrought iron and curling ivy, while a huge dining room set from the seventies took up the rest of the room. I barely had enough space to wedge myself around the table on any of the four sides. Thank God I'd worn my rattier jeans just in case I got hung up on something.

"This all has to go except the adorable white set.

Isn't it cute?" She lovingly ran her hands over the curlicue back.

"Absolutely."

She smiled and nodded as if I'd answered the million-dollar question right. "It's a model for how I want to redo the inside of the coffeehouse once it's mine."

I nearly choked. Gina would have a fit if this woman tried to turn her homey café into a mini bistro. Who was I trying to kid? Gina would have a fit if the woman even approached her at this point at all. I couldn't think of a way to tell Michelle to let go of her dream without announcing the fact that I knew Gina, so as frustrating as it was, I had to keep my mouth shut.

"So, a lot of changes for you in the new future. Did you take a class or something on changing your life and just decide to do it all at once?"

A soft, breathy laugh answered my question. "Oh, girl, you have no idea. Things are changing here because I want them to. I've held on for too long to things that no longer serve me."

"Interesting. Breakup?"

"Death, actually. And I need to move on, or I'll be mired in grief. I can't afford that—you understand."

"Ah." I didn't know whether to offer my father's services, but Jeremy beat me to the punch.

"I own a funeral parlor if you need help making final resting plans, Mrs. Johnson. I understand it can be hard to face all these decisions at once."

She eyed him up and down in a way that I found to be less sensual and more like an assessment. "I'll give you a call. Thanks." She turned to the dining room with her arms outspread. "All of it goes. In fact, everything goes except the kitchen. The kitchen is mine." And she walked away, hips swaying and step sure.

So much for getting a chance to ask her pointed questions—but I still had a couple of hours.

Those hours flew by, as the house was stuffed to the rafters. Not with anything valuable, but not quite a hoarder's paradise either. Just stuff, lots and lots of stuff that Uncle Sherman grumbled at me about as he made his fifth trip out to his truck.

"You'd better be paying me handsomely for all this manual labor," he said as he came back into the house. "I run a fire company, not a moving company."

I pretended not to hear him and kept going through all the men's clothing in the closet looking for any clues. It had worked before, a random receipt here, a threatening note there. But I found nothing. Absolutely nothing, and I still didn't know what Michelle thought she had on Gina that would pin her for the murder.

It was time to get down to business. Jeremy was heading out with the last load for Sherman.

I found Michelle in the kitchen, a smell wafting from the stove that nearly curled my nose hairs.

"Uh, we're almost through here. Good luck with everything, and not that I want to sound like I know everyone, but if you need somebody to look over the books for your husband's business before it becomes yours, my boyfriend is a tax consultant." I didn't mention the government thing since this wouldn't be an official inquiry, and I assumed he probably wouldn't take any money for it. I didn't know the rules, but I was sure he would, being the Taxinator that he was.

"Wow, you should open some kind of Death Boutique. Clean the house, lay out the body, work through the financials. You could be a full-service grief handler."

God, no, never. I answered nicely, though, since I still wanted to pick her brain. She'd stayed one step ahead of me for the last few hours. Always moving to the next room as soon as I found her. "Thanks for the idea. I'll definitely give it some thought." Of course, the answer would be no since I didn't plan on cleaning forever, and I certainly didn't want to work for my dad anymore than absolutely necessary. "If you need anything else let me know."

"You're from across the river, right? Is there any way you know a Gina Laudermilch?" The question seemed innocent enough, but there was an underlying tone that I didn't care for.

Time to come clean. "I do. We grew up together."

"And you're her best friend." She tapped her chin with her index finger. "I just realized where I'd seen you before. I can't believe you felt okay coming to clean for the woman who wants to see your best friend rot in jail."

"A job is a job," I said through clenched teeth.

"Well, here's another job for you. Tell your precious Gina that I'm coming for her and her shop, and it would be so much easier if she'd just give in and do what I want. There's no telling what can happen when my plans are thwarted."

Still clenching my teeth, I now also clenched my fist. This woman was going to have to get through me before she thought she could take down Gina. "That could be taken as a threat."

"Not a threat, just a warning. She's not going to be around to run the place anyway, and I have far more innovative and forward-thinking ideas of what can be done with the coffeehouse. Make sure you tell her that, too."

She turned away with her last words and waved to me over her shoulder as if she'd already won the war.

We'd see about that.

"You don't think I should tell Gina about the threat on the Bean just yet?" I snuggled in with Max on the single couch in my studio apartment. When he wasn't here the place sometimes felt like an okay space with just me and Mr. Fleefers, the roamer, in it. But whenever Max was here, I wished I had something bigger, something more like a real house where we could grill out on a wonderful night like tonight, or sit in the backyard and play cards under the moonlight. Since we had an incinerator in the back where we did the cremations, and the back drive was where they delivered bodies, sometimes late at night, I did not think that was the most romantic of places.

I gave Max kudos for even wanting to be here. I kissed him on the cheek just because I could.

He pressed his hand to his jaw when I moved back. "What was that for?"

"Just because. Thanks so much for helping today."

"Of course." He took a moment to look my face over. Running his fingers along my jaw, his lips curved into a soft smile that I wanted to nibble. And then he was all business. "Now back to your question.

I don't think it's a good idea. She already knows that the woman used to measure her store and that now she wants her cuffed and shot at dawn for killing Craig. Telling her the woman actually wants to offer for the coffeehouse would just send Gina over the edge. Leave her some kind of ledge to hang on to."

I sighed, burrowing into his side. "You have a point, but I'm going to tell her by the end of the week just in case Michelle decides to walk in and offer."

"Unless she has a ton of money of her own, she can't do anything until the estate is settled."

"But she could still try to rattle Gina by making the offer, knowing how much it would irritate her." That was my main worry.

"She could, but why don't we at least sleep on it? You can make a decision tomorrow morning." He nudged me to move down the couch, then took my feet into his lap and rubbed them. The word "keeper" flashed into my head.

"True, and it's late." I glanced out the window. All the lights were out across the way at Gina's. Burton had told her she could go home finally. I still didn't know why the word around town had been that he was planning to arrest her, but I was thankful he hadn't. She'd be up early in the morning to open even though we'd all told her that she could take a few days off. Especially since Laura would probably not be in again tomorrow. I'd stopped by the house on Marble on my way home and Mrs. Farrell had only told me the girl was still "indisposed."

The idea of closing for the day was protested long and loud. In her mind, Gina had to make as much as she could now. Eventually, people might get bored coming in when nothing new happened and then she'd just go back to her regulars instead of the crush she was currently enjoying. There were several people who had come in and out numerous times for coffee who had never been there before. She'd gotten names, but they flew out of my head now when I tried to think of them.

I'd written them down on my notepad just to make sure I had all the information I could get in one place. Glancing over at the counter where the notepad sat, I sighed again. It didn't have anything truly useful on it yet. I was beginning to feel like I was failing even though it had only been a day.

Max distracted me from my funk by digging his thumb into my arch. He might be a whiz with a calculator and numbers, but his true calling had to be rubbing my feet.

Mr. Fleefers jumped up on Max's lap and demanded his own rubbing.

"Down. You are not taking one of my magic hands away."

As always, the cat ignored me, purred deep in his throat and butted his head against Max. The man could never resist the cat, and so I lost one hand to a cat belly rub.

That was okay, though. I was back in thinking mode. I'd wait until tomorrow to tell Gina about the impending offer. Surely Michelle would wait at least that long to spring anything on Gina. For all we knew, she might wait and have a signed and sealed envelope delivered, since she wasn't allowed in the Bean regardless.

I drifted in a haze of contentment and almost sleep with Max rubbing my one foot and Mr. Fleefers purring rhythmically. Not a bad way to drift, if you asked me.

I was nearly asleep for real when my phone chimed with my older brother's ring tone. I'd given him the *Addams Family* theme song because it made me giggle and him roll his eyes. Kid sisters, no matter how old they are, often can find the fun in all kinds of ridiculous and tiny jabs.

I considered continuing to loll there on my warm couch with my wonderfully talented boyfriend, but my phone continued to ring long past when it should have gone to voicemail.

"What on earth do you want?" I was not exactly nice in my answering.

"Get up and get downstairs. Your precious Michelle called about a half hour ago and has decided to have a memorial without the body because she doesn't want to wait that long if they're going to keep Craig as a murder victim."

I sat up straighter, removing my feet from Max's lap. "Wait. What does this have to do with me? I'll set things up for her to come make decisions tomorrow if you want, but we could've talked about this in the morning, not at ten o'clock at night."

"Except that she wants it tomorrow morning."

"What?" No way. We'd never pulled something together this fast. I'd be up all night, battling the demon computer in my dad's office.

"Yeah, get your clothes on and book down those stairs. We have freshening up to do. Bring your boyfriend with you. Make sure he's dressed, too."

"We're both already dressed, Jeremy. Don't be a punk."

"Pity, but that means you should be down here in

about sixty seconds, when Dad shows up and starts handing out those to-do lists you hate."

Fantastic. Any lull that I had been enjoying was now totally gone. It was off to work I went. As I dragged Max down the stairs it did occur to me that a memorial might be the perfect place to look over Craig's acquaintances and see the widow in action. I had a feeling the performance would be much different than today's. I would finally be able to tell if she really was a good actress, or if she really was that hot and cold.

Chapter Six

"Are we ready?" Jeremy paced in the front foyer in his best suit. The charcoal gray was muted and the blue tie matched his eyes. His short blond hair was perfect, and he looked like someone you could trust. And he was someone you could trust now. Back when we were younger not so much. As evidenced by the time I was a preteen, not so bright girl, infatuated with fairy tales, and he had a frog that he thought I should kiss to become a prince. It was disgusting and I didn't trust him with anything he told me for years after that.

"So much for your vacation, huh?" I patted him on the head and he flinched out from under my hand. "I'm not going to mess up your hair, for God's sake. You have more gel in that small thatch of blond than most people use in a decade."

That got me a glare, but I was only trying to lighten the mood before the locusts descended. Or rather, the Johnson clan and friends.

"Yes, well, this is better. Working is good. My plans fell through anyway. It wasn't meant to be."

"I'm sorry to hear that." And I truly was. Everyone needed some time away every once in a while. As much as I loved to tease my brother, I still thought he worked too much. There had to be more to life than dead people. "What were you supposed to do?"

For just a second he looked over my shoulder in the direction of the Bean, then gave his head a miniscule shake and brought his gaze back to mine. "Nothing to mourn over."

"Was that a joke? Did you really just make a funeral joke?" I laughed and Max joined in, but quickly turned his laugh into a cough when Jeremy glared at us.

"We have no idea what this is going to be like." The glare did not lessen even as he straightened his already straight tie. "I did not get to meet with the widow other than when I was moving a dining room table out of her house. Everything was done over the phone. This is highly unusual. I don't even know who might show up since the deceased is from across the river, and they had no notice."

Ah, the joys of living in central Pennsylvania. You either lived on the West Shore or the East Shore, and some of the older folks wouldn't even cross the bridge into Harrisburg, talking about the trip like it was a thousand-mile trek, across a mountain range, on foot, with no shoes, instead of a short drive over one of the seven bridges spanning the Susquehanna River.

"I'm sure it will be fine." I tucked my clipboard and list under my elbow as my dad walked in from the yellow parlor. He, too, was in a charcoal suit, his tie a deeper blue and his hair gel-less since he didn't have enough to actually need hair product.

"We're all set. Your mother secured some light fare for the memorial. She also made her famous punch."

I didn't know that I would call fruit punch from the freezer and clear soda famous. Maybe it was the rainbow sherbet she added to the mix.

"We have a program thanks to Tallie."

The printer and I had a love-hate relationship, but last night it had worked for me flawlessly when I ran off a hundred of those babies while I had Max fold them. They weren't as lovely as some of the other ones I'd made, but considering the philandering, womanizing subject I had to work with, I had done the best I could. Of course, I'd never say that to my father. To him, all the dead were equal and deserved the utmost respect when being laid to rest. I believed that to a certain extent, but this guy had hurt Gina, and I just wasn't at the forgive-and-forget portion of the program yet.

"We have flowers thanks to Monty." Dad placed two big check marks on his own clipboard. I swore that the man would be buried with one when his time came. Along with a list of all the things he wanted to be perfect on that day.

"We have all the chairs out, the floors cleaned, and the mantels dusted courtesy of Max and Jeremy."

I looked around the rose carpet on the floor and noticed they had even done the trick that made it look clean but didn't leave lines. I'd add vacuuming to my list of things I admired about my man. I nodded to him and he winked at me. Be still my heart but he was something else.

A car pulled up out front and the show was on the road, or in the funeral home, as the case may be. Max looked divine dressed up in a tie and shirt he'd borrowed from Jeremy. He had a fancy suit that he'd shown me but it didn't fit the requirements of the funeral home for this kind of ceremony. Though it did make me wonder why he had brought something like that with him. Did he plan to take me out to dinner somewhere fancy?

We hadn't discussed much other than just hanging out and being together. It had been weeks since I'd seen him last. I'd have to search through my closet for something non-house-cleaner and non-funeral-parlor-girl-Friday later, just in case.

At the moment, though, the people were coming through the double doors in throngs. I didn't know anyone and that made it easier to escort them to seats. I'd set out plenty of tissues for the people who might have forgotten, or had gone through all the ones they'd brought with them. But instead of there not being a dry eye in the crowd, I couldn't find even a vaguely moist one.

Gina had called an hour ago to tell me that a lady from the library had come in to the Bean sobbing that all chances of her having a real relationship were over. She'd ordered the biggest mug of hot chocolate Gina could give her, with a mound of marshmallows and whipped cream, to mourn the loss of Craig. If she had tears there, why didn't we have tears here?

That stayed true for the next ten minutes, until a wailing woman in a teal dress streaked through the door and threw herself at the foot of the twenty-by-twenty-four picture of Craig that I'd had blown up first thing this morning at the local printer's.

"Oh, Craig. Oh my God. You'll never get to meet our baby now," she said between sobs, stopping the whole room in its tracks.

Well, everyone, that was, except me. I ran to her side. Not only did I want to get her out before the widow came in, I also wanted a chance to talk with her about her claim and maybe find out just a little bit more about this other, other, other woman. Gina's hot chocolate swiller made two, and this one was now three. I was going to have to find a notebook like Burton's to put in my pocket to keep track of everyone.

Back to the kitchen we went. I swear I was spending more time in this room in the past week than I had in years. I didn't want to risk taking her into another parlor just in case someone wandered into the wrong room in their grief. Nor did I want to use the downstairs office since it held quarter ends of caskets, heavy furniture, and gravestones on the wall along with shelves of urns. I didn't think that was an appropriate place to take someone who was obviously grieving.

So the kitchen it was. I put down a mug of my herbal tea and a plate of my mother's famous snickerdoodles. She must have made more last night. I had depleted her stash significantly over the last couple of days, but now it was full again. They'd cure what ailed you if you let them.

This woman didn't quite look ready to be cured, but she did take a cookie, then a sip of her chamomile tea.

She pushed her brown bangs off her forehead and tucked a hank of hair behind her ear. Brown eyes swam in tears, but no more fell. "Thank you for this. You've gone above and beyond, but I really should go back out there and pay my last respects to the man who had promised me the world and only left me with a piece of himself."

Yikes. Did she know about the wife? And how hard it must be to be left to raise a child all on your own? Although, even if he had lived I had my doubts that he would have supported this poor woman.

If she'd seen the notice in the paper, then she must have seen the part about being survived by his wife, Michelle.

"Um, I think it might be better if you stay in here and collect yourself. You can have a private viewing later, if necessary." My dad would probably have a fit about that, but it was the only way I could think of to keep her here instead of putting her directly in the path of the widow, who had shown herself to be unhinged.

One tear spilled over. She swiped it away with her fingertip. "Oh, I couldn't do that. Craig meant too much to me to not be here for his final farewell. I want to fix this moment in my mind for the lonely years ahead."

Seriously? Okay, she must not know about the widow, so this would be tricky territory, especially since she was pregnant and I did not want to upset her more than she already was.

I handed her a box of tissues while also holding her hand in mine. "Sweetie," I started, then realized I didn't know her name. "I'm sorry, what should I call you? I feel like if we're going to have this discussion I should know your name."

"It's Brenna. Brenna Johnson. I had it legally changed last week. Craig and I weren't married yet, but when I found out about the baby, I wanted to be sure that he or she would legally have his or her dad's name. At least until his divorce went through and we were free to be together."

Wow, okay. So she did know that he was still married, but wasn't aware that Craig was still very much tethered to his wife before he died. How hard was this going to go down? Maybe I should have added another spoonful of sugar to that cup in her hands. "So, Brenna. Here's the thing. I don't know how else to tell you this, and I don't want to upset you in your delicate condition, but I don't think there's any other way to do this."

She looked at me with glistening eyes, making me unsure how to even start. I plunged in because nothing was going to make this better. Craig was a jerk through and through and no sugar coating was going to change his sour into sweet.

"Brenna, Craig was very much married. He was still with his wife the day he died. He left the coffee shop with her as soon as she came to get him. I can assure you she is taking her role as widow very seriously."

"Widow." She snorted, setting her cup down with a solid *thunk*. "They were separated and had been for years. She couldn't bear him children, and he didn't want her anymore. But when he tried to leave her the last time, she threatened to kill herself. He was making sure she was stable and then we were going to be together. If I really am pregnant, I know he would have left her for good, no matter what."

"Wait—are you not sure if you actually are pregnant?" What kind of farce had come storming into my town? We had our problems, but this seemed almost as bizarre as the stories Mama Shirley loved enough to tape.

"I can feel the baby inside me. I know it! I would

only be two weeks pregnant, so it's too early to take the test, but I know it in my heart. I was so excited to tell him, and now he's gone."

I itched for my pad and paper just to write down this latest lie. Did he keep a note card of all the ones he'd told so that he could keep them straight and not blow his own cover? I wondered if that might be what Michelle had that she felt would damn Gina to jail. I almost wished that we'd found some kind of secret room like I'd found in Darla's house all those months ago. It would make this so much easier, plus it would give me a list of other women I should seek out. But I had none of that, and my long silence had brought tears to Brenna's eyes again.

I quickly patted her hand. "I wish there was a way to make this easier for you, but the wife was most definitely the wife, and you aren't the only one he made promises to. He was on his way to deliver flowers to another woman when he died. And the wife is the one who scheduled and paid for the memorial. She loved him."

I wasn't entirely sure of that, of course, since she'd seemed pretty much over her husband even though he'd only died three days ago. But now was not the time to get into that.

"I . . . I . . . I . . ." She gasped, and I grabbed her a glass of water.

"Head between your knees."

"No." Gulping, she sat back, then took a swig of water. "No, that's okay. It doesn't come as a complete surprise. I thought he might be too good to be true, but I never thought he'd do this to me."

Gina had said something similar. How many women now thought that? "I'm sorry."

"It's not your fault." After sitting up straighter, she smoothed her shirt down, ran a hand over the shoulder-length hair she'd slightly mussed with her crying jag, and then stood. "I think I'll skip the funeral. I find myself not as grief stricken as I had originally thought."

A quick changeover for sure, but having been in the funeral business for years, I knew that things could change in the blink of an eye. I'd once had a guy come in to plan his wife's funeral only to find out that she'd spent all their money on bingo and not the burial services she'd told him she was paying for all those years. After one beat of silence, he went from wanting the most extravagant send-off to telling us to burn her and put her in a cardboard box. Later he'd changed his mind, but it took time.

This might take time, too. I wouldn't be surprised if Brenna came back at some point and wanted to at least sit in the room where she would have said good-bye to Craig if she hadn't been so angry.

"Why don't you finish your tea first?" I said gently. "We still have people coming in, and it might be better if we wait until everyone's seated so there's no chance of you running into anyone you don't want to see."

"Can I have another cookie?" Her voice was soft and those brown eyes pleaded as she sat back down at the table.

I couldn't turn down her hopeful face, not with the full understanding of how addicting my mother's cookies were. "Of course."

I handed her a snickerdoodle, congratulating myself on a crisis averted, when my dad stepped into the kitchen doorway and frantically motioned me to come out.

Turning to the woman, who was munching around the edges of cinnamon and sugar goodness, I said, "I'll be back as soon as everyone is seated, Brenna. Don't leave without an escort, okay?"

"Sure thing. A few more cookies might help me have something to do."

I smiled at her as I put the jar on the table. Mom could always make more.

"Phew," I said to my dad as soon as I closed the kitchen door behind me.

"Come with me."

Bud Graver didn't sound happy, and that could mean one of two things. Either he wasn't happy with me, or not happy with the situation. Then again, it could also mean he was in business mode, and I was just taking it as him being not happy. Really anything was possible.

I totally should have gone with my first instinct.

As we entered the aforementioned office filled with places to put your dead in or under, he gestured to the guest chair while he remained standing and then began to pace.

Stopping in front of me, he crossed his arms. "You can't walk away from your post like that. More importantly, I can't be running after you when I need to care for our patrons."

He paced back and forth once more, then stopped in front of me with his hands clasped behind his back and his belly sticking out. I remained seated because getting up would be seen as some kind of rebellion, and I was not in the mood to go through those motions right now.

Schooling my features into the best neutral I could, I drew a slow breath in through my nose, then let it out. He was concerned for his business—I got that—but this was one of the reasons I would never work here full time. He didn't trust that I knew what I was doing.

After another breath, I felt I could talk without yelling. "I was containing a situation," I explained, hanging onto my patience with my fingernails. "Perhaps you didn't see the woman wailing by the big picture of the deceased—the woman who most definitely was not the deceased's wife—crying about the deceased never getting to meet their unborn child."

He opened his mouth, then he snapped it shut with a *clink*. Knowing the way his mind worked, I figured he was trying to come up with a way to save face for his assumptions and chastising me when he had no idea what I had done or why.

I continued before he came up with a way to weasel around his error. "I took her to the kitchen because I didn't want anyone walking in on us by accident—plus it has the bonus of having an exterior door that I was going to walk her out of as soon as all the bereaved showed up, so that I could keep her out of a mess that I was sure you did not want in the funeral home. She's fine in there, eating Mom's cookies. You wouldn't have had to run after me if you would trust me every once in a while."

So much for the kudos for making the programs and getting everything taken care of this morning by the crack of dawn. Working here at all looked less appealing with every word out of his mouth, every scowl. I was about at the end of my rope and didn't want more strife. No thank you very much.

"I . . ." He cleared his throat, tugged on his tie, then opened his suit jacket and put his hands on his hips, flaring the jacket out to his sides.

"I think the word you might be looking for is 'sorry.'" I did get up this time and skirted around him. "I accept your apology." At the door, I turned back to find him looking after me with squinted eyes. "I'll walk our guest out just as soon as the talking gets started and hope that we can keep this all under wraps."

There might have been some sputtering behind me, but I was not ruining my exit by going back to see if he was okay. He could take care of himself.

I found Max at the entrance to the kitchen with his hand on the doorknob.

"I was just looking for you," he said. "We're out of tissues."

And here I had thought the crowd was dry-eyed. I guess I had been wrong there at least.

"They're in the closet around the corner. Take as many as you think we might need. I'll be back in a moment."

"Is the wailing woman still in there?" He kept his hand on the knob.

"Shh, and we'll talk about it later. Craig had his fingers or other parts of him in far more pies than we thought. Let me take care of this, and then finish the service. Once it's over, we'll get some dinner and talk." I'd missed breakfast with getting everything ready, and I was famished. I hoped Brenna had left me at least one cookie to still the gnawing hunger in my belly.

But when I opened the door, she wasn't there anymore. I really hoped she had followed my advice and slipped quietly out the back so as not to be seen by anyone else. If not, then at least I'd tried.

The ceremony itself was quiet, though many were crying and not being discreet about it. And far more people had attended on such short notice than I had thought possible. Hopefully my mom had made enough of her famous punch.

The majority of the attendees were women, which wasn't unusual, but the number of unattached women was. I didn't recognize anyone, though several looked vaguely familiar. Once I thought I might have seen Laura from the Bean, but when the woman turned around it was someone else entirely. I would have to look over the surveillance footage my dad recorded during these things to see if I could match it with any of the people Craig had on his list of likes on those dating sites.

It was going to be a long day.

There would be no moving everyone to the gravesite, or a party afterward to celebrate his life. Michelle had nixed both of those ideas and wanted everything to happen here. The other parlor had been set up with the cookies, small finger sandwiches, and the famous fruit punch to be served after this ceremony—if you really wanted to call it that.

In my black skirt and pale-peach shirt, I stood at the back of the room, watching for anything that seemed out of the norm. At first, I didn't find it curious that Michelle and Drake sat together. Craig's wife and his business partner had the most to lose between them with his death.

The more I watched, though, the more I got a vibe

that made me look closer. Drake had his arm around her and touched her as often as he could. For a grieving widow that might have been a comfort, but it appeared Michelle was trying to get away from him yet smiling the whole time. She smiled through the eulogy one of Craig's old college buddies gave and through another given by Noreen, the secretary.

My ears perked up and my attention did not stray from Noreen when she said, "Craig was like a best friend, an older brother, and yet the man I trusted most with my heart and my love. He made me who I am today, and I wish he was here one last time so I could hug him and tell him how much he meant to me as I never did while he was alive."

Now, that could be taken as a secretary who adored her boss. But it felt different, the delivery more like a love lost than a good boss. I must not have been the only one who thought that, since Drake shot out of his chair, almost tipping Michelle over, and pretty much ran Noreen out the side door.

I hustled after them like I was going to intercept the two before they went wandering around. Of course, if I happened to stand behind a pillar and listen to their conversation for a minute or two before announcing myself, I could just chalk that up to trying to give them the illusion of privacy.

"What did I tell you?" he said as they ground to a halt in front of the closed parlor doors directly across from where they had just exited.

"I had to do it, Drake. His body might not be here, but I had to say good-bye."

He blew out a disgusted breath. "You're being ridiculous. He never wanted you, and now you've just made a fool of yourself in front of a whole room of his family, friends, and our clients. Don't be surprised if Michelle ends up wanting your head on a platter and demanding you be fired."

Noreen gasped and then began sobbing. I couldn't see the body language, so I had no idea if he was comforting her, but I had a feeling the answer to that was no.

"Pull yourself together. I think it would be best if you left now instead of later. You don't need finger sandwiches, and maybe I can smooth Michelle's feathers before she comes after you." He paused and sighed. "I'm hoping that things will now go the way they were supposed to before that asshat Craig showed up in all our lives."

She sniffled. "He wasn't a bad man, just unhappy, and he didn't know how to get away from that she-bitch." The vehemence in her voice was enough to set me back a step.

"Don't you ever call her that again. She is wonderful and has been dealt a bad hand here. You will not treat your new boss, and the woman who means a lot to me, like that."

Holy crap. So the office had been a love *square*? Noreen wanted Craig and Drake wanted Michelle and no one got what they wanted except Craig, who apparently could do no harm in Noreen's eyes and could do no right in Drake's eyes.

I made mental notes of everything being said since I wouldn't be able to make actual notes for quite some time. I should have brought my little spiral notepad with me. Or even better, I should have used my checklist with the clipboard. But that was tucked into a filing cabinet, so there was no way I could get to it. I also didn't want to miss the rest of the conversation.

Although now that I tuned back in, it seemed no one was saying anything.

I peeked around the round pillar and came nose to red-patterned tie with Drake. Slapping a smile on my face, I tried to look like I was still in motion from having just come out the door, instead of standing there the whole time as an eavesdropper.

"Do you think you heard enough?" His brows showed deep grooves over his narrowed eyes.

"I just came out of the room. I'm not sure what you're talking about."

"Yeah, and you weren't snooping when you came around to my office trying to get me to build something in a house that's not even yours. I highly doubt Daddy would let you have the attic remodeled."

"Of course he would."

"Should I talk to him about it now, then?"

I backed down, not wanting to have him ask my dad about that when he was already trying to circle his way out of wrongly accusing me of doing something un-employee-like here at Graver's. "No, that's fine. I've decided to go with a less . . . angsty firm, but thanks anyway." I eyed him up and down even though I was shaking just a little bit in my low-heeled black pumps. "If you'll come back in to the room, please? We don't want people getting lost in here and there are certain places that are off limits." I motioned back toward the parlor where Craig was having his final good-byes.

"I have my eye on you, Tallie. Don't doubt it for a

minute. And if you try to pin anything on anyone in my circle, I'll show you all about being lost."

What kind of threat was that?

I didn't have a lot of time to worry about it though, because my dad came out just as Drake was walking back in. Well, at least he couldn't yell at me for actually looking like I was doing something. Even if it wasn't exactly what he thought I was doing.

I smiled at my dad as we walked by, but he just frowned at me. Okay, so I might get yelled at anyway. It was worth the new lines in my journal and a better understanding of the players on this stage—a whole lot more players than I had originally thought.

Jeremy was up at the podium making final remarks and directing people across the hall. That was my cue to open the previously locked doors to the second parlor and have one last glance around to make sure all was ready.

Using the key in my pocket, I turned it in the lock and threw open both doors at the same time.

I had to jerk around with my hand over my mouth to keep the puke back. There was Brenna, laid out on the powder-blue rug, with her knees to the side. Her eyes were wide open, but she stared at something I could not see—and she couldn't either, since she was most definitely dead.

Chapter Seven

I stood there for a second, holding a scream back along with the puke. I heard people moving around in the other room, chairs creaking and footsteps.

I had to do something *now*.

Backing out as quickly as I could, I pulled the doors closed with a snap. I then locked them. My dad came out of the parlor. He was always the first one so that he could shake hands and offer condolences. I frantically motioned him over to me, hissing his name.

His frown spoke volumes, but I was not going to be deterred. "Keep them all where they are. Don't let anyone come out."

"Tallulah!"

"Trust me, Dad, please. Just trust me and keep them in there."

An exasperated sigh was all he gave me. But he did turn back around and made an announcement that the refreshments were going to be a few more minutes, and if everyone could just stay where they were for the moment everything should be ready as soon as possible.

Yeah, it wasn't going to be that soon.

He walked back out of the parlor and closed the doors behind him. As he stalked toward me, the thunderclouds across his face could have been the forming of a tornado.

"This had better be good."

In answer, I unlocked the doors and dragged him through, then locked them behind me.

I knew the moment he saw the body.

"Damn."

My dad didn't swear often, but when he did he always seemed to find the right word the first time.

"I waited to call the police because I didn't know how you wanted to handle this. Do you want to make a personal call to Burton while I gather everyone to move the food to another parlor?"

"Jesus, Tallie. No, we can't have people eating food that has been around a dead person. Whether or not it's safe doesn't matter. That's not how I run my business." He rubbed his forehead and paced the powder-blue carpet.

"Please tell Burton I didn't touch anything this time. I didn't even touch her at all. I don't want to get yelled at again by him." I hadn't even checked for a pulse before I'd gone to get my dad.

"You should have at least checked her pulse, Tallie."

One more fail for me. But who was counting?

My dad did bend down to check her wrist. He jerked his head around to look at me with fear in his eyes. "Call an ambulance now! She's still got a pulse." He kept his voice down but the urgency was there. I grabbed for my phone but realized I didn't have it because of my dad's rule regarding no cell phones while working.

Fortunately, there was a phone on a cherrywood credenza along the wall. Grabbing it up, I explained the situation to Suzy while my father spoke softly to the woman on the ground, who had begun to bat her eyes furiously.

No other part of her moved, though. It was as if her whole body was paralyzed. What on earth had happened between the time I'd left her and finding her on the floor in here? And how had someone locked her in here and also locked themselves out? How had anyone gotten through the lock in the first place?

Questions for another time.

"Is she going to be okay?" I held for Suzy to get back on the phone with me and wanted an update when she did.

"I think so. As long as the ambulance gets here soon. Go meet them at the back entrance, Tallie, and tell your brother to keep everyone contained."

Suzy got back on the phone and let me know Burton was on his way and so was an ambulance. I put the phone back in the cradle, then stood there, knowing what I was supposed to do but unable to get started. "Anything else? What are we going to tell everyone?"

Cupping his forehead, he blew out another breath. "I don't know how you stumble upon these things over and over again, but I will put in that call to Burton and you call Gina. See if we can at least get some food set up over there. I'll pay her whatever is necessary."

"Um . . ."

"Just do it, Tallie. I don't have time for whatever you're about to say. I have a crisis and a funeral and this whole day has been so far out of the norm that I can't take anymore. Please just do as I asked."

I nodded, knowing Gina was going to have a fit and that I would have to be at my most convincing. The way things were going, though, anything was possible.

He took his cell phone out of his pocket, and I chose not to nail him for not following his own rules. He stood against the door with his cell phone against his ear while I remained at the credenza to dial Gina at the Bean. I paid attention to what he was saying just in case it became important as I waited for Gina to pick up on her end. I had no idea what I was going to say but desperately hoped something brilliant would come to me before I messed it all up.

"It's a great day at the Bean!"

She sounded happy and like herself again. I was about to ruin that.

"Gina, Graver's needs your help."

There was a brief pause that I couldn't interpret.

She growled, and that was easy enough to interpret. "Isn't today Craig's memorial? I'm not even supplying one cruller for that bastard, so don't ask."

Yeah, this was going to be a tough sell. "Um, it's not that exactly, though your crullers are amazing."

"Don't try icing me up like a freaking cinnamon bun—just spit it out."

I rolled my eyes and counted to three. Neither worked to find the right words. "Fine. You asked for it. Craig had a mistress who thought she might have been pregnant, which she wailed in the middle of the ceremony. I hustled her out before she could do anything else, but now I just found her paralyzed and initially unresponsive in the room with the food. The service is over and we have to have something to feed people, but we can't do it here anymore, and my dad and Jeremy were wondering if you could maybe let us all come over there." I finally took a breath.

And was blasted with anger. "I can't even believe you would ask."

"I'm sorry. I really am, and I wouldn't have if this wasn't an emergency. My dad asked me to call and you were the one he thought of first. Is there any way? Please?" Maybe that would soften her just a little bit to our plight. I knew what this would cost her, not financially, but emotionally, but we had a need here, and she could feed it.

"Take it to the firehouse."

Or she could throw me out despite the need. I didn't blame her, but I still had to convince her. "But they aren't ready for us. I'm sure the floors are dirty. My dad will have a fit if I have to tell him that."

"Tallie."

"Gina, please."

"I don't want her here. I don't want any of her friends here, either."

"I know that, I do, but I don't have any other options. What if you go in the back and have Laura serve everyone? It would still be money in your pocket but you wouldn't have to talk to anyone."

Some growling occurred along with some cursing and some more growling. "Laura didn't show up again today. I'll have to deal with her later." A sigh came across the line. "What about the office over there?" Desperation instead of anger crept into her voice. I wasn't proud that I was wearing her down, but this had to work.

"That won't work."

"It's big enough. It's got that huge table and the beautiful memorial pieces on the walls. I can bring some stuff over and then get out before anyone else comes in."

"Give me a second," I said, as Jeremy called through the door at my back and my dad moved me to be able to unlock it, let him in, and then immediately lock it again.

"What is . . . ?" He trailed off as he spotted the woman on the floor.

"I've called the police," Dad said. "And Tallie is supposed to be talking Gina into letting us have refreshments over there."

I put the phone down against my leg and hoped it was enough so Gina couldn't hear. "Gina can't do it."

"Can't or won't?" Jeremy asked, raising an eyebrow.

I ignored him. "She said she can bring stuff over if you want to put it in the office and have people eat from there. It is a really pretty room, Dad. I think it could work."

"And what are we supposed to do about the paramedics coming in? And the way things are around here, I wouldn't be surprised if we had the police coming in with their investigation tools and cameras, gathering evidence, too," he answered.

I hadn't thought that far ahead.

Jeremy stuck his hand out to me for the phone receiver. Gina wasn't going to like it, but we didn't have time to mess around. Maybe I was willing to do more for this business than I had originally thought.

I didn't have time to explore that particular avenue at the moment as I handed over the receiver.

"Gina, this is Jeremy." He listened for a moment. "I understand, but I'd like to propose that we look at this as a business deal and with the added incentive that we'll talk about compensation afterward over dinner tomorrow. I'll make both worth your time."

My jaw dropped open. He was trying to entice her with dinner? With him? They were barely speaking to each other. I didn't think dinner with him was going to turn the no to a yes.

Shock overtook me when he thanked her and handed the phone back to me.

"There," he said to our father. "We'll head over in five minutes. She's getting out everything she has and starting pots of coffee. Mama Shirley is at bingo, so I'm going to go over and help her and take Max with me." He turned to me. "Close your mouth, Tallie. Gina is a businesswoman and knows when to let personal issues slide to be able to provide a service. Now call Max and tell him to meet me over there." He barked a short laugh. "After all this I think we might actually have to give the guy a paycheck for all he's done around here in the last twenty-four hours. I doubt he knew what he was getting into when he decided to date you."

I was quick to hit the numbers for Max's cell because I was going over with Max and Jeremy to make sure Gina was really okay with this.

My dad cut me off before I could connect the call.

"Tallie, you stay with me and talk with Burton when he gets here. I'll let the paramedics in. I hear them now."

Sure enough, a siren wailed from behind the building.

With a nod, he turned toward the door, then looked back over his shoulder. "I'll walk everyone across the street, and then as soon as you're done giving Burton the facts, get over to the coffeehouse and make sure everyone's cup is full."

He left the room like a battle sergeant. I had my orders so I followed them.

When Max picked up on his end, I told him what was going on. "Where are you?"

"In the parlor with a bunch of guests wondering what the heck is going on," he whispered.

"Okay. Can you discreetly leave and meet Jeremy at the Bean? He'll explain everything there."

I didn't give him a chance to answer because my father escorted the paramedics into the parlor and Burton walked in through the double doors right behind them. After a short greeting, Dad left with his eyes narrowed at me over Burton's shoulder, not locking the doors again.

Looked like the show was all mine with the man who thought I was always interfering and was frequently irritated with me. This was going to be as much fun as shaving my legs in the dead of winter with no heat in the house.

With his little notepad in hand, Burton looked me up and down with a sober and stern expression on his face. Right, so this was not going to be easy or pleasant. Not that I'd been expecting that, but sometimes it was nice to be surprised with a different experience every once in awhile.

"I'll start off by saying I was nowhere near this

when it happened. You can ask anyone and they will tell you I was out in the other parlor attending the memorial for Craig Johnson."

"You know, Tallie, I'm hardly ever worried that you actually did it so much as I worry that you're any-where close, and that you'll get involved in things that have nothing to do with you."

I couldn't exactly reassure him there.

"And don't even try to tell me that you're not in-volved here already. I had a call from Craig's partner telling me to keep an eye on you and Gina."

That rat fink! I wished I had that note with his let-terhead with me right now. I'd hand it right over along with the info about the love square at Johnson and Fuller. But it was two floors up, I had no proof about the love square, and the paramedics were work-ing to keep Brenna alive on the floor before taking her to the hospital.

They put an oxygen mask on her and checked to see if they could get any other response from her rigid body, other than the eye blinks. As far as I could tell, nothing else moved. What had someone done to her?

I turned away because I couldn't watch them intu-bate her and stick a needle in her arm. "I have some-thing for you about that later. At this moment, I think there are more important things to discuss."

"Fine. Let's deal with one thing at a time. Do you know who this is and what the story is?"

I was only too glad to be able to help out in the open this time, instead of hiding and not being sure what to reveal and when to reveal it.

I gave him the rundown on the possible but not probable pregnancy and the affair, Craig's many women, angry wife, and his habit of giving gifts to so many women I had no idea how he kept them all straight in his mind.

While I was talking, I made a mental note to ask Monty, the local florist, about how many bouquets Craig picked up on a weekly basis. And there had to be other florists in the area. I wasn't sure why he came across the river to get them. Maybe he was concerned if he ordered that many flowers in his town that never got delivered to his wife, he'd look suspicious. The information from Monty would give me an idea of how many other women there might be out there.

But now I had business with Burton. I wasn't going to try to direct him this time. I knew the score. He would only scoff at me and tell me to mind my own business. Again.

Once I was done with my monologue, he rubbed his head and then made a few more notes in that little book of his.

"You know, I was only looking for the info that had to do with this particular incident."

"Oops. Sorry."

"No, no." He sighed. "I didn't have over half of that, so it's fine."

He needed me in on this but he was still going to fight it. I could feel it in my bones.

"For all the information, I'll tell you this one thing and then you're out of it altogether," he said, his face stern and his voice forceful. "Agreed?"

I couldn't agree to that, but I nodded anyway.

"Craig broke his neck on a fall down the stairs, but we don't think anyone pushed him because it sounds like he was already dead when he toppled backward. He'd been poisoned."

"Poisoned? So Gina's off the hook?" That would be awesome if it could be that easy. I would still probably try to figure things out, but at least the pressure to save Gina would be off.

"You weren't listening. Depending on how the hemlock was administered, it could be long-acting or quick as a breath. In theory, it could have been administered at any time during the day and hit him late that night. The coroner thinks later in the day, but we can't rule anything out. Not even that it wasn't given as he stood at the top of the stairs. Because Craig had probably been lying at the bottom for hours, we have to do more tests. So, no, Gina is not off the hook. She could have followed through on her threat to poison his drink. That *was* her initial threat, wasn't it?"

Dammit. I knew that comment from Gina was bound to bite her in the ass. I'd felt it in my gut when she'd uttered the words.

I still had to try to convince him that she would never do something like that. "And what would get Gina off the hook?"

"Don't even ask me that. Leave it in the hands of the professionals, Tallie. I'll try to give you what I think you need to know. Anything more than that and I might just haul you in for obstruction of justice."

He could do it, too, but if anything, he'd just made it even easier for me to commit myself to finding out who this murderer was and bring the person to justice. I was not going to let my friend go down for something she didn't do, and I knew she hadn't done it. Not a single doubt in my mind.

"Well, then, that's all I have for you," I said, instead of fighting with him. "I'll leave you to it and see if I can go help at the Bean for the after-memorial party. Unless you still need me for anything?"

He barely nodded at me as he used his pen to write more notes. I hadn't seen any strangle marks when I was standing with the victim earlier, and there wasn't any blood that I could see. The paralysis really bothered me. Had someone done this to Brenna or was she prone to seizures? Either could be possible, but with the timing, I just couldn't buy that this wasn't deliberate, that it wasn't done by someone after her scene in the parlor. It would be way too much of a coincidence for her to randomly fall over at the funeral after announcing she was pregnant. This was not a coincidence.

We just had to find out how and then who. I'd leave the how up to Burton, but I was about to get elbow deep into the who across the street.

I chose to walk around the block and in through the back door of the Bean. I wanted to be able to scope out the scene before I entered the main room. As far as I knew, whoever had done this had been in the parlor with everyone else and that meant the person could very well be here now, mingling and drinking soda or coffee or tea as if he or she hadn't just tried to end a life. Or two.

I definitely hoped that Burton would let me know if Brenna had been pregnant. From the way she and

I had left it while she munched on cookies, I had the distinct impression that she hadn't actually been pregnant but was more looking to make a spectacle for being left alone. However, I would feel much better having my theory confirmed.

Even without time to properly decorate the Bean, Gina had really pulled things together. The counter was set up to look like a buffet, with a variety of pastries and a coffee urn along with a teapot. Gina was behind the counter beside Jeremy, making hot chocolate and filling sodas as needed.

My Max wandered through the crowd making sure everyone had everything they needed and that they were comfortable. He was a natural. And if I had any doubt that he owned a part of my heart, the smile he gave me when he noticed me peeking out from around the door jamb would have thrown the notion totally into a tailspin.

He excused himself from the elderly couple he'd been listening to and made a beeline for me. "Hey, did everything go okay over at the parlor? Your dad said he left you with Burton. I wish I could have been there to help."

"It's okay." I pecked him on the cheek, wanting to kiss him properly but also knowing that this was not the appropriate place or time for that. But then he backed me around the corner and laid one on me that made me curl my fingers into the front of his shirt.

He stepped back with a sly smile this time. "So now that we have that out of the way . . . How did it go over there?"

"Well, she definitely wasn't dead when the ambulance took her, so that's good. I've about had my fill of dead bodies. I'm hoping she'll be able to tell us who did what to her. I have no idea how anyone had time to hurt her or how they were so quiet about it. We should have heard something, yet I heard nothing at all."

"Was Burton grilling you?"

It hit me that he hadn't actually grilled me and had in fact handed me information that I didn't strictly need to know. Plus, there had been no heavy sighing, which was much different from our usual encounters. "Strangely enough, no. He, of course, told me to stay out of it, but he wasn't grilling me—I think because I had already given him everything I had, which was apparently more than he had in the first place."

He kissed me again. "My Lady Detective." Circling his arms around my waist, he pulled me in closer. "So I guess there's no way you'd back off if I asked you now?"

"Gina's still not in the clear." I stepped out of his embrace because the chatter was getting louder out in the room, and I wanted to make sure everything was okay. Plus, I didn't want to get caught with my boyfriend if anyone walked back. It shouldn't have mattered, but it did in the town where most people knew me and everyone who did immediately reported to my father. Not to mention the fact that I was still technically working. My dad would have a fit if he found me in Max's arms when I should be out making sure that everyone was comfortable and engaged.

And I needed to be out there trying to find out

who could have hurt poor Brenna and if it was the same person who killed Craig. Did we have a serial maniac on the loose?

Two incidents so close together was not a good thing in any way. And while they had something in common, I didn't know who was out to get Craig and now someone who had shouted that she was pregnant. Was it an acquaintance? Someone he'd dated? His widow?

Time to do some canvassing of the crowd. It would be easy enough to talk to everyone while they had coffee and hopefully reminisced about Craig. I was interested to hear some good things about him since I had only heard bad things so far. He couldn't have been all bad or he wouldn't have had all these women throwing themselves at him. But I hadn't seen much to recommend him as of yet.

Grabbing a pot of coffee, I started making the rounds.

I stopped at the first table and poured while listening to chatter about the beautiful houses and buildings his firm had made, how he worked hard all the time to make sure people got what they wanted under budget and with as many extras as he could possibly give them.

The next table talked about the way he gave to charities and always came around at food drives to make sure everyone was taken care of.

Saint or sinner? I wasn't sure, maybe a little bit of both.

The next table held Craig's parents.

"My boy, my poor baby boy. He had so much life and love left in him and now it's all snuffed out."

I had tissues in my pocket from the memorial, so I handed a few over while I poured Craig's mother some more coffee. Mr. Johnson held his wife's hand and patted her back.

I knew none of these people. And that was going to be a problem when it came to trying to ferret out information. I was used to my town where everyone knew someone and someone could help. I might have to consider finding an insider. Then the trick would be in getting them to talk things up and see if I couldn't put the pieces of the puzzle together myself with the extra information.

It was worth considering, and I did just that as I continued around the room with a pot of coffee.

I found one woman sitting by herself with a sad smile on her face. Perhaps she could be my first try at getting a mole.

"So sad to see him go," I said, pouring the coffee and sidling up to her lone chair against the wall of the old case of apothecary items that Gina had inherited when she purchased the shop.

The woman gave me a weak smile. "Yes, it is. He was very generous with his time when he was alive. I don't know what we'll do without him at the club."

"The club?"

"Oh yes. It's a gentlemen's club across the river. He was a frequent visitor to my girls. He spent money often and we'll miss that."

"Of course. Well, I hope you find another patron." It wasn't the smartest thing to say, but then what did you say to someone who ran the local nudey bar lamenting that her best customer was no longer alive to shove dollar bills down ladies' G-strings?

Moving on, I went to the next grouping of people. There were enough bodies in here that seats were rotated out. As one person got up to get something else to eat or to talk with another group, someone else would take the vacant seat and strike up a conversation. They seemed to all know each other in some capacity.

If only I could find an in.

My next likely candidate had been in the middle of a group of men dressed in business suits. When she rose from the chair, she looked like a goddess. About my age, if not a little younger, with long, flowing black hair and china blue eyes. She was striking and I wondered if that was why all the men were around her.

Then one called out, "I expect a call next week for a meeting, Amanda. Don't disappoint me. I want in on that construction deal as soon as possible."

Businesswoman, perhaps a savvy one. I didn't know if I'd get her to talk to me, but it might be worth a try as she walked over to the small line waiting for the restroom.

"Can I get you anything while you wait?" I asked, hoping she might say no but that we could still talk.

"Oh, no thanks, sweetie. The last thing I need is another drink with my bladder this full. Although if you could talk our lovely barista into getting me another one of those fabulous cinnamon rolls, I certainly wouldn't object."

The line moved up and she turned away to follow it. My chance at her was lost in the line and the conversation she struck up with the woman in front of her.

I was not batting a thousand here today. I had to find a way around the insider stuff.

Who did I know on the other side of the river who I could tap for information?

After wracking my brain, I couldn't think of anyone, but then the front door opened with a tinkle and my cousin Deandra was standing in the doorway like a light. She moved in this circle. She was an interior decorator and would probably know everything I could ask for. I tried to make my way over to her, but was pulled up short by a woman who looked like she should still be in high school except for the wrinkles at the corners of her eyes.

"Do you mind finding out when this is all supposed to be over? I don't want to overstay my welcome, but it's so comfortable and cozy in here that I don't want to leave sooner than I absolutely have to either."

Her smile carried right up to her eyes. The red hair piled on top of her head made me think of a doll, and the perfect porcelain skin made me want to check to see if she had troweled makeup on or if she really was that flawless.

"I'm glad you like the atmosphere. Gina works hard to make sure everyone feels welcome here and doesn't want to leave until they have to."

"Well, you tell Gina she is doing a marvelous job." She smiled at me, crinkling those eyes, and then stuck her hand out. "Lily Kellerton."

"Tallie Graver." We shook, her hand dry and firm. A good handshake, not overpowering. Also, not one of those where I felt like I might break her, or that maybe I should lean over and buss the back of her knuckles like visiting royalty.

"Is that her?" Lily pointed over my shoulder.

I turned my head and found Gina coming out of

the back with a grin on her face. That smile fell, and so did mine, when I also saw Michelle heading her way.

Now, Michelle could have been looking for Gina to thank her for opening up the coffeehouse to hold the wake since the parlor was currently under investigation. But I didn't feel that vibe coming off her, especially with the sickly sweet and completely smarmy smile she was aiming at my best friend.

"I should go and make sure everything's okay," I said to Lily. Without waiting for a reply, I hightailed it over to Gina's side just in time.

"I don't understand why you won't let me buy it, Gina. It's a perfectly good deal and even gives you a little something extra so that you can find your true calling."

"This is not the time, and it's certainly not the place." Gina's voice was low in contrast to the high, happy voice Michelle was using. The exchange gained attention, and I braced myself. I waved to Max to turn the low music up a little bit and circle with food to distract. Not that it would probably work, but at least I would have tried.

"I think it's a perfectly good time, and this is the perfect place. I want your coffee shop. As far as my lawyer and my accountant are concerned, I have the money to not only buy it, but also to turn it into what it should be instead of what you've made it."

That was not going to go over well. I admired Gina for keeping her voice down even though her hand was fisted.

"I don't need or want your money, and the place is not for sale. If you want to buy something else and set up a competing shop, then I say go for it. You can get all the equipment you need, and the customers, and the food, and coffee presses you want, and you can make a go of it. Some. Where. Else."

"Hi, ladies." I inserted myself between the smiling buffoon and the angry best friend.

"Tallie, let it go." Gina kept her gaze on Michelle. "I can take care of myself. I believe Michelle was just leaving."

"Well, you believe wrong," Michelle answered, taking her bravado and riding it like a dying horse. "I'm not going anywhere. You're not going to kick me out of my own husband's wake, are you? That would be ludicrous, and you might not be smart, but I don't believe you're ludicrous."

My new acquaintance, Lily, came up to stand next to us. I tried to tell her not to get involved since there were already too many people paying attention, but that wasn't to be.

Lily, with her young-girl looks and her perky smile, walked right up to Michelle and smacked her across the face. We all stood there stunned, the crack was that loud.

"I'd like everyone's attention please," Lily said to the room at large. Since no one was talking after that slap, there wasn't much quieting to do. "Thank you," she continued. "I know that I'm a stranger here, but I'd just like to introduce myself." She turned to face Michelle, who held her hand against her cheek and was shocked enough from the slap to not have moved yet. "Twenty years ago, Craig Johnson and I were married. He never divorced me, which means that you, my dear, have been living a lie. You're not the widow, because I am."

Not a peep could be heard. I didn't even dare to breathe and neither did most of the rest of the room.

"If you think you have the money, or especially the taste, to remake this beautiful café, you are sadly mistaken," Lily continued. "In fact, I believe you probably have no money at all. You might want to take that into consideration before you start trying to bully people with your checkbook."

Chapter Eight

Silence reigned supreme. It was like someone had hit the mute button. And then Michelle ran from Lily as if she had set the whole place on fire. Chaos erupted in every corner. People talking and muttering, a few women yelling and swearing. Gina leaned back against the counter with her arms crossed and a small smile on her face.

"Gina," I whispered, hoping no one else would hear and that the wailing of Michelle would be enough to cover up our conversation.

"Yes, Tallie."

"Do you think it's true?"

"Oh, I wouldn't doubt it at all. Just think what that does to Michelle and her precious plans. I don't think she's going to have a pot to piss in when this woman is done with her. Have at it, Lily. Go get her."

Oh, I hadn't thought of that. Michelle had been a thorn in my side this whole time with her accusations against Gina and her bitchy, mightier-than-thou attitude. This would certainly bring her down a notch. Especially for her to think she was superior to all the "other" women only to find out that she herself was now one, too. That had to be brutal.

She deserved every second.

But she shouldn't be doing it in the middle of Gina's coffeehouse. Plus, maybe she was so rattled that she'd talk in hopes of finding a sympathetic ear. I wouldn't be sympathetic, but I certainly could listen to any story she wanted to tell. "Don't you think maybe we should give the grieving former widow a place to collect herself outside the public eye?"

Gina snorted but then she sighed. "Yes, we should. Go get her and I'll open up the office."

I threaded my way through the crowd, only to see Michelle facing off with Lily in the middle of the room. I was waiting for someone to throw the second punch of the day.

Before that could happen, I grabbed Michelle by the arm, escorting her away a few feet. Lily looked overjoyed to have put Michelle in her place, but still perfect in every way. Michelle, however, looked like she and her perfect hair had been through a wringer set on tornado speed.

Michelle took three steps with me before she realized where I was taking her.

"I do not want to go any further into the bowels of this hellhole. Someone needs to take me home right now. I don't feel well. I need to lie down."

Jeremy was there, Michelle's keys in hand, and with Max right beside him.

"I'll drive you, Mrs. Johnson, and then Max can drive me back."

Salvation in a charcoal suit. Her whole body language went from angry and combative to relieved and thankful. "If you don't mind."

"Not at all. It's part of the service at Graver's. We'll get you home safely."

I waved to Max's and Michelle's retreating backs as they headed out. Lily looked like she wanted to follow them, but Gina had a firm grip on her arm. I wanted to follow them, too, as I watched my chance to grill the woman slip through my fingers.

With the spectacle, and the woman who we all thought was the widow, gone, the party broke up pretty soon afterward, with most people walking out in clumps talking among themselves. The talk was all about this turn of events and how it might affect things in general. And now they had the whole day to gab since it was only eleven-thirty.

I had seen Drake across the room a few times, but had stayed away from him just so he wouldn't level any more charges at me. I was in enough trouble with Burton all on my own.

I avoided him again by ducking behind another gentleman when he tried to come my way. The man grabbed Drake's arm and gave him a quick shake. "You'd better fix this. I'm counting on you to get that inheritance through Michelle."

"Not here and not now." Drake narrowed his eyes at me. "There are little intrusive ears everywhere; be careful what you say."

The other man zeroed in on me. He looked vaguely familiar.

"If you're talking about this trash back here, my sister already knew how to handle her, and when Michelle told you she could handle it, she could."

I did not take kindly to being called trash no matter what the circumstances, but these were even worse.

And who knew someone could spawn two nasty people from the same family. One viler than the next.

"I think the two of you need to leave now." I said it very calmly and coolly while underneath I was steaming. I wanted Drake and Michelle's brother out of here now. "We're closing things down. You can finish your discussion elsewhere in the town or in even your cars. Not here."

Michelle's brother looked like he was ready to burst. That, fortunately, was not my problem. Drake, on the other hand, gave me the same smile he'd laid on me before handing me that fancy note on his letterhead telling me to back off.

Two could play at that game, and the first chance I got, I was giving that letter to Burton.

While I didn't want the whole world to fall apart, I found myself okay with maybe just Drake's world falling apart. My only hope being that he didn't take everyone else with him.

"You might want to watch out for that Lily." I used my nice voice, giving the illusion that I cared. "She looks sweet enough, but I feel like there might be a core of steel under that girlish exterior. Hopefully she doesn't take Craig's part of your business and dissolve it. I'm sure that would be a shame for you, especially if it's true that you're not making the kind of money you needed to in order to support your expansion. Maybe instead of flirting with the not-real Mrs. Johnson, you should take your charms to the new Mrs. Johnson."

I left Drake with his jaw clenched and his temper rising in his eyes. I turned my back on him and retreated before he could say anything to me, and I called that a win all the way around.

* * *

With everyone out of the Bean, I cleaned as best I could while listening to Jeremy talk to Gina. I was eavesdropping again, but it was for a good reason. I wanted to know where they were going to dinner, and if I might be invited, too. I highly doubted that last one, although if I knew the destination maybe I could just talk Max into taking me to the same restaurant.

Either way I wanted to know what was going on. That seemed to be a theme in my life right now, and a parallel theme seemed to be that everyone was keeping me out. How was I supposed to get anything done if no one would tell me what the heck was going down?

Jeremy shot me a look and waved his hand at me to tell me to leave. Fat chance of that.

"So where are you guys going to dinner tomorrow?" Since no one was going to tell me voluntarily, I had no other recourse.

"You're not coming, so don't expect an answer. This is between me and Gina. It does not need your interference at all."

I huffed because of course I wasn't going to interfere. I was a noninterfering kind of woman. I just wanted to know what was going on so I could be prepared for any contingency.

I was also lying to myself. I wanted to know because ultimately, I was just that nosy.

I did have other things to do, though, with this new twist of a real first wife, which left the current wife a mistress instead of a wife. Michelle was probably having a conniption fit at her house. If it was even still her house. I saw a lot of research in my future.

What was already complicated had just become convoluted. And I just wanted Gina off the hook for Craig's murder. There was no way she had hurt Brenna, and if Burton even hinted that he thought Gina had, I might just do him some bodily harm. To hell with the consequences. Once everything was cleaned and soaking, Jeremy left and Gina said she just wanted to rest. Neither of them would tell me where they were going to dinner tomorrow. The dinner I was not invited to.

Since I had time on my hands after snagging a sandwich for lunch, and Max had gotten a work call that he was taking in my apartment, I decided to head down to the station.

Suzy sat at the front desk in the police station. The second she saw me come in the front door, she buried her head in a novel.

"Come on, now, Suzy. I'm not going to go away until you tell me where Burton is. I have info for him, and I'd like to see if he has any info he wants to share with me."

She rolled her eyes as she set the steamy romance down. I approved of her tastes and might have to find a copy of the book for my own, if only for the hot guy on the cover.

"You know he's not going to tell you anything," she said. "He's going to want to have the info coming in, not going out. Why do you have such a hard time understanding that? Burton is a private man and likes to solve things himself. And, well, you tend to step all over his toes."

Censure was not a new thing to me. As always, I just barreled over it. "And yet I still want to see him, and he's going to want to talk with me. Right about now would be good. I'm just saying." Repeating myself was not my favorite thing, but she hadn't moved, so I persisted. "I have info, and he's going to want it, and I'm not leaving it at the desk."

She did some hemming and some hawing of her own. I took note of the effective technique to add it to my repertoire for my car ride with Max as we looked for restaurants, and my brother, tomorrow night.

In the end, she called Burton in his office, and I literally heard him growling my name all the way at the front of the building. He could deal with it.

Straightening his tie and looking right at me, he made his way up the hallway. Maybe he had tried to hang himself with it when he heard my name. Who knew? And I didn't care.

"You might as well come on back. I have ten minutes. You can have five of them. No more."

Looking at the clock on the station wall, I wondered where he was going at twelve-thirty in the afternoon. Not that it was any of my business. Maybe it was lunch, but maybe it would have to be on hold once I told him everything I'd found out.

I mentally composed what I was going to say, and how I was going to say it, to cram it all into five minutes. Spitefully, I decided I'd watch the clock and at five minutes I'd stop totally and make him ask me nicely to continue.

After five minutes, I had just gotten to the point where Lily had announced that Michelle was mistaken about her widowhood. . . . And then I trailed off and didn't say another word.

"That's it? You can't leave me hanging like that."

"My five minutes are up. I don't want to take any

more of your time. I'm sure you have other, more important things to do than figure out the murder. Actually, I guess this really doesn't have anything to do with the murder, and so I shouldn't have brought it to you at all." Would I ever live down the irresponsible person I'd been when I was Mrs. Walden Phillips the Third? Burton and I had had run-ins before, but the way he dismissed my ideas made me think I would never get through to him.

I expected a big sigh from him or the pinching of the bridge of his nose, maybe even rubbing his chin or covering his eyes. What I did not expect was for him to laugh out loud. A really long laugh that nearly shook the walls and definitely shook his shoulders.

"You've got me. You have totally got me. And it would make sense that you would be the one to best me. I knew years ago, way before Waldo, that you'd be a thorn in my side."

"So glad to not disappoint." I sank back into my chair, completely defeated.

"Now, don't go getting all pouty. It's meant as a compliment. Do you remember when you wanted the albino squirrel that ran around your backyard protected? You wanted color-accurate road signs posted so that people wouldn't think it was a fly-away trash bag and accidentally run it over. It was so important to you that you started a petition and had over fifty signatures. I ordered a deer-crossing sign, then tacked a drawing of the squirrel to the front of the sign."

God, that had been forever ago, maybe when I was about five. I was definitely precocious even at a young age. I still hadn't figured out exactly why I had agreed to marry someone who had wanted to cut that part out of me, but I might never know.

"So, yeah, I knew what I was up against from the beginning. You just went astray with that jerk Waldo. Now that you're back, I'm going to have to remember that the thorn in my side can also be what gets me back on the right track."

I was quite honestly speechless. Who had taken my Chief Burton and how did we keep the old one from ever coming back?

"Not a word from you, huh? Okay then. Let's do this. You write out all the things you know. Give it to Suzy, she'll make a copy. I'll look it over tonight, then tomorrow we'll talk about it."

I finally found my voice, though I had to dig hard for it. "Are you really serious, or are you just pulling my leg to get all the info? I'll give this to you, then you won't talk to me at all and fine me for obstruction of justice or framing someone, or something else that will get me out of your hair?"

He shook his head. "No, I'm really very serious. I can't have you helping in an official capacity, but if you happen to bring the facts to me and we talk about it, then I guess that's the way it's just going to have to be. Although I have some restrictions and some rules."

"I'm not going to like either one of those, am I?" I sat forward in the chair, no longer feeling the need to shrink away from his displeasure.

"Maybe, maybe not, but you have to follow them if you want to help. Look, I love Gina. I've known her since she was little, and Mama Shirley and I are cousins, which makes us blood. But I have to find the person who did this. I have to look at all avenues. This job is about serving the community, not favoring my relatives and looking the other way."

This was not new to me. I had plenty of relatives who wouldn't give me the easy way out. But that usually involved making the sauerkraut for New Year's Day or poking fun at me when I finally left Waldo. This was murder, and Burton had to know that his cousin once removed would never do something like that. Frowning at me, he leaned forward, breaking into my thoughts. He must have said something I had missed in my musings.

"Sorry about that. Just trying to remember if I fed Mr. Fleefers today."

"Right, anyway. Rule Number One, and this is a big one—you do not put yourself in harm's way."

I was quick to agree. "I can do that." My last brush with a killer had not exactly been a picnic. I was in no rush to repeat the whole hiding-in-a-drop-bottomed coffin thing. I didn't fear tight spaces, but I had feared I wasn't going to be quick enough to escape before it became my real coffin.

"Number Two. You can bring me things you find, or happen to overhear, as a concerned citizen, but you are not an investigator. I do not want you violating other people's rights by sneaking around in places you don't belong or pretending to be something you're not."

I opened my mouth. Ignoring me, he kept right on talking over me.

"These are nonnegotiable, and this is on a case by case basis. I don't need you out there being an amateur sleuth. You want to do something like that, then go join the police academy and get hired here like everyone else."

I paused to think about the possibilities there.

He shook his head. "Don't even do that. Your dad

would kill me and your mother would take my head as a trophy. I remember when Dylan wanted to get into the police academy. Your parents absolutely forbade it. That's why he took up landscaping. Don't tempt them to put you on lockdown, even if you are technically an adult."

"Can I talk now?" I asked after a long pause where he just stared at me.

"I suppose."

"I appreciate your vast belief in my accomplishments, but I can't promise that I'm not going to ever get in trouble or fake something to get information. You guys do it by the book, but don't you think that you have a unique opportunity here to let me do my thing and hand stuff over to you through the proper channels?"

After a pause, he shook his head again. "No, I don't, because some of the stuff you think you might get could be thrown out in court." He rapped his knuckles on his desk.

"I suppose that does make sense." I still thought my idea was better, but I wasn't going to argue about it. I had other, more important things to tell him. "So, it turns out that the widow isn't actually the widow since she was never legally married to the dead guy."

"*What?*" He rose halfway out of his chair, then settled back down with his arms crossed over his chest.

"Yep. Right after we got to the Bean I was talking to a woman named Lily Kellerton, who walked over to Michelle, slapped her, and told her that she was not going to inherit anything because it all belongs to this Lily, whom no one knows anything about."

"Good Lord, so the plot thickens. This means I

can't talk to Michelle anymore about the deceased, or about anything having to do with him."

"I don't think she cares." Wailing erupted from the lobby of the police station. "Or, I didn't think she cared," I said.

It was definitely Michelle. She must have gotten herself back together quickly since Jeremy had only driven her home an hour ago. Or at least together enough to drive back into town intent on chaos. Currently, she was throwing a tantrum of monumental proportions. Again.

I thought it might be a bad idea for Michelle to see me. I didn't want to make her lose her mind even more, so I stayed back in Burton's office after he very pointedly told me not to touch a single thing or the whole deal was off. I sat on my hands just in case as I listened to Michelle plead her case.

I almost felt sorry for her as she started the sob story of her non-widowhood. Almost. Until she slammed something into the counter and went on a tangent.

"I want that bitch, Gina, tested for those poisons. I want every cabinet and drawer searched in her store. I think she poisoned him. I think she put something in his coffee, something that killed him that night, and I want her taken out and hanged for her crimes against my husband."

Who was going to be the first to tell her that they couldn't talk to her anymore?

Dead silence for at least a minute as I leaned further and further forward in my chair. I could hear the clock tick down the hallway and the low hum of the computer on Burton's desk.

"I'm very sorry, ma'am, but in light of recent discoveries we can't talk to you about Craig Johnson's case."

"What? What did you say?" There was a scrambling noise, then something fell, and when Burton spoke next, he was out of breath.

"Do not come over the counter at me like that again. I will have you arrested for assault and then you can sit in my jail until I'm done with you."

I moved around the desk to see if there was a clear visual shot to the front and found that there was a camera feed on Burton's desk. I sat in his chair and leaned in to catch everything on the visual as well as hear everything from down the hall.

In Technicolor, he straightened his shirt, then ran a hand over his hair. "Now, you either stay over there or I will have someone restrain you. Are we clear?"

She snarled at him, her lip rising over her teeth.

"I'm going to take that as a 'no we don't understand each other' and have my deputy come in unless you answer me in five, four, three, two—"

After throwing her hands up in the air, she tugged on the ends of her hair until they looked like they would break. "Fine! Fine, I'll stop, but I want you to explain to me why you can't talk to me. The man is my husband. I demand you let me know what you've been able to uncover."

"I'm so sorry, Michelle, but the question of your status as the wife is a problem. Until we figure that out, I can't share anything with you."

"But I have the marriage certificate," she screamed. The hands came off her hair and waved around in the air. She was going to hit something, or someone, whether she meant to or not, if she didn't calm herself down. "You can't take the word of some crazy woman who just walked into town. We've been married for years. Years! And now he's dead, and you're trying to take him from me."

That was a far cry from the way she had been speaking when I cleaned her house the day before the funeral. Then, her determination to eradicate him overpowered any other emotion. She'd wanted to get rid of all his stuff just so she could redecorate and forget he'd ever existed. Maybe it was grief, but I doubted it. I was pretty sure she was possessive now because if he was dead, and they weren't married, then she had nothing at all.

Burton stood with his arms crossed, not giving an inch. "Bring the certificate in. I'll get a hold of this other paperwork, and we'll see what we can do. I understand that's not what you want, but it's the way it has to be. I'm sorry."

In the monitor, I saw Michelle's head droop and her shoulders with it. What did she expect? She wasn't the wife unless she could prove it. And not being the wife put her in a position of absolutely no power.

"I still think you might want to look at the apothecary cabinet that Gina has," she said in a far more subdued voice. "The poison had to come from somewhere and there are a lot of different bottles in there that have been there for years. You don't know what she could have done. She was mad enough to say she was going to boil him in coffee. Poisoning his coffee would have been easy enough for her."

I ground my teeth in Burton's office as he answered.

"I will certainly look into that. I know you're concerned. We are as committed as possible to finding out what happened to him. I'm just not going to be able to discuss the details with you other than as a concerned citizen. Now, please go home. See what you can find in your paperwork. Bring it back to me so I can start one of my guys on a search. We'll figure this out."

"You'd better, and if it's Gina, you'd better bring her down hard before I get to her." The snarl came flying back, her head erect, the veins in her neck straining.

"I wouldn't go bandying around threats like that if I were you." Burton didn't move, yet even I could tell his patience was thinning.

"You're not me. I'm not even sure who me is anymore." She buried her face in her hands, making me shake my head.

I probably should have felt sorry for her for possibly losing everything, even her name, but she was trying to throw my best friend under the bus for something she didn't do. I couldn't, let's be honest, I wouldn't, forgive her for that. She'd made her bed; now she'd have to snuggle on into the mess that was her life and leave Gina out of it. Something had to give here, and I knew precisely what I needed to do. I just had to wait for Michelle to leave. I didn't think she'd want to see me at this point. I knew for a fact I didn't want to see her.

After waiting ten minutes, watching the small monitor in Burton's office, I quickly jumped out of his chair when he disappeared from the screen. He came into the office with narrowed eyes.

"You were awfully quiet back here. I didn't see a single piece of you peeking around the corner to get a better view of what was going on."

"Just staying out of the way like you told me to." I threw out as much of an innocent vibe as I could muster. "And I could hear her all the way down the hall, so there was no need to come find out what she was saying."

"Okay then. This poison thing. I'm going to have to look into it."

"I know. I'll let Gina know." My stomach hurt and my head started pounding.

"You can't let her know anything, Tallie. I already sent one of the officers over to get into the cabinet. I can't have her hiding anything because she had prior notice."

Gina was going to be pissed, but there was nothing I could do about it at this point. "Okay, so do you really think that might be what happened? Someone took something out of the cabinet and dosed his coffee?"

Gina had an old roster of everything that was in there. As far as I knew she hadn't opened the thing in years and many of the bottles were empty. It was just for show, after all. And Gina was the only one with the key that unlocked it. I needed to get to Gina now so we could start gathering our own evidence and finding names and reasons that the culprit would have been anyone but her. I couldn't remember if she had any hemlock in that cabinet. I hoped she knew and could show very clearly that the bottle was empty and had been for years. What would it take for them to believe it wasn't from her place if there was even a trace of the poison in an old glass bottle?

When I asked, Burton told me he couldn't answer that. "Just report anything that's out of the ordinary. I'd warn you to not go looking for stuff, but since it seems to find you regardless, I'd be an idiot to not have you tell me the things you learn."

Not the most ringing of endorsements, but not a no either.

Okay, I'd have to go about this the old-fashioned way.

I left the police station, intending to call my cousin Matt, who was with the police, as soon as I got far enough to pull over and make a call. He'd tell me what he knew and then we could get on our way with looking for clues. But when I got to my car, Michelle was standing next to my passenger door looking as if the weight of the world was sitting on her shoulders.

It was so tempting to just get in the car and leave, to ignore the fact that tears streamed down her face and if she hunched her shoulders anymore her chin would be tucked into her belly button. It had been an extremely long day already and it was only two in the afternoon.

"Oh, for heaven's sake, spit it out. What do you want? Another go at Gina? Another session of blaming her for Craig's shortcomings?"

"No." She gulped and spoke louder. "No, I need you to find out who did this, and I want to know who this new woman is."

"Look it up on the Internet. I'm not sure what your game is, but you've thrown Gina under the bus every chance you get. My best friend did not kill Craig. She had no intention of seeing him ever again. He's the one who came by her house and threw flowers

at my boyfriend thinking he was there for Gina. He's
the one who somehow snuck into Gina's stairwell
and then fell down the stairs to his death. She had
nothing to do with any of that. She thought she was
meeting a nice guy off the Internet and instead she
got this."

"I know, and I'm sorry."

I snorted.

"No, really I am." She moved around the hood of
the car to stand in front of me. I opened my door just
to keep something between us. She could go from
hot to cold in an instant. I'd seen it happen before. I
didn't know what, if anything, she had with her. She
could still be the killer, trying to foist it off on everyone else simply because it was the easiest way to
deflect attention from the fact that she'd finally had
enough and had killed her own husband.

"And how do I know you didn't kill him? You could
have just as easily slipped something into his dinner
or something into a drink."

She shook her head so hard her hair flew around.
"Never. I loved him."

"That's not exactly the way it came off when we
were cleaning your house."

Tears ran down her face and they looked real this
time, real distress and real heartbreak.

"I was so distraught and thought I just wanted to
move on without him because of the way he'd looked
at Gina. He never looked at me like that, like he
thought I was everything. When I found him in
the coffeehouse I've wanted for years, eyeing up the
owner with those roses that he used to bring me

before we got married, I lost it. I wanted to throw everything out."

Now that I could understand.

"Is that why you keep blaming Gina? Because you want her to pay for him looking at her like that?"

Using the heels of her hands, she dug into her cheeks to get rid of the tears. "Yes, I'm sorry, but yes. It still hurts, and I want someone to pay. I swear to you I didn't kill him. I don't really even think Gina did. But someone poisoned him, and now I might never know who because the police won't talk to me anymore because they're not sure if I'm his real wife or just another 'other' woman." A sob broke free. "My God, I don't even know what to do. She could take everything we have."

I let her sob it out. There was nothing I could do for her, and I didn't know if she would want comfort from me. It did put a little hitch in my anger toward her as I watched her, though. I wasn't completely heartless. I ended up patting her on the back. Before I knew it, she was hugging me tight and shedding tears all over my shoulder.

She backed away after a few moments, obviously trying to compose herself. "I'm sorry. You don't even know me, and until a few minutes ago, I hated you almost as much as I hated Gina."

So much hatred and angst. She lived in a world where she never got what she wanted. I tried to imagine myself there and couldn't. My life might not be awesome right now, but I had a lot of good things going on and I was thankful for every one of them. I softened, just a little, not enough to feel bad for her but at least enough to feel pity. "Maybe you should go home and see what's there."

"Will you come with me?"

Well, I certainly hadn't expected that. And yet, it could give me just the access I had been looking for.

"Of course." That mental calendar I kept in my head was whirling through the things I had to do today. I had two houses to clean this evening, spaced hours apart. I had the time.

At this point, I'd make the time if I had to. No one was off the hook completely until we found out who had killed Craig and hurt Brenna. It could be the same person, or two separate ones, but someone was responsible for the pain caused to both parties. I didn't want any more to happen before I found out who had come to town with vengeance on their mind and poison in their pocket.

Chapter Nine

I made a quick call to Gina to update her while Michelle got into her car.

I still didn't trust Michelle completely, but what she had said made sense. I'd have to go with my gut on this one, praying I wasn't wrong. Being at the house would at least give me the lay of the land and I could find out what Michelle thought she had on Gina that would prove her guilt.

"I'm working on it," I said after Gina warned me for the fourth time to please be careful.

"I know that, but this is not all about you figuring it out. I want you safe more. This has gotten out of hand. I can't believe the police are here taking those old bottles out of the cabinet. Some of that stuff is over a hundred years old. They could harm someone just by opening the stopper."

I hadn't considered that. "Hopefully they're being careful. I don't think they really believe you did it, but they have to follow all avenues while I can just get right to the pieces that will make this whole picture fit."

"Fine, but you'd better not come back dead."

"Thank you so much for the warm wishes."

"It's what I do." She hung up before I could shoot a zinger back at her.

We pulled up in front of Michelle's house only to find that there was no room for us in the driveway. A huge moving truck took up half the driveway and a small compact took up the other half because of the way it was parked.

Stopping my car at the curb behind Michelle's, we both got out and convened in front of my car.

"This has to be her." Anger was a mild word for the venomous tone in Michelle's voice.

"Yeah, I don't think there's much doubt about that, but how did she get in?"

I saw no evidence of anyone outside. Inside, though, there was plenty of noise. Did we knock on the door? Or just walk in since Michelle did own the house, too?

"Is your name on the mortgage?" I asked, hoping she'd say yes.

"No," she whispered. "Craig thought it would be better if everything was in his name so that it could all be a tax write-off."

Oh man. I didn't say that out loud because I didn't want to make her even more upset. The tears sparkled in her eyes again, and I thought she might need a drink of water soon, just to stay hydrated.

"Okay, let me call this in to the police. We'll see what can be done."

I didn't call the local police in Harrisburg, even though they would have been the smart choice and probably the right one. I highly doubted Burton had any jurisdiction over here across the river, but I at least needed to know what my options were.

"What do you have for me now, Tallie?" Burton rattled out as soon as he picked up. "And it had better not be another dead body."

"No, I promise, it's not that." I turned away from Michelle and lowered my voice. She could probably still hear me, but at least I was trying to be discreet. "Michelle and I are at Craig's house and there's a huge moving van and a car. People are moving around inside. Michelle says she didn't authorize anyone to go into the house. What can we do?"

"Sit tight, don't move. I'll call a buddy of mine and have him come out."

"You want us to just stand outside here and hope no one sees us? That no one comes out for a confrontation?"

"Your mind is a terrifying place. They probably don't even see you, and it's a public road. You could be going to the bookstore across the street. I saw it when we had to go tell Michelle about Craig's death. In fact, why don't you go there? Don't worry so much. Someone will be there in a little while. Just keep your cool until they show up."

Of course, not thirty seconds passed after I hung up with Burton that Lily came floating out of the house as if she were greeting party guests.

"Tallie, and dear Michelle. Is there something I can do for you?"

"You can get out of my house!" Michelle marched up onto the small front lawn with her hands on her hips. I was moving before I could stop myself and got right in between them. I did not want Michelle throwing any punches when the cops got here.

"Oh dear, we have a problem. You see, this is my house," Lily replied.

"Why can't you just stop?" I moved to the right

a little to block all view of Michelle behind me. I wanted Lily to focus only on me. "He just died. Michelle had no idea about you and within hours you're taking over her stuff. This can't be legal. Even if it is, you could at least give her a chance to get her own stuff out before you go steamrolling through. There has to be a law against this. You have no idea if Craig divorced you without you getting paperwork for it. You have no idea if your marriage is even still legal. And you certainly can't think that everything in this house, including the house, is yours."

Despite my vehemence, she just laughed in my face.

"You don't think I would have checked all of that out before I came winging in here? I've got the papers to prove my marriage. I already spoke with the Harrisburg police and plan on dropping them off to your chief of police as soon as I'm done here."

I'd have to ask Burton what they said when he got them. I pulled myself back to the conversation because she was still talking. I didn't want to miss what she had to say.

"I ignored Craig for years. But I decided I wanted a real divorce, to make sure that I was free of him because I have new plans of my own to make happen. Was it coincidence or fate that I come into town just as he dies and everything I've already made sure is mine is actually mine?" She smiled.

I laid a hand on Michelle's arm to keep her from pouncing on the other woman.

"Now, dear Michelle, I was going to talk with him about divorcing and splitting everything in half so that he could marry you for real. I wanted my share, though. I built my own life hours away where we had lived together after marrying. I started keeping my eyes and ears open for any sign of him about a year ago when I realized that I should be free to pursue my own dreams and life. Early on it was convenient to stay a missus and let him do whatever floated his boat, but not anymore. So I started looking for him in earnest. I knew about his roving eye from our early years together and figured it would get him into trouble at some point. Who knew that it would happen just as I was coming in for the kill?" She covered her mouth as she giggled. "I guess that's probably not the most appropriate way to put it. Freudian slip. I didn't really kill him, but I was going to take him to court for half of everything I should have had all these years after he walked out on me. And now what's his is mine."

She broke eye contact with Michelle to lock gazes with me while she continued to smile. "So no, I don't think I will wait. This is all just falling right into a neat little plan, and now I don't have to pay for lawyers. I don't have to try to split things evenly. It's all mine. And unless Michelle earned any of the money that went into the buying and stocking of this house, then I say she has no right to anything."

That last part was apparently too much for Michelle. She came around me swinging and knocked Lily right to the ground with a left hook that I was both horrified by and mightily impressed with.

And it didn't surprise me in the least when that was the moment the cops pulled up with Burton right behind them.

* * *

"Why is Michelle here in your jail when her crime was committed across the river?" I sat in Burton's visitor's chair, flipping a pen around and around my fingers.

"Because that police department had some sort of drug bust last night. They don't have any more room until they process everyone. So, she's our guest for the moment." Stacks of paper sat in front of him. He'd sign one, then move it to another pile, sign another and move it to a different pile. Who knew police work involved so many dead trees?

"Why didn't you tell me Lily had let you know her marriage license was coming to you?"

"Because it didn't concern you."

"And yet it did."

"Point taken, but we are still operating on a need-to-know basis, and I had no idea she was going to swoop in like that and start cleaning out the house."

I made a disgruntled noise, but kept going. "Did you take Michelle's statement already?"

Burton's forehead creased as he continued to stare down at the papers. I wasn't sure I wanted him to look at me with that scowl on his face. It might freeze me for eternity.

He smoothed out his brow before lifting his head and clasping his hands together in front of him on the desk. "Yes, Tallie, I processed her. I asked her for her statement. I even gave her the one phone call, but she wanted to call you, and since you were already here I thought that might be unnecessary."

"Does Michelle want to talk to me?" I nearly bounced in my seat. "Maybe she'll admit something she hasn't already."

His eyes narrowed. "There is nothing more to

admit. This is a separate incident from Craig's death at this point. I still have to try to find some information on the woman who swore she might be pregnant. Which she wasn't, by the way. It was a ruse. She doesn't even have the parts to be pregnant."

"What? Was Craig making time with men and women? How did he ever get any work done?"

His disgusted sigh should have aggravated me. Instead, it made me smile.

"I'm sorry. You left yourself wide open for that one. I'm assuming you mean that she's had a hysterectomy or something."

"Yes, she doesn't have a uterus, so there's no way she could have been pregnant. Which means that if someone hurt her thinking she was pregnant, it's an even more senseless act than we thought."

"Oh man."

"Right. So now I have a death and two assaults. I'm a little busy here right now for you to sit in my chair and play with my pens. You have to have something to do. Clean a house. Get a funeral going? I can't have you sitting in here all day and distracting me."

"Sure. I get it. Can I talk to Michelle before I go? If she wanted to call me, I really think there's value in at least seeing what she has to say. I'm surprised she had no one else to call. I would have thought she would have at least called Craig's partner, Drake. Or her brother."

"No, no call to Drake Fuller. In fact, I asked her about that, and she said she just wasn't ready to deal with him and his issues when she had so many of her own going on. She was even more close-lipped about her brother."

Interesting. I figured I might have to talk to the

brother eventually but truly didn't want to. Instead I added Drake to the list of people I should talk to in between house cleanings tomorrow. I would make sure my customers got their money's worth, but there would be no extras. At this point, maybe I'd need to take Max up on his offer to help, since we could be done that much sooner.

With everything that had gone on today, I wasn't going to get a chance to just hang with Max until much later.

For every step forward I might have taken, I kept getting rocked back at least fourteen. And instead of just one murder and one bad guy, now I had this convoluted mess to unravel before I could even begin to figure out why someone would truly want Craig dead. It could have been his partner who wanted his wife for himself, the secretary who wanted Craig for herself, the woman who was willing to fake a pregnancy to claim a man who was never going to be hers, one of the scorned women coming after him for lying about being single. It could have been Michelle, who thought she was a wife and who wasn't, or the wife whom no one had known about and yet probably was. Maybe even Michelle's brother, who had threatened Drake at the funeral after-party. That last one I wasn't sure about, but he had seemed nasty and that was enough to make it on my list at this point.

I really needed my pad of paper, but there was little hope of having time with it until after my jobs were done. I needed something portable to take with me, but I'd have to come up with an alternative for that later.

I called Max and asked him to meet me at Buffy Hoffington's place at four-thirty. Timing would be tight, but it was a weekly cleaning job and Mr. Hoffington usually picked up after himself. No socks crammed in the sofa would be nice.

Arriving at Buffy's, Max and I emerged from our cars at the same time. My Lexus had seen better days, but at least it ran nicely. Max had an SUV that could probably hold a football team. I had never understood why he needed that much room for one person, but who was I to question his vehicle of choice? I knew he wasn't compensating for anything, so maybe there was another reason he felt the need to drive what looked like a bus on oversized tires.

He grabbed me up in a hug and kissed me on my cheek. Someone swished the curtain at the front window, so I pushed away from Max.

"You are too much. This is a small town and people like to talk."

"So let them talk. What do we care?"

"We don't, but technically I'm on a job and you're my help. The boss shouldn't be messing with the employee."

I laughed at the dumbfounded look on his face.

"We can go back to just boyfriend and girlfriend after we clean up at the Hoffingtons'."

"As long as you promise."

"Absolutely."

He patted me on the butt on our way up the walkway. I let that one slide since no one would have been able to see it. Buffy opened the door before I could knock.

"Is this the young man I keep hearing about? Quite the step up from Walden."

I blushed. I didn't quite know why, except that I

disliked talking about my former, and now dead, husband in front of Max.

When Max was with me I tried to keep things light and fun. We were still in the beginning stages of this relationship and it was taking longer because of the distance between us. He lived three hours away, so we weren't in each other's circles constantly. We didn't know what life would be like if we lived in the same town and frequented the same restaurants with friends, or wound up at the grocery store at the same time. I didn't think I was ready for that just yet, so I hadn't encouraged Max to move himself up here, and I wasn't ready to uproot my life once again to move down there. Plus, I wouldn't have work down there, nor would I have any friends. When the time came, I guess Max would move up here, but working for the government the way he did, on a tax task force, might not be a telecommuter position.

Which is why I tried not to spend much time thinking about it.

"This is Max and he's going to be helping me out today so that we can get the job done quickly for you. Sorry I'm later than usual. I hope I won't mess up your dinnertime."

"It's not a problem at all, dear Tallie. I've heard you're out there putting yourself in danger again to try to solve another murder."

Where did people hear these kinds of things?

"Not that it's any of my business, young lady, but you need to watch yourself. You have far more to live for now. You don't want someone to snuff you out just because you couldn't keep your nose out of things that the police should be taking care of."

I started to form a rebuttal, then I remembered Buffy was Burton's aunt. Not worth going there with her.

"Thanks for the warning. The only reason I'm helping this time is because someone is trying to make it look like Gina did the deed, and I know it wasn't her."

"Oh, that Gina makes the best café au lait. Don't you agree, Max?"

"Absolutely, ma'am."

"And he's a gentleman," the older woman cooed.

"Yes, a gentleman who's going to come in and help me clean your house as soon as you let us in the door." I smiled but really I was itching to just get in and get this done so we could move on. The partner, Drake Fuller, was on my list as the first person I wanted to talk to. I wanted his side of the story about Michelle. There was no way that a woman like her would have been unaware of his interest in her. I wanted to know how far things had gone, or if she'd rebuffed him, and he thought the only true way to get Craig out of the picture so that life could go on the way it should have before Craig had shown up was to take Craig out of the equation permanently.

We swept, we vacuumed, we cleaned dishes and wiped down counters. I did find one sock on the staircase to the second floor, but that was far preferable to the house being a mess that I not only had to straighten first but then go back through and really clean afterward.

Buffy followed Max around wherever he went. Fortunately, he was good about it, engaging her in conversation. Talking to her about investments and showing a far larger working knowledge of the stock market than I had even known existed. Mr. Hoffington was into the stock market and that was how I had met them when I was married to Walden Phillips the Third.

Waldo had ended up being a dirty dealer, but Mr. Hoffington was always on the up-and-up. He and Max got into a spirited discussion about the index, and I just kept on cleaning. I wasn't planning on paying Max, anyway, so anything he did was just one more thing I didn't have to do in the long list of cleaning chores.

Finally, an hour and a half later, we were done. I had to practically drag Max out of the house away from both Hoffingtons.

"You and your beau should come for dinner one night, Tallie. We'd love to get to know him better and reacquaint ourselves with this very different version of you." She smiled when she issued the invitation.

The smile made me feel better about my transformation. There was still more work to do, but her words gave me hope and added oomph to my optimism. "That would be wonderful. Let me see when Max will be back in town, and we'll get something set up."

Holding hands, Max and I walked back to our cars.

"Well, that was unexpected," I said as we neared my car. Max trotted around the fender to open the door before I could get there. "Thanks."

"Of course. I'm a gentleman, after all." He laughed. "They seem like really nice people."

"I think they are, and I think I underestimated them because of how far up in the sky my nose was thrust when I was a Phillips the Third. I'm glad they liked you, and by extension I like that I'm liked again."

"Maybe this Tallie is the real Tallie and the other one was just trying to find her way."

"Maybe." His insight made me think for a moment. Maybe that was what had happened. It could be that I was looking for something and only found it when I was myself instead of who I thought I wanted to be.

He kissed me on the tip of my nose. "Well, I really . . . like this Tallie."

There had been a hesitation there, one I was almost sure would have led to a different *L* word if it had been another time and another place. My heart sank a little that I might just be being fanciful, but I couldn't help the little spark of hope. Of course, there was no saying that I couldn't be the first one to declare my love.

All in good time. My hope was that we'd have years together. Saying "I love you" at this very moment, outside someone's house where we'd just been up to our elbows in bleach to clean toilets, might not be the big romantic gesture that I hoped I might get some day.

I jumped to the next subject because I didn't want to think too hard about this one right now. "It's six. Do you think we should go talk to that partner of Craig's? I have a few questions, and he must be ready to talk a little bit more since I can't imagine he'd been aware of a first wife, either."

"And there you go, straight back to work. I like that about you, too."

He kissed me on the nose again, tucked me into the car, then shut my door. Many people thought chivalry was dead, or they didn't need someone to open or close a door because they were fiercely independent.

For myself, I knew I could do it myself, and I was still fiercely independent, but also knew that Max enjoyed opening my door. And it didn't hurt me to let him.

He patted the top of my car, then jogged over to his own. We got on the road with me leading the way to the construction offices of Johnson and Fuller. We'd see what we found there, or if Drake would even agree to see us. Time would tell. But I didn't have a lot of time left before Burton had to at least look like he was close to catching the killer, who had already taken a life and possibly almost taken another. There was no way Burton could blame Brenna's injuries on Gina, but he could certainly try to nail her with Craig's death just to make it look like he wasn't being negligent.

The offices of Johnson and Fuller sat on the corner of Third Street and Capitol Avenue. They too were across the river. My great aunt would have had a heart attack at how often I was moving back and forth, but really it was about a fifteen-minute drive.

I needed to get something to eat soon since the sandwich from earlier was wearing off. For my stomach's sake, I'd have to make sure I kept this brief and to the point.

I found a parking spot and Max parked right next to me. Almost every space was taken, but that was likely due to the woman-centric gym next door. I checked all the tire sizes on the cars with a glance just in case I saw any big ones. Mama Shirley's description of the car the night of the murder hadn't helped so far, but I was leaving no stone unturned.

Entering the building, though, I was pretty sure no one was next door sweating off cheeseburgers, because it looked like every car had dumped out its people in here.

It took me about ten minutes to sort out who everyone was. Some of them initially refused to tell me their names. To be honest, I was a little surprised that anyone actually answered me. In the end, even the refusers decided to jump in with their names because they didn't want to be left out. It wasn't like I had any authority, but once Max started asking questions as a tax agent of the government, people babbled to keep up with what all he wanted to know.

Finally, we ended up standing in the middle of an attorney for Michelle, two for Lily, another for the company, and a fifth for Drake personally. Three accountants stood in the room also, and poor Noreen sat at her desk looking around at everyone as if she wasn't quite sure what to do or whom to offer coffee to first.

"Can I ask why everyone is here at this precise moment?" Max asked into the suddenly quiet room, once the introductions had been made.

The lawyer for Michelle, a Peter Skandish who was very proud to let you know he was an esquire, pulled the lapels of his charcoal suit down to straighten them. "I'm here to make sure that the interests of my client are not overlooked as everyone else goes about squalling for what they think is theirs. Michelle Johnson worked and lived with Craig for ten years. While she might not have had a direct hand in the making or running of this business on paper, she still supported Craig for years as his fledgling company became a thriving business. She will not be left out."

"Except that she was never legally married to Mr. Johnson." This from Walter Masterson. He wore a deep blue suit with a red tie and had a mane of white hair. He was one of the two lawyers representing Lily. "Without a legal marriage, she's entitled to nothing. My client has been married to the deceased for twenty years. She spent a lot of that time trying to look for him and possibly reconcile. The fact that he is now dead means that the chance for reconciliation is gone and so she will have to make do with inheriting his business. She is the only one legally able to step in and take things over."

"None of you are dividing up anything," Drake chimed in finally. I'd watched his face turning redder and redder and his knuckles get whiter and whiter where he gripped the edge of the desk he was leaning against. "Craig and I talked about it and his will very clearly states that all shares go to me. Nothing but the house goes to Michelle. He was planning on leaving her anyway, and while he didn't want to leave her destitute, he was not planning on providing for her for the rest of her life. He left her enough to start up the coffee shop she wanted and the house. The rest is to come to me. I pay her a portion of what we make every month and that's it." His eyes took on a fierce cast. Added to the fact that I knew he thought Michelle walked on water and probably had loved her for years, this must have been a blow *and* a blessing for Drake. Now he could have the woman he loved and take care of her financially, but never have to worry about her selling his company out from under him if she decided she was tired of footing the bill for a construction firm she had no part in.

I wondered if he still wanted her now that she was being accused of assault—and now that he might have to kowtow to another partner.

"You can't do that," the second lawyer for Lily said. I didn't remember his name but I felt like it might have rhymed with jerk. His nose in the air and his pointy shoes shined to an almost blinding sheen, he got right in Drake's face. "Unless you have proper documentation with Lily Johnson's signature on it, a husband cannot sign away his entire fortune with the widow still alive." He shot his cuffs as he backed up. "We won't go down without a fight. Everything Mr. Johnson promised is on the table due to the fact that he operated without the consent of his true wife. The deceased may bequeath certain things to others, but the control will be in the spouse's hands and the spouse here is Lily Johnson, not Michelle Franks. Beyond that, I've seen no will and there isn't one registered in any of the attorney offices I know of. Would you care to produce it so that we might have a look?"

"I'll get it for you," Drake said, but his eyes had a desperation to them that told another story.

"So you know where it is?" the other man pressed.

"I said I'll get it for you. Tomorrow is soon enough." Drake's hand went into a fist. I knew I was probably the last person he wanted to deal with, and certainly not about personal matters, but I felt the need to step in.

"Max," I whispered, "can you keep them busy with questions while I take Drake away? He's riled. I bet he'll talk about all kinds of things right now, but not in front of all these goons. You know enough about this, and I know nothing. Let's see if we can divide and conquer and then share notes."

My answer was a slight nod of his head.

Drake had walked over to Noreen's desk to get a glass of water. I took the opportunity to corner him.

I jumped in before he could back away. "Look, I know you don't like me, and you don't trust me, but Michelle has asked me to help her find out who killed Craig. I'll leave Max to look into everything else, but I need some information from you. Can you at least give me ten minutes to try to figure out what's going on before you shut me out?"

He stared at me for a long minute while Max continued his question and answer session. I heard some numbers being thrown around that made my eyes want to pop out of my head, but I kept a cool face.

"My office, ten minutes. Noreen, let everything go to voicemail. Take notes on the things they're saying here and then hand them to me when it's all done. I have to figure out what in the world is going on, and what we're going to do, but I need it on paper so that I can start getting a grip on the situation."

She looked at him with sad eyes and bit her lip.

"You can do this."

"Okay, Drake."

He led the way to his office, no one really seeming to notice he'd removed himself from the conversation. Good for Max for being such a sparkling conversationalist that no one missed Drake's presence.

I stepped into the room I had sat in two days ago trying to convince Drake that I really wanted the attic refurbed at the funeral home. The more I thought about that, the more I actually did like the idea, but that was not a concern for now.

Now, I had to get to the meat of things so we could get to the bottom of this murder.

"You're not going to be happy about this, but I have to ask if you and Michelle ever had an affair."

"Wow, you come shooting straight out of the gate, don't you?" His laugh was harsh, not really a laugh at all.

"Sorry. I just don't know how much time we have, and with Michelle sitting in jail, I can't afford to mince words."

"She's in jail?" His whole face paled.

"Yes, she hit Lily. Clocked her actually. I bet that's why the lawyers are all here. Lily was pissed and wants Michelle put in real jail for battery and assault and then sends her goons over here to tie up these loose ends. And I'm not even sure she and Craig were actually married. If they only lived two hours apart, how is it that they never crossed paths? Why did she wait so long to pounce? The coincidence of him dying and her showing up at the funeral the next day to announce her wifehood all seems a little too pat for me. And the fact that she's already trying to take over Michelle's house and put her out on the street just sent Michelle over the edge, so Michelle punched her."

That finally got a real reaction. He seemed to just be sitting through the rest of it like what I was saying interested him but not enough to move him. But that last part was apparently the straw and his back was inundated.

"How dare the vile woman!" He spat the words out and then he chuckled. "Good for Michelle."

"Keep your voice down, and don't you make any threats. Those are lawyers out there, and while they might be dressed nice, at least two of them would be just as comfortable swimming in the ocean with gills and row upon row of teeth in their mouths."

While he didn't sit down, he did pace instead of running his mouth, which was something.

"Now, did you and Michelle ever have an affair?"

"No, we didn't. She would come to me when things weren't going so well with Craig, or when she found out about yet another woman that he thought he loved more than her, but nothing untoward ever happened. She was better than that. I wanted her to be my wife. I didn't want to be a side piece of beef like Craig had so many of."

Made sense to me and ran true with the character I'd seen in Drake already. "Okay. But does she know you're interested in her?"

Finally sitting, he leaned back in his chair with his hands gripping the arms. "That I'm not sure about. She knows I care for her, but I've tried to be discreet about my affection for her to honor her marriage. Also, to not piss off Craig. He might have seemed like a really nice guy, but he had a streak in him that ran deep and ugly."

"Did he really leave you the company and a stipend for Michelle?" This was the crucial question because if Drake tried to dig up some phony paper saying that and tried to pass it off, things could get worse.

"We had talked about it but I don't think anything had ever been solidified or notarized. Damn." He ran his fingers through his hair.

"So no will? That's a game changer. And what's Michelle's brother going to say about all this?"

"I'll deal with him." His frown got more intense. "He doesn't have her best interests at heart anyway. He wants the money and the easy in when I've worked my ass off for this whole place."

"But he seemed sure that he was getting that in and now he's not going to have it. Would he have killed Craig to be a part of your company?"

"He doesn't have the guts to do that. He's a free-loader and has wanted a handout since Michelle married that bastard. He won't get it from me and I was going to block him from getting it from her as soon as the dust settled around the estate. He wouldn't have had a leg to stand on."

"One last question, for now."

He looked at me head on, unnerving me. I didn't know any other way to say it, so I blurted it out.

"Did you have the guts to kill Craig?"

Chapter Ten

I was never so happy to walk out of an office in one piece before. That had been worse than getting a pelvic exam. At least during one of those you knew everyone was out for your best health. In Drake's office I was sure they would have loved to tear anyone apart limb from limb as quickly and efficiently as possible.

"Thoughts?" I asked Max when we stopped at the local diner to get a bite to eat before my stomach ate itself. I shoved a corner of my grilled cheese in my mouth, then dipped a fry in gravy while I waited for him to formulate whatever he was going to say.

"What I don't get is what you were trying to accomplish by asking him if he'd killed Craig. It's rare someone is going to just come out and say 'yes I did,' and now he knows you suspect him. Don't you think that's showing your hand a little early without any kind of facts?"

"Yes and no. I wanted to see his reaction to me suspecting him. I also wanted to see if he'd try to talk me out of my suspicion and what he'd offer to get me to stop thinking he was the one who had killed his partner."

"And did you get all that? You left me out there with all those stuffed shirts so I didn't hear what was going on."

"Yeah, sorry about that, but I didn't think I was going to be able to get them to leave, and I wanted to hit Drake with the questions when he was feeling out of control. I even asked him about Michelle's brother while I had him on the hook."

"Do you watch too many crime dramas, or do you just come up with this stuff on your own?"

Now I laughed. "Probably both. I just remember that if I wanted my brother Dylan to admit that he'd done something, I'd accuse Jeremy, and the little guy would confess right away because he didn't want to see anyone else get in trouble. I also told Drake that many people think Michelle is guilty, and he was quick to defend her, but I could see in his eyes that he wasn't that sure."

More fries were dipped into more gravy. I absolutely loved the stuff, but never made it for myself. They didn't exactly make gravy servings for one at the grocery store, and I certainly didn't need it hanging around in my refrigerator, tempting me to keep eating it every day.

"And what did that accomplish?" He snatched one of my fries, and I let him. Now that was something I'd never done before. Maybe this really was love.

"Are you playing devil's advocate here, or do you really think I did the wrong thing?"

"Definitely the first one." He took another fry, and I did not stab him with my fork.

"It accomplished getting him to think about who

might have done it. Also, I wanted to put him on alert in case he wants to go to the station and talk to Michelle about how we think she might have done it, too. I might have deliberately planted the notion that we're considering the idea that maybe they did it together."

He took another fry and I let him again. But that was going to be the last one because I was almost out of fries.

"I see where you're going with this, hoping that one of them will rat the other one out. But what if it was neither of them? What if you're going after the wrong people?"

"Well, it's not like I have to deal with them on a daily basis, so I don't see a downside as far as going on with life goes. But it also gets them to thinking and maybe coming to me, or even going to Burton, to defend themselves with facts about how it wasn't them. Neither of them has an alibi except that they were sleeping." Burton had told me that, and I'd scoffed at him. Michelle did have footage of her garage from a security cam that clearly showed only Craig's car leaving at ten at night and hers resting, turned off, in the second garage. I believed she was not the one who did it, but rattling cages could be the way to go on this one.

"Any other suspects?"

"I don't trust Lily. She has too many reasons to cut Craig's life short. She says she wanted to come and get her half of things, but why did she wait so long? And what is she going to do with her half? She also swooped right in on Michelle's house and refuses to let me in. At least I got Burton to close the house off and make them both get out until the issue of the marriage is settled." And that had taken some fancy footwork and was one of the reasons Michelle was still in jail. She had nowhere else to go and the bank accounts were now frozen, so she had no money either. No matter how mean she could be, I was starting to feel just a little bit sorry for her. To lose your husband, even if he was a cheating bastard, and to lose your home and everything you thought was your life in one stumble down the stairs must be devastating. I no longer had my husband or my house, but I'd walked away from both of them in my own time.

"Anyone else?"

"I'm still not sure about Michelle's brother. Drake said that he was going to cut him off as soon as the estate was settled, but could he? Would Drake really be able to do that if Michelle agreed to give the brother money or have him run the part of the business she thought she would own?"

"Are you going to set something up to talk with him? The brother might not be as open as Drake. Why would he kill his sister's husband, or supposed husband, and then hurt a supposedly pregnant woman?"

One last fry. I dipped and savored before answering. "There have been coincidences before. I'm not ruling them out this time. I just can't."

"Well, at least you're not keeping things back from Burton this time. And you have his blessing to bring him what you find. He did, however, ask you not to go and seek things out, and I think going after Drake today might count as seeking."

"We just won't tell him then." I pushed my plate away and grabbed the check. This one was on me, even if Max had eaten several of my fries along with his own dinner. It was the least I could do since we were going to clean Mildred Forbes's huge Victorian this evening with its fourteen cats.

"I don't know how you do it." Max literally toppled onto my couch at ten, scooting it a few inches across the floor with his size. "I could not do that every day. I hope you get paid well."

After dropping my keys off on my kitchen counter, I sat on the floor near his head. "Poor baby, do you need a back rub? I get paid just fine. Mrs. Forbes pays double because I am willing to come in so late to accommodate her schedule. It's all in the timing."

"And you don't want to pick up more hours here at Graver's? Jeremy was telling me that they could really use you more around here and would love to have you full time."

I scooted back. "Jeremy needs to keep his mouth shut. And no, I don't want to work more at the funeral home. You don't know what it's like to be under your parents' thumb."

He closed his eyes. "No, I guess I don't."

That had been a crappy thing for me to say. He'd been shipped off to his grandmother's when he was a teen, the grandmother who was a tyrant and one of the reasons he had valued my parents so much. I'd had no idea that they'd gone to his graduation from high school and college and that they'd stayed in touch with him over the years. It wasn't until he'd come back nine months ago that I even remembered him from my childhood, trying to tag along behind him and Jeremy.

And look at us now.

"I should have thought before I said that. I just

don't want to be beholden to them for everything. I already live in their building, they helped me with the move, my mom refuses to cash my rent checks, and if I also only work here and nowhere else, then everything I have and do is wrapped up in them. I love them, I do, but I have to have some independence. I hope that makes sense."

He rolled his head so he was staring at me. "It makes complete sense. I shouldn't have phrased it like that."

I leaned forward to kiss him and all was right in our world even if things not so far away were in turmoil.

"Tallie, I need you." Gina's call came at eleven that night. The words alone would have had me moving, but the tone set me in my sneakers before I could completely comprehend what was happening.

Max and I had fallen asleep on the couch after snacking on leftover orange chicken and beef with broccoli. My quick movements woke him up.

"What's going on?" He rubbed his eyes, pulling his T-shirt back down over his firm stomach.

"I don't know yet, but Gina's in trouble." I went back to the phone. "Where are you?"

"Jail."

Good God. "With Michelle?"

"Yep. Please come down here and help me out. No one will listen to a word I say. I don't think I need a lawyer yet because Burton hasn't charged me with anything as of right now, but I need you here. Maybe you can talk some sense into the man."

"I'm on it." And if Burton didn't like it, then he could just suck it up.

"I'll go get ready." Max lumbered off the couch and headed for the bathroom.

"Why don't you just meet me down there? I have to go. *Now.*"

He changed directions in midstep to head for the door to the stairway. "I can just use the bathroom there, I guess."

"Fine by me."

By the time we got in the car, and I maneuvered my way around the hearses, then opened the gate at the front of the tunnel, then closed it again behind me, I probably could have walked there. Could have, but I didn't want to walk home in the middle of the night.

As Max and I entered the police station I didn't hear any yelling, so that had to be a good thing. Max headed to the restroom and I approached the desk even though I wanted to head back to the cells without any help from the man at the counter. Maybe they had put Gina and Michelle into two cells far away from each other, or at least as far as possible in our small station.

But when I was escorted back to them by the very nice deputy, I was surprised to find them talking through the bars to each other. Calmly, quietly even, and having a decent conversation. Would wonders never cease?

They both looked at me as I approached.

"We were just comparing notes," Gina said before I could ask.

"Okay then."

"Since we're both in here, we thought it might be

best to try to go over all the things we know about the people around us and see who we think could have killed Craig." Michelle sat on her flat bunk with her hands between her knees and tears in her eyes.

"Have you come up with anything?"

"Not really, but I'm glad we got a chance to talk. I believe that Gina would never have gone after Craig if she'd known he was married, so that at least makes me feel better. And the evidence I said I had that could have linked her to the murder was a total lie."

Well, that certainly made me feel better. Now to figure out how to get them both out of jail and find out who had really done this. I wanted the real killer jailed in the worst possible way so he or she could never hurt another person again.

But where to start? And how to get the information we needed to nail this person? First I was going to ask the question I'd only gotten part of the story about from Drake earlier.

"What about your brother, Michelle? He and Drake appeared to be having quite the discussion at the Bean right before your brother called me trash."

She shook her head, a look of disgust on her face. At least this one wasn't aimed at me or Gina for once. "We don't talk often. He irritates me and he's an idiot. Before Craig was even cold, my brother approached Drake about letting him come in to the business. Drake was going to allow him to think whatever he wanted until the will was read. The arrangement Drake and Craig had worked out leaves no room for a new partner. I didn't want to get involved. I wasn't involved from the beginning in any of the business of the firm." Her eyes narrowed for a second and then cleared. I didn't know what that look meant, but she was on a roll and I didn't want to stop her. "Anyway, he was in Texas with his wife until the day before the funeral. I really thought he wouldn't make it back in time, which was fine with me. He's been after me for years to let him be a part of Craig's business, but I always hid behind the fact that it wasn't my firm, so it wasn't my decision."

Max joined me at last. "He had no opportunity then, but he would have had a motive to kill Craig if he wanted in and you weren't making it happen."

Brilliant deduction from my Taxinator.

Michelle shook her head, though. "My brother wouldn't know motive if it jumped up and bit him in the brain. He lacks ambition. He wants everything handed to him the easy way. I think you're looking in the wrong direction."

I took that under advisement and went with my next question. "Did either of you come up with a name, then?"

"Lily," they said at the same time.

Well, at least that was somewhere to start. Maybe solving this marriage thing was step one and we'd go from there.

"Why are you in here, anyway?" I asked Gina.

"Because we found a bottle in the apothecary case, the one only Gina has a key to, and it has traces of the exact same thing that killed Craig. Hemlock." Burton spoke from behind me. I hated when he snuck up on me like that. Why hadn't Max warned me?

"You have got to be kidding me." I turned around and poked my finger into his chest. "You can't really believe she did this. Someone is working hard to make it look like she did, and you're falling for it."

After staring down at where my finger was still

drilled into his chest, he looked back up at me and gently moved my finger out of his personal bubble. "I'm aware that someone is trying hard to get her framed for this murder. I also can't just go on gut instinct. I have to follow the rules. With the bottle, that means Gina's in here for the moment."

"And are you also keeping Michelle? I thought you'd cleared her."

"Yes, and not yet." He moved away from the cells and waited for me to follow him. Max stayed where he was, talking with the two women. "Look, please, I don't need you to tell me how to do my job, Tallie. It was one thing for me to let you help if you have any info I might need or can't get, but it's another for you to walk in here like you think you own the place and start bossing me around."

"I am not." I didn't say anything else, though, because I had sorta done that. Not only that, I'd also made him explain himself to me when I should be letting him do his job and should be out of his hair. "Okay, then, sorry. Can I take Gina home now?"

"Yes, you can, but she can't leave town. I'm trying here, Tallie, but my hands are tied. I need something concrete if you have it. But don't get hurt. Your Uncle Sherman already doesn't like me, and sometimes I get the side eye from your father, so the last thing I need is to tell them that you've been hurt running around town trying to play amateur detective."

"You got it." A giddy bubble rose in my stomach. He had called me an amateur detective again. That wasn't exactly a compliment, and I knew that it had come out grudgingly, but I was deliberately looking on the bright side.

Max and I signed Gina out but felt bad leaving

Michelle. There wasn't much I could do about her situation. Burton wouldn't release her to me anyway. Then a thought hit me. I should have considered it sooner. I bet I could get him to release her to Drake, or at least I could ask.

"Go on out front, Gina. Take Max with you. I'll be right with you two."

"Okay." She raised an eyebrow at me and Max did the same. I just waved them on. I didn't want Burton to feel pressured by two females and a male. I also didn't want to lose face if he said no.

"Burton, can I have a second of your time?"

"You've already used up hours, Tallie. I don't know if I can handle anymore."

"Don't start. I have a question I want to run by you. I even sent Gina and Max up front so you don't feel pressured. I want points for that."

A genuine smile broke out on his face. "I'm listening."

"If I can get in touch with Drake Fuller and have him take custody of Michelle, can I take her with us and drop her off at Drake's?"

His forehead crinkled. "I'd need to talk to him, too. And I don't want you to say anything to Michelle until it's all sewn up."

"You got it. Can I use an office?"

He pointed me to my cousin Matt's office and I promised myself not to touch anything.

I called the number for Johnson and Fuller. On the voicemail, Noreen spouted out a cell phone number for Drake in case of emergency. I figured this counted as an emergency.

I was honestly surprised that Drake wasn't down

here already, but maybe Michelle still hadn't called him, or maybe she had and hadn't told him the severity of the situation. But I'd told him she was in here earlier. Had he never tried to see her? That seemed strange for someone who professed to love the woman.

He picked up on the first ring.

"Drake, it's Tallie. Before you hang up on me, or accuse me of doing anything, I have to talk to you about Michelle."

"Do you know where she is?" Urgency made his voice vibrate with tension. "She told me she was getting out of jail hours ago. And I've been trying to get a hold of her ever since. I have no idea where she is. I know she can't stay at her house, and she doesn't have money for a hotel."

"Actually, she's about twenty feet from me in a jail cell." He roared, and I held the phone away from my head long enough for him to wind down before asking if he was done.

"What is she still doing in jail? Why did she lie to me? Forget it. I'm going to nail that Burton to a wall."

I'd like to have seen him try. "I told you before that she attacked Lily. She should be in a Harrisburg jail, but they didn't have enough room so Burton brought her here, where it was safer. Plus, he also knows she has nowhere else to go and was going to keep her until she could make arrangements. I called you to see if I could bring her to you, but I hadn't realized she'd already told you she was out." Why would she have done that? What was the purpose of lying to him?

"All right, maybe I won't nail him to a wall."

"I think it would be best if you just let that thought go right now. I was calling to let you know I asked Burton if I could bring her to you. He agreed as long as he can talk to you first."

"Fine then. I definitely won't nail him to a wall. Put him on the phone."

I did as I was asked and watched Burton talk to Drake. Burton tried to scoot me out of the room, but he was out of luck, and there wasn't much he could do about it since he was tethered to the desk phone.

I only heard his side of the conversation.

"Yes, you can house her overnight, but make sure she doesn't go anywhere."

He paused, scratching his chin.

"I don't want her anywhere near that other woman. You have to make sure there is no contact."

Pause again.

"Yes, Tallie does always seem to be where she isn't wanted and where she's not supposed to be. We've had a talk about it, but either she didn't hear me, or she thinks she's above the law."

I sputtered. He smiled a sharky grin. Eavesdropping never got me anywhere when I was eavesdropping on a conversation about myself. It was rarely, if ever, flattering.

"Fine, I'll have her transport Michelle to you. But remember that she must stay with you."

He hung up, then crossed his arms over the chest of his blue uniform shirt. "You can take her directly there. Do not deviate. And if she tries to talk you out of dropping her off, you tell her that it's the only condition under which I'm willing to let her go from here."

"You *had* to say that part about already talking to me."

"Yes, I did. And you're lucky I didn't respond to everything he said about you." Uncrossing his arms, he strode out of my cousin's office. "Now, come get your entourage and get the heck out of here. When I said I'd deal with you, I didn't think it was going to be twenty-four hours a day."

And I hadn't thought that he would arrest my friend over and over again. I guess we had both been wrong.

Still, I was getting out of here before he could change his mind.

Walking back to the cells, it had been strange to see Michelle and Gina sitting on opposite sides of the bars and talking. After that scene in the Bean that first day, I was sure they'd never speak to one another ever. Some things could change, though. And now if I could just clear my best friend, I'd be happy as a clam and ready to enjoy the rest of Max's vacation with him.

The ride to Drake's took about half an hour. He not only lived across the river but through the woods, too. His house was a stately, two-story, stone dream. Situated on a large plot of land, it looked like it had been a farm at one time but now had houses on all three sides and fronted the road. He must have made a pretty penny if he was the one who had sold the land to a developer.

I pulled into the driveway, lined with old-fashioned streetlamps, then around the back of the house, which was lit with soft ground lights shining onto the stone. The front didn't look like it got much use. When I commented on it, Michelle told me the real entrance was at the back of the house. The front was just for show.

How often had she been here? Had it ever been alone? Drake swore that they'd never had an affair, but why had Michelle stayed so long with a man who cheated on her constantly in the open and without remorse?

Yes, *I* had stayed with Waldo for a while when I knew he was a jerk, but I also didn't have anywhere else to go and thought that I could put up with his crap as long as he kept paying the bills. Shallow, I know, and thank God I wasn't that person anymore.

But Michelle didn't seem to have that much in the way of money and little if any respect for herself as a woman. Was that why she had stayed?

If we were closer, or hadn't been trading insults just a handful of hours ago, I might have asked. But it wasn't my place, and I certainly wasn't going to judge.

Maybe she had said something to Gina, though. That I would have no problem asking.

Drake was waiting at the back door when I pulled up behind the house. He stepped out onto the deck, haloed by light spilling from the house, and hesitated. I could almost see his brain working. Should he come out? Wait for her to come to him? Would she be angry that she was here instead of her own house?

Not that she could go to her house anyway. Burton had said it was off-limits until they sorted out whom it belonged to.

Surprisingly she had been silent after I'd told her where we were going. She only gave directions in a soft voice and seemed to scrunch in on herself in the front seat.

She wasn't afraid of him, was she? I hadn't even thought to ask that. Right then might not have been the best time with him standing on the deck, but I had to take the time.

"Michelle, I have to ask before you get out of the car. I don't want to make you uncomfortable and I know we're not exactly friends, but will you feel safe with Drake?"

"Great time to ask that now, Tallie," Gina chimed in from the backseat. I glared at her, then turned back to Michelle.

"No," Michelle said on a sigh. "I'm not afraid of him. It's just that we were almost something a long time ago and I think he's never forgotten it and wants to rekindle it. But he doesn't know me. And I think he just likes the idea of me, not the real me."

Boy, did I know that one like a song that wouldn't get out of your head.

"Maybe being here with him will change that." It couldn't hurt, anyway.

She stared at me for a moment. "I'm recently widowed, as in four days ago, in case you've forgotten, and I don't want another man. I want that bitch out of my house and I want my life back. Craig might not have been the best of husbands, but at least I knew what I was getting in the end."

What a sad way to look at life. But again, I wasn't judging. I'd had no idea what Waldo was like, and I'd left him when I'd found out for sure. Michelle had chosen to stay through who knew how many girlfriends. There must have been something there that I just couldn't understand.

"Well, we'd better get you out of the car before Drake comes for you."

"Yes, I suppose we should." She unhunched long enough to open the door and step out. But as soon as she stood up from my low-slung car, her shoulders rounded back down.

Drake met her at the bottom of the stairs leading up to the deck and put an arm around her shoulders. She stepped in to him and began to sob.

Maybe it was the stress of the day, or the last few days. Maybe it was finally being in the arms of someone who you knew was not a jerk. Maybe she was just letting it all out now that she was out of jail and at least would have a warm bed and food that didn't come out of the microwave. Whatever it was, I left it there on Drake's driveway as I backed the car up and did a nine-point turn to get out.

"Do you think they did it together?" Gina asked. She'd remained in the backseat, along with a very quiet Max, making me feel like a chauffeur.

"I wish one of you would have moved up here, and no, I don't think they 'did it together' as long as the 'it' we're talking about means murdering Craig."

"Of course. I don't want to know about any other 'doing it' at this point. I just wonder if they decided to kill him together. Then Drake would get his company back under his own hand and not have to pay for a ton of dates and flowers. And Michelle could have been done with always being left behind."

I thought of how Michelle had said that Craig

hadn't looked at her like he'd looked at Gina. Ever. I supposed it could be possible that she had hooked up with Drake to remove the jerk.

However, I was leaning more toward the actual wife. It was awfully convenient that she'd waltzed in mere days after her husband was dead and knew enough about him and his estate and holdings to think she could swoop in and take it all without being contested. How had she known that they definitely weren't divorced? And if she only lived two hours away, why did she take so long to make contact?

I thought about those questions and about a hundred more as I made my way back to my apartment.

Gina and Max sat silently in the backseat. Actually I was pretty sure I heard Max snuffle out a snore. It had been a long day. A long four days. I think we all just needed the chill time and the silence. I didn't even turn the radio on for once, and instead rolled the windows down and stuck my hand out to ride the current of high-speed air going past us.

Whoever had done this had to have access to poisons and the knowledge of how to use them. What they were capable of. And in the case of Craig, how long it would take them to react. I highly doubted they'd actually gotten the poison from Gina's cabinet. They were just trying to make it look like it had come from there to more solidly point the finger at her.

I wished that Brenna would wake up so I could ask her if she'd seen who had hurt her. She was still in a medically induced coma last I had checked with the hospital. The hemlock the person or persons had used was not something commonly seen, and the antidote wasn't exactly orthodox. They were working as fast and as hard as they could to get her well enough to be able to talk. After she was stable, hopefully she could blow the whistle on this whole thing.

Until then I was still on a mission to find out everything I could and bring the killer and the attacker to justice. I had to, for the friend sitting quietly in the back of the car.

Chapter Eleven

The next day was filled with cleaning and other non-sleuthing things. I did try to do my own research on the marriage of Lily and Craig but got nowhere. While Max and I had lunch, I tried not to fret that I didn't have any new leads in the murder case. After eating, I called Gina to see how she was doing. Apparently, she'd opened the Bean, where business was brisk, then went for a walk around town until it was time for her to go to dinner with Jeremy. She still refused to tell me where they were going, drat her.

Once Gina left for her dinner date with my brother, I did my best to talk Max into following them, but he nixed the idea and instead presented me with other, more enticing things to do.

I was still awake when Gina came in late. I saw her lights go on across the street but she refused to answer her cell, even though I called her seven times.

I got up the next morning, groggy but filled with purpose. I would make progress on who had killed Craig today even while I cleaned. With that in mind,

I dragged Max with me to the cleaning job I had scheduled for one of the old guard.

Mrs. Smythe had to be nearing ninety, and she still refused to even go out and get her mail without full makeup and heels on. Sometimes she forgot the clothes in between, but her daughter lived with her to remind her to put them on before she stepped out the door.

"Now remember, she likes them young, so be careful what you say or she'll have you in her boudoir in two point three seconds," I said to Max.

I wasn't talking about Mrs. Smythe but the daughter, Miss Smythe. She'd gone back to her maiden name after getting rid of husband number four. I could honestly say that if I couldn't make it work three times I probably wouldn't go for a fourth. I admired people with that kind of optimism, but I was not one of them.

Heck, I wasn't even sure I wanted to get married a second time. Miss Smythe, though, was an over-achiever in the marriage department and somehow they always seemed to die on her. Then again, that wasn't so hard to believe since she tended to only marry men who were much older than her. If she wanted to fool around, she always went for the younger guys.

To each his or her own, I suppose.

When we arrived at the grand house on the hill, I stepped out of my car and stretched. I hadn't slept well last night, even with Max beside me. Not being sure what my next move might be had kept me tossing and turning.

Where did I go from here? I had put in a call to my cousin the interior decorator, but she hadn't yet called me back. If I didn't hear from her today I was calling her mom to see what I had to do to get an audience with her highness, the queen of sheers.

And if that didn't work, then I'd go track her down myself. I needed the skinny on the people in a circle I was most definitely not a part of, and I needed it now so I could parse through the info and try to figure out who else had something to gain by offing Craig.

Although the more I thought about it, the more I wondered if it wasn't someone in our town. It would have had to be pretty random for someone to be in town at the same time as Craig and poison him before he got to Gina's.

I was baffled, and I didn't like it one bit.

Max carried my tools of the trade up the front walk. Miss Smythe opened the large, carved, oak door with a smile and not a lot else.

Had she stripped down when she'd seen me pull up with Max? I sure hoped not.

"Miss Smythe, how nice to see you." Nearly all of you, I thought, keeping my eyes on hers. "This is my boyfriend, Max. He'll be helping out today." Better to lay the law out right from the get-go instead of letting her get any ideas in her pretty head.

"Oh poo. Boyfriend? I thought maybe you had hired a crew to help with this monstrosity."

"Boyfriend," I said firmly. "And he's only here for a vacation. I had him ride along to help so we can get out of here early and spend some time together this afternoon."

"You know what you're doing. I'll just leave you to it." She pulled the see-through wrap tighter around the short silk dress and sauntered off toward the kitchen.

"Good Lord," Max said from behind me. "Did she really think that the hired help was going to fall into bed with her without even exchanging names?"

"Keep your voice down," I whispered, but ruined the stern tone when I snickered. "And yes, she would."

He laughed, patting me on the shoulder. "I'll remember that if I ever need a different job than the Taxinator."

Blushing was not something I liked to do, but I couldn't help it. I didn't realize he had remembered I'd called him that.

"Anyway," I said, "let's get this done. There probably isn't much since they do have a day maid. I'm only here because she doesn't like to do the high places or the corners."

An hour later, I was bopping along with my music in the kitchen while Max cleaned out the cobwebs in the dining room next door.

"Oh, Tallie, did you hear? That wonderful Craig Johnson died!" Miss Smythe came into the kitchen fully dressed this time and looking far more distraught than I'd ever seen her before. "Oh, you might not know him since I doubt you're in a place that you can remodel. You're still at your father's above the funeral parlor, correct?"

"I did hear that. And yes, I still live there." Had she really just heard or was she trying to let me in on gossip she thought was important? I didn't remember seeing her at the funeral, but maybe she had not gotten an invitation.

She had always been a gossip. Even when I was

vapid and ridiculous I had at least known enough to stay away from her as much as possible.

I wanted to keep my cards close to my vest here. Craig would be about the age she liked, and he would have probably been perfect for her. Was this another one of his girlfriends?

"I'm devastated. Absolutely devastated." I saw no tears forming in her eyes, but everyone dealt with devastation differently, I guessed.

"Were the two of you seeing each other?"

She laughed gaily, a high-pitched trill. "Oh heavens, no. He had a bevy of ladies after him. I might change husbands as often as some people change their hairdo, but I like mine unmarried and not quite so polished."

She leaned against the counter I'd just scrubbed and idly ran her finger over the top, lifting it to her face. To check for dirt or dust? She wouldn't find any. I was good at my job. That was why people hired me.

"I'm devastated because he was going to remodel our house. That man had ideas like you wouldn't believe. You would have thought he would be more masculine, but some of the things he wanted to install, and the way he seemed to almost read my mind about the little feminine touches, were astounding."

Feminine touches? I had taken Craig for a man with an eye for the ladies. But one never could tell about these things. I had never seen any of his work that I knew of, and his Web site had been strangely devoid of any finished project pictures.

"Well, hopefully you can find someone else. Does he have a partner that could maybe still do the job?" Yes, I was playing dumb, but this could be information

I could use if she knew things and had worked with them before.

"Ah, yes, Drake. Now, that man is magnificent to look at but not so wonderful with the designs. I was scheduled with him first." She mock shivered. "His ideas were far too blocky, too masculine."

"Did Craig do most of the designing?" With my rubber-gloved hand in ammonia, I kept scrubbing the silver as we talked.

"Oh, I think he did a fair amount. Drake was mostly the one who would follow along behind him with the hammer and nails. A strange partnership if you ask me, especially with the way everyone knows Drake wanted Craig's wife."

Everyone but me, until recently.

"And how did Craig seem about Drake wanting his wife?" An outside opinion could go a long way to seeing the dynamics in a totally different light. Especially since I had not known Craig when he was alive and had never seen him with his wife except for when she was pulling him out of the Bean that fateful day.

"Unconcerned. It was curious, but I would not have been surprised if Craig was actually gay. He showed all the feminine qualities of my friend Roger. Do you know Roger?"

Yes, I knew Roger and had enjoyed chatting with the flamboyant man who always had a laugh and smile on his face while he wore silk smoking jackets with cravats that were perfectly arranged. I had loved Roger, but as far as I was concerned he was nothing like Craig. "Roger and I used to get in debates about the theater." Long ago, when I was married to Waldo, Roger was one of the bright spots in any party I had to go to.

"Oh, the theater. He can't ever stop talking about that. Anyway, I just always thought Craig might be more of a man's man, if you know what I mean." And then she winked at me.

And now I had a whole other thing to think about. How many women that he dated did Craig sleep with? All? Or was it all just flowers and showmanship? Was he gay? Could it have been a man who'd killed him? One who'd seen him go into Gina's house one more time? I put it into my mental file, but I had doubts. Coming from this particular source, I had to wonder if the theory had more to do with Miss Smythe failing to capture Craig's attention and so blaming it on something that had nothing to do with her.

Thoughts whirled and swirled in my head as I continued to wipe down counters and make sure the stove was clean. I couldn't wait to talk with Max about the whole thing. And Gina. I couldn't dismiss it altogether but I had my doubts. I'd been witness to Miss Smythe being turned down before and then suddenly the guy who'd turned her down had hair plugs, or a fetish for women's underwear. You weren't safe if you rebuffed her.

Still, I was tempted to call Michelle and ask about her sex life with Craig, but we weren't exactly friends. Even I knew where to draw the line sometimes.

Max and I went to Farrah Chance's house for its once-a-month cleaning next, and I swear the woman had not lifted a single finger in the thirty days I wasn't there. I'd tried to talk her into letting me come more than once a month. I'd even offered her a discount to let me come in once a week. But she didn't like intruders and was only happy with the once a month.

I'd had to keep Max close at hand for that one since his jaw kept dropping every time we went into a new room and he saw the many, many dead animals Mr. Chance liked to display on every wall.

Once we were done there, I gathered Gina and Max in the back of the Bean.

"Did he really hunt all those things?" he asked, now from one of the comfy chairs in the break room. We all sat in chairs with mugs of plain coffee. After working through the big houses today, I didn't think I would be able to stay awake with a latte. I needed the strong stuff, and Gina had pulled out the big guns with her double-brewed high-octane coffee.

"No, he didn't shoot them all. He actually buys them off the Internet already stuffed." I took a sip and hummed. I needed this caffeine. It was only two in the afternoon and I already wanted to go to sleep and stay there until morning.

"What is the point of that? Does he like all those blank stares? I would be scared out of my mind to get up and go down the hall to the bathroom."

Gina and I laughed and it felt good to let the tension go for just a few minutes. I was going to have to bring the subject up soon, but I let the steam rise from my cup for just a few more seconds before I got into the info I'd heard on my cleaning journey today.

"Spill," she finally said, looking at me over the rim of her cup. "I can almost hear your brain firing on all pistons. If you want to ask a question, or need info I have, just spit it out. I want off the hook, Tallie. My mom wants me off the hook, too, and I barely kept her from grilling you about how long this is taking."

"Why does she want to grill me? I'm not the police. If she wants to grill someone, have her talk to Burton."

"She's not speaking to him right now, and she's afraid if she goes after him that he'll just pin it on me to shut everyone up."

"I don't really think he'd do that. He might not have a clue sometimes, and I know he's going to want to shut down the case, but I really don't think he'd pin it on you if he knew you hadn't done it."

"That's the problem. With the bottle from the cabinet and the fact that Craig died in my stairwell with no one else in sight, he might have to take me in for more questioning. I don't like that little room with the two-way mirrors. I like even less that I don't have answers."

"I don't like that we don't have answers, either, but I also am doing my best. This is not a science for me. I'm not even good at solving puzzles in the news-paper. Last time with Darla and Waldo I'm beginning to think I just got lucky. This time nothing is making sense."

Max patted my hand. "If you think you're in over your head, then no one is going to blame you for just letting the police take care of it."

How little he knew. If Mama Shirley wanted her daughter cleared, I would never hear the end of it if I let her go to jail and just cleaned my houses and got ready for my funerals. I just kept feeling like I was missing something. Something important.

But first I wanted to get Gina's take on the Craig being gay thing.

"So today I heard something interesting." I hoped that I'd be able to introduce the topic without sound-ing like an idiot.

"What was that?" As always Gina didn't fall for my nonchalance. It was the problem with being friends for so long.

"Miss Smythe seems to think that maybe Craig was gay."

Gina rocked back in her chair and took a big gulp of her coffee. Because she was nervous? Because she knew something I didn't know? Because she was offended?

I hoped not on that last one. Last time Gina and I had talked about anything like this, she hadn't judged.

"It would almost make a strange kind of sense, wouldn't it?" Gina closed her eyes and wrapped her hands around her mug. "He was so attentive and always seemed to know the right thing to say. He never got handsy and *I* had to kiss *him* on our third date because he never made a move toward me."

"Then again, he could have just been a gentleman," Max said. He sat in the chair opposite me and had been sipping on his own coffee. "I know plenty of men who aren't Neanderthals. It doesn't have to be anything but that. From my perspective, I think Craig was just always looking for something he didn't have."

I so wanted to ask Max if he'd found that something in me, but I didn't have the guts just yet. Instead, I focused on Gina because I still wanted her impressions.

"Miss Smythe said that he was very into remodeling her space and had all kinds of feminine ideas that she would have never thought of."

"Meh, he was just good at what he did." She waved a hand in the air. "I don't think he was trying to hide anything. I think he really was just a womanizer. Nothing more, nothing less. Why add to your available suspects when we have plenty of people with motive if not the means? I think you're barking up the wrong tree."

"Should I ask Michelle?"

"Ask her what?" Gina sat forward in her chair with her elbows on her knees. "You cannot seriously be thinking about asking that poor woman, who just lost her husband, if they had a good sex life, or if they ever did it at all."

"Well, I wasn't going to say it quite like that." I was affronted that she would think I would have so little tact.

"I'd ask Drake," Max said. "He'd know, and he's mad enough about all this with the first wife that I bet he'd spill if he knew something."

"No, I know who I'm going to ask. He'll know better than anyone."

A trip to the flower shop had been on my list of things to do, anyway. I would just move the time table up a little and make sure I waited around long enough to get Monty alone.

Walking into the fragrant store, I took in the displays Monty had put together for summer bouquets. Flowers bloomed, grew, and looked fantastic in the small area Monty called his own.

He'd been in business for almost forty years, and for all those forty years he'd been here in our small town delivering bouquets, making clutches, corsages, and funeral sprays. Baby showers remained one of his favorite things to do, and he had a whole box full of baby carriages and booties and little teddy bears dressed up as boys and girls.

He took pride in what he did. I'd never been disappointed in anything he'd made, and I'd never heard of anyone else being disappointed, either. If you needed flowers you came here, even if you lived out of town, apparently.

I wandered the shelves, touching a bloom here and a leaf there. I had never been able to grow anything, not even Christmas cacti, which were supposed to be almost indestructible. I'd killed one a year for three years in a row until Monty told me I wasn't allowed to buy them anymore because he couldn't face handing them over to me knowing they were just going to perish.

But he had always been happy to make me arrangements when I was Mrs. Phillips the Third. He'd even made me a couple since I was just Tallie Graver. Not the big expensive ones that I'd displayed around the house for parties and daily brightness in the gloom that was my life then. Recently I'd only asked for simple little clutches of posies that made me happy and brightened my room on the third floor of the funeral parlor.

I traded nods with the three people walking around the shop, too, wishing that I could tell them to leave. I had already cleaned two houses today and had another to clean this afternoon. Which meant I did not have a whole lot of time to be here. But this was important. I needed to get him alone before I had to go to my next job.

Finally, they all left, happy to either have flowers in

their arms or deliveries on the way. I pounced before he could get caught up in anything else.

"Fair warning, I have several questions, and I'm not sure you're going to like any of them," I said by way of hello. I had business and fifteen minutes in which to conduct it.

"I'm glad to see you're well, and yes, I'm doing fine, too. Thanks for not asking." His words were accompanied by a sly smile, so I gave him what he wanted.

"Okay, okay. Hi, how are you? Doing great? That's great. Now, on to my questions."

"By all means, chat away, but do so softly. I'm trying to coax these orchids back to life. Loud noise is not what the plant doctor ordered."

"Okay." I drew the word out, and he just raised an eyebrow at me. "Question one: can you give me a list of all the women Craig sent flowers to or bought flowers for over the last year?"

The other eyebrow went up. "He may be dead and God rest his soul, and I may be out of a ton of weekly money, God help *me*, but I really can't share that information with you. Besides," he went on when I opened my mouth, "unless he asked me to deliver them I was never privy to whom he made his cards out to. It could have been the same woman over and over again, or it could have been a different one every time. I have no way of knowing."

"You're lying to me." I could tell from the way he avoided my gaze. "You had to have some kind of list so that he could come in and tell you to make a specific kind of bouquet. You work like that. I know it."

"You've got me there, but I'm still not telling you. Some of the women may want to remain anonymous."

"Married women?"

"You know, Tallie, not everyone cheats. And I'm sure most of them had no idea he was married. For heaven's sake, I didn't know he was married until he died. He'd just come in whistling a tune about a new woman, and how maybe this one was the one, and then he'd tell me to pick out flowers and be on his way."

"Wait. What do you mean when you say he asked you to pick out flowers? Didn't he do that himself?"

"The two times I set him loose on the store he came back with horrible ideas that did not go together. The colors clashed and the design was all wrong. Finally he left it up to me."

"But he was a home remodeler and supposedly had the most amazing ideas for color and design and could make all the women deliriously happy with his ideas. But he couldn't pick out flowers?"

"I don't ask, sweetheart. I just sell. But I certainly wouldn't have had him decorate anything in my home."

I wasn't sure what to do with that information since it went against everything I'd been told by many people. And yet it would make sense. His home was not well decorated and Michelle had lamented the way Craig put things together. But how had he soared as a designer if he couldn't even put colors together? Even I could do that.

I asked Monty that very question and he shrugged. "I have no idea. It takes all kinds, I guess."

I let that sit in my head, thinking I really should find a house he'd decorated and see the end result. But first I still had questions on these bouquets. "You really don't know whom he was sending them to? Or how many women were the recipients?"

"There were repeat bouquets, but I am being totally

honest when I tell you I did not keep those preferences anywhere but in my head. Besides, he had code names for them."

"Code names?" What was this? *Mission Impossible?*

"Yes, he'd say 'Make me the sunshine bouquet' or order a dozen pansies for the 'Lady in White.' He never got specific, and since it is most definitely not my place to judge he who gives flowers, or she who gets flowers, I didn't ask."

"Dammit. I was really hoping you could help me get a list together so I could see if anyone else had the motive or the means to kill Craig. Someone did, and I know it isn't Gina, but Burton needs more convincing."

Monty broke the stem of one of the orchids and cursed. "I'm so sorry, baby," he cooed to it, stroking the petals and laying it aside. "You have got to be kidding me." He said that to me this time in a much angrier voice.

How come I always got the anger and inanimate objects got the petting? Probably because I always seemed to be the one asking the tough question, not just sitting there and looking pretty like I used to.

"I'm not kidding. He had her in jail last night because one of the bottles of medicine from the apothecary cabinet in her shop had traces of hemlock. They think it might be the hemlock that Craig was given. Burton released her to me, but if he doesn't start making progress on this soon, or if I don't hand him the killer with a bow, then he might go after her again."

"I was wondering why Burton came in and bought a bouquet for Shirley."

"He didn't." "Aghast" was the closest word I could think of for how I felt.

"Oh yes, he did, and since he wouldn't normally do that for his cousin except when he's in trouble, I bet she wants to bite his head right off. He should have spent more money."

I let that roll around in my brain for a moment. Mama Shirley did love her flowers, and Burton probably did not want to be on her bad side. If buying her some posies would keep her from hitting him with her infamous rolling pin for going after her daughter then he'd buy them. I would have to explore that more later. Right now, I was running out of time, and I hadn't asked my second question yet.

"Okay, so you can't help me with names."

"Well, this might be a little different. Let me have the afternoon to see what I can remember or dig up. I don't want that girl in jail. She worked here to learn business smarts, and she's one heck of an owner. I won't see her go down for something like this because of a scum bag like Craig."

"Language." I laughed as I said it.

"This situation calls for language." He huffed and patted some dirt around the remaining orchid. "Now, what's the next question? I'll see what I can do."

There was no easy way to ease into this, so I just went straight for the gut. "Was Craig gay?"

Out of all the responses I had imagined, I certainly didn't expect Monty to guffaw so loud and long, smacking the countertop until the orchid almost fell off the glass surface. But he did, and I waited him out, at least as long as I could. I had five minutes before I had to be on the road for my next job. I did not have time for hilarity, especially when I didn't know what was so darn funny.

He wiped his eyes with a fingertip. "Before I answer, you have to tell me if you heard that from Miss Francesca Smythe."

I drew myself up to my full height of just over five feet. "Yes, as a matter of fact I did. She lied because Craig turned her down, didn't she?" Now I felt kind of stupid for even asking when I'd known better. But no stone could go unturned.

"Oh, don't get ruffled. She lies with the best of them. I've even believed a few myself. She can be very convincing when she wants to be." He chuckled again. "Anyway, she frequently tells everyone that any man who doesn't jump at the chance to be with her is gay. It's her thing."

"It used to be hair plugs."

"Yes, well, she's moved on to sexuality now instead of cosmetics." He stroked the petals of the orchid. "She came in wanting to know if Craig had a girlfriend. She waited out on the sidewalk around the corner until he left. I have these CCTV cameras so I can see three hundred and sixty degrees around the building."

I would have to remember that if Max and I ever decided to stop for a quick kiss near this place. What else had Monty seen over the years? I would have to ask him about that later.

"So Smythe hid around the corner until Craig left. Then what?"

"She comes strolling in, trailing her hands all over everything in the store, and all nonchalant asks if the man has a girlfriend. I told her I didn't know, and if I did it wouldn't be right for me to talk about it. She tells me she appreciates my discretion but wants to meet the man who comes in every day like clockwork."

Every day? No wonder he lived frugally in a small house. The man must have been spending a fortune on flowers alone. Not to mention the money involved if he ever bought other gifts. Then you had to figure in the cost of taking these women out on dates. I really wanted to get my hands on the books for his business. Had he been expensing the flowers? It wouldn't have surprised me.

"And did you introduce them?" I asked.

He narrowed his eyes as if the memory was not a good one. "Yes, I did. How could I not since she showed up the very next day, back in here trailing her fingers over things in a low-cut dress? She gushed all over him, and he barely looked at her. She waited about two seconds before asking him if he'd like to go get a cup of coffee. He was just as quick to turn her down flat, telling her he was already seeing someone who made the best coffee ever."

Gina. He'd been seeing Gina. And married and pursued by other ladies. How on earth did he keep them all straight?

"I will tell you that once he started getting those multicolored roses, he only bought small arrangements for other women. Like he knew he had to keep up appearances but he really thought the coffee girl was the one."

"And was that coffee girl Gina? Because that was who he was seeing."

"Gina? I was making all those flowers for Gina?" The shock and anger in his voice set me back a step.

"I thought you didn't judge."

"Don't throw my words back at me, young lady. I'm

not offended as I make Gina flowers as often as possible. She's my protégé. However, if I had known they were for her, I would have warned her off him in a hurry."

"Interesting. Then he really wasn't gay. It could have made sense that he saw all these women to keep up a masculine front."

"No, he wasn't gay, Tallie, and there are plenty of men who aren't gay who go in and get their eyebrows waxed, too. It's called grooming, and believe me there are just as many gay people out there who dress like slobs."

My time was up. I had gained some information, but not nearly as much as I had hoped for. No list from Monty meant no ideas of other women who might have poisoned Craig. But with the sexual orientation thing off the table, at least I didn't have to try to find any men he'd led around by their noses, which could have doubled my possible list of people he'd romantically misled.

"All right then. That wasn't so bad, was it?" I asked.

"No, not nearly as bad as I thought it was going to be." He peered at me over his flower. "I guess you're looking into Craig's murder to get Gina off the hook?" he went on again as I opened my mouth. The man had a habit of cutting me off before I could even get a word out. "Let me rephrase that. You had better be looking into this, because Gina will not go to jail on my watch."

"On my watch, either." I bit my lip. "I know you can't tell me too much, but if you see anyone suspicious or have seen anyone suspicious on your CCTV, will you let me know? Especially the night Craig died? It could be important."

"I'll look over the footage. You're lucky because I was about to use that tape today. I recycle them."

Thank God, I'd caught him in time. At least one thing had gone right today, even if I still had no clue who might have killed Craig, and I was no closer to naming that someone to keep Gina out of the clutches of the law.

Chapter Twelve

Next stop: Taylor Fromm's house. Taylor was a yoga teacher and kept her home pretty clean, but she also had a very particular way of doing things, along with her own cleaning products that she made herself. I had tried a few at my own home, but the overwhelming smell of vinegar and lye were a little too much for me in the small area I had. She also liked to burn incense. For about the thousandth time since I'd started my cleaning business I was so thankful not to be allergic to anything.

I waved good-bye to Taylor and headed back to the Bean. Gina was standing behind the counter surveying the nearly full shop. Saturdays Gina closed earlier than any other day. Everyone had a cup in front of them and seemed engrossed in what they were doing. I hoped she hadn't been using the time to mope about her situation. At least I could tell her some good news.

Sidling up to the counter, I accepted the cup of hot chocolate she'd poured for me when she saw me come through the door.

"Iced coffee might be good to put on the menu. It's sweltering out there." I took a sip of the hot chocolate and, no matter how hot it was outside, this remained awesome on my taste buds.

"I've thought about it," she said. "But I don't want to be the same as any old chain coffeehouse. I want different."

"You could make coffee slushes."

"Now, that I might be able to get on board with." She made a note with the pencil behind her ear and then pressed her hands to the counter in front of her. "I don't want to push, and God knows I'm so happy you're helping me at all, but any news by any chance?"

I took another swallow of the hot chocolate and sucked a tiny marshmallow off my top lip. "You'll be pleased to know that Smythe was just angry that Craig wouldn't give her a second glance and that the information she tried to snow me with was completely incorrect."

"That doesn't exactly make me feel better. I think I almost wished she would have been right so I could just think he was using me. Instead it seems I was the one being snowed by a common womanizer."

I reached out to touch her hand where it had clenched on the counter. "We'll figure this out and make it all right, I promise. The other piece of news is that Monty has CCTV." I whispered the last part because I didn't know if anyone else knew. I didn't want to blow it for him.

"He does?"

"Yes, and there's a possibility that the lady whom your mom saw driving around the block three times could be on it, as well as anyone else if they tried to slip out of your street without being seen." It was a long shot but it was possible. And the smile on Gina's face was worth the tiny stretching of what may or may not be the truth. I didn't go anywhere anymore without looking at tires and was surprised at how few cars around here had oversized wheels. We were a bunch of economy-car-driving folks, apparently. But I needed to find the car and maybe then I could find the culprit. I would keep looking.

And then her smile fell into a frown.

"What?"

"I've kissed people behind Monty's store. Oh my God, I let Tommy Hellman feel me up back there when we were in high school."

I laughed and laughed and laughed. Until I realized that I had done the same thing. "Wait, when were you with Tommy?"

"Eleventh grade."

"Month?"

"I don't remember, Tallie. That was years ago. Right before school let out, I think." She shrugged. "Like I said, it was a long time ago."

"Huh, well, he still might have something to answer for because that was about the time I was with him, too. Why didn't you mention him?"

She laughed, a real one this time, and it was so good to hear. "Why didn't you?"

"I was embarrassed."

"Yeah, me too. He wasn't exactly a prize, and I swear he had like seven hands."

"No kidding."

The bell above the door rang and we both looked to see who had entered. Tommy Hellman. Gina's glare matched my own. Tommy had no idea what he'd just walked in to.

* * *

I hung out for a little while after we grilled Tommy. He'd stumbled over his words a bit, saying something about being young and dumb, but if Gina wanted to give him another chance he'd definitely take her up on it. She handed him his coffee in a Styrofoam cup even though he hadn't asked for it to go. Without another word, he scooted out the door, obviously smarter now than when he walked in.

"What do you have planned for the evening?"

"Nothing much." Gina swiped at a spot in front of her. "Did you want to hang out? I want this figured out but I need a break from all of it."

While I certainly didn't want to turn her away, I also wanted some time with Max before he had to go back to DC. "Of course," I said. Tallie Graver, best friend and least selfish person in the world. That was me.

Laura, the still relatively new girl, came bustling out from the back, tying her apron on as she walked quickly.

"Hi there," Gina said, stopping her in her tracks. "I wasn't sure you were coming in today. Do you feel better?"

Laura nodded. "Yeah, sorry about calling out like that yesterday, but I had a migraine. I couldn't even stand to see light, much less deal with the noise and activity that happens here."

"No worries. Take it easy if you have to today. We're pretty slow at the minute."

Laura nodded again and went to clean a table that looked like it might have a few specks of sugar on it.

"How's she working out?" I asked. Gina and I had

been so wrapped up in clearing her name that I hadn't asked about the new girl.

"So far so good. I don't like when people call off in the first week they're working, but Laura sounded miserable yesterday. I'm not paying her much more than minimum wage because I can't afford it yet, so I can't complain. If it keeps happening we might have to talk about it, but at this point, I'm willing to let it slide."

"She seems like a nice person."

"She is. I've known her aunt for years, so she came highly recommended."

"Good enough then." I sipped the last of the cocoa, then put my glass back on the counter. "I should get going. Let me know if you hear anything that could help us."

I hugged Gina over the counter and turned to go when the bell rang over the door again. This time it was not someone we could razz about things from high school. It was Burton, and he looked entirely too serious for my liking.

I hadn't yet moved my hand from the bar, intending to use it to push myself out and up to leave. Gina clamped her fingers tight over mine and whispered, "Please don't leave yet."

"Of course not." I said it loud enough so that Burton could hear. Not that he'd know what we were talking about, but he might have gotten the hint when I sat back down and crossed my legs and arms. I was not going anywhere. He'd have to go through me to get to her.

"Tallie, you're like a guard dog and a demon all wrapped into one."

"Call me a hellhound and let's get this over with."

"Jesus, I'm not coming with bad news. Would you give me a break every once in a while?"

"Possibly, if you'd start making some headway and leave my best friend alone. Or are you going to have to buy more flowers when this is all said and done?"

He narrowed his eyes at me. I probably shouldn't have blown Monty's secret like that, but I was not the happiest of campers. I was willing to drag Burton down into the mud with me. Only too happy to do it.

"I'm here to let Gina know she can get back to her house tonight. She doesn't have to stay with you again. We have some new information that makes me comfortable having her on her own. Now it's just a matter of putting all the clues together to make a full picture."

Whoops, I hadn't realized that when Burton said I could take her with me that she should have actually stayed with me the whole time. I wasn't going to be the one to tell him she had gone out to dinner with my brother and slept at her own house. That information was on a need to know basis, as he liked to say, and he didn't need to know.

He turned to me as Gina smiled. "See, not bad news at all."

"And how close are you to figuring things out?" Because I didn't have a clue and wanted him to tell me that he knew all, saw all, and I was no longer needed to get my friend off the hook he'd so conveniently put her on.

Instead of reassuring me he had it all under control, he scratched his head and twisted his lips.

"I'm getting there. These things take time. I heard from the hospital today that Brenna is coming around.

She's next on my list to talk to, but I wanted to give
Gina the good news first."

A group of four walked into the Bean, laughing
and joking with each other. Where the place had
been almost too quiet before, now it was loud. Dishes
clattered and conversations soared. Somehow those
four made the whole place seem full. They jockeyed
around the place and must have knocked into Laura,
because there was the distinct sound of a dish hitting
the floor and then her profuse apologizing as she
ran for the broom.

"I should head over to the hospital to see if Brenna
needs anything," I said with all the nonchalance I
could muster. "I feel like I owe it to her since I found
her, and I was the last person to see her upright,
other than the person who hurt her, that is."

"No." Burton's tone was stern, but I'd heard worse
from my father.

"Sure thing." I could lie with the best of them, too.

"Why do I have a feeling that you're not actually
agreeing that you shouldn't go to see her?"

"I have no idea. And now that you've delivered this
fabulous news to Gina, you should get on your way."

He shook his head at me but left nonetheless.

"That was good news! We're almost there." I patted
Gina's hand.

"Are we? I want whoever did this caught. Until they
are, they might still try to do more things to point the
finger at me."

"It's going to be okay." Or at least I hoped it was.
No need to burden her with my doubts.

"And I'm still having trouble with the stairwell.
Last night I was too tired to care, but I hope I'll be
able to go up there without seeing him at the bottom

over and over again. I had a hard time the first night before Burton threw me in jail and then released me to you."

"I think you'll be okay. It might take a while, but I also think that once we have resolution for this whole thing, the memory will fade faster. Could you go up the back stairs?"

"It's blocked by boxes."

"And here I have a handyman who would be willing to move those for you. Or we could ask Jeremy. I bet he'd be happy to come over and help, especially if we promised him dinner. This is supposed to be his last night off and we should do something that will make him happy."

"You are not trying to hook me up with your brother."

"Hmm, no. I *was* wondering how dinner went the other night. You know, the one I wasn't invited to?"

She blushed and turned away. Ah-ha!

"Anything you want to tell me?" I nudged her with my elbow.

"Nothing you want to hear." The look on her face was a mix of chagrin and smugness.

Yeah, actually, I probably didn't want to know where that came from or what it meant.

"At least tell me if it's still going to be awkward to have my brother come to your house for dinner and a couple of board games. We have to do board games. They help me think."

"It won't be uncomfortable for me, but he might shy away. It's what he's good at."

"Okay, maybe I do want to hear this," I said. "The Mighty Jeremy doesn't shy away from anything."

"I don't know what it is about me, but he runs hot,

very hot, warm, and cold. We'll see if he even decides to show up tonight. I think I might have him on the run." Now the smug won out over the chagrin. Interesting.

"And do you want him on the run?"

"I'm not entirely sure yet, but in the meantime, it's good to be with a man I can trust. Someone I've known for years, so there's that. I didn't think I'd ever be interested in anyone from our town. Not really, anyway, because there's so much history. But history can be a good thing when you're looking for someone who isn't living a double life and who doesn't have a wife at home waiting for him to walk in the door."

"You're not wrong. Just don't break his heart. Please." I didn't want to push her here, but I did want her to take this at least a little bit seriously. I didn't want my brother hurt by having him shoved into the role of rebound boy.

"I promise, Tallie, I won't break his heart."

"Well, maybe you could just a little—to bring him down a notch?"

"You are trouble." She gave me a smile, the one I'd been missing lately with all this stuff going on. "Now what should we make for dinner? I'm thinking I want to actually cook, not order out again."

My mouth watered just thinking about her cooking. Gina made a mean coffee and her crullers were to die for, but when you let her fly in the kitchen, she became absolutely divine.

A year ago, when she and I had first started reconnecting, I had desperately wanted to know why she hadn't gone full bore on a restaurant with the food and the wine. She could still make the coffees, the pastries, the sugary goodness in a full restaurant. But she'd said it was too much pressure and the hours were too long. That I understood and was only too happy that she still made me food. Bring on the dinner and games!

After the boxes blocking the back entrance to Gina's apartment were moved by Max and Jeremy while we ladies sat on the couch and sipped wine, we got down to the eating portion of the evening. Throughout our conversations, I kept catching Jeremy sneaking glances at Gina. She, on the other hand, openly admired him and even winked at him a few times. The boy was totally on the run, and I was going to have fun watching him be caught. *If* that was what Gina intended.

I did worry a little, because if they each hurt the other I wouldn't know whom to console and whom to hit upside the head. I shrugged to myself—guess I'd just smack and hug them both.

Over chicken marsala and fluffy rice pilaf, Max groaned and looked at me from across the table.

"Can I compliment the chef without hurting your feelings?"

I laughed. "Absolutely." Toasting him with my wine-glass, I started. "Gina, that was magnificent. If I could cook like that I would not fit down your stairs and probably not through any regular-sized doors around here. You are a kitchen goddess."

"Well, forget it now," Max said with a smile. "I won't be able to top that, but I will say that is the best meal I've ever had, and I've eaten at some five-star restaurants in Washington DC. It was wonderful."

DC. Where he lived and I still hadn't visited. I might need to seriously consider fixing that. At least make an effort to get to know some of his friends. I mean, it wasn't as if I didn't want to be in his life more than a weekend here or a week there. It's just I was also very comfortable in my little town and I liked knowing everyone. At least for the most part.

But effort would be good, if I really wanted this thing to work.

Jeremy was curiously silent, but he had a look on his face that reminded me of the time he'd taken one of my dolls and cut her hair off, then burned it because he said he was a Viking making a sacrifice. Yes, we had been under ten, but I still remembered that doll and mourned her loss.

"Why the smirk?" I asked, not very politely. Little Cammy Cozy, with her long blond hair that I'd loved to comb while I sang to her, was fresh in my mind.

"I just enjoy a great meal, and Gina's cooking is even better than our mom's."

Glee filled me. The unholy kind. "Oh, I am so telling her you said that."

He sputtered and jerked in his chair. "Don't you dare. I'll never hear the end of it."

"Precisely." My wicked laugh rang through the house.

"Now, Tallie, don't be mean to Jeremy. He can enjoy my food without getting in trouble because you told. Isn't that right, Max?"

Oh, double whammy. Maybe I didn't want her dating my brother if she was going to take his side and rope Max into agreeing with her. I grumbled to myself, but in truth, I liked the easy smile on Jeremy's face and even more the one on Gina's as she looked at my brother. It wasn't the goo-goo eyed, smarmy, smitten one she'd had for Craig. This was more real and more appreciative. Equal footing.

"Games," I said before I could get too far into the wine or my thoughts. My brother and Gina did not need me as a matchmaker, and I had too many things to do to worry about their love lives.

"What are we playing?" Gina asked.

"Rummy tile." It was my turn to pick the game, but I knew the reaction I would get and anticipated it with a smile.

Max groaned and so did Gina and Jeremy. I rocked this game and it would help me think.

Twenty minutes later, I'd run the table a few times, stealing pieces from other people's tile arrangements to make my own and racking up the points. "Right now, we have a guy who died and no real clue who did it. Several women and at least one man have the motive and possibly the opportunity." I stole a four from Gina and made a set of three of a kind.

"Okay, but who was the woman who circled the block while my mom was here? And did anyone ever find out what time Craig actually died?" she asked.

I still hadn't found those oversized tires. And the thought of him lying down at the bottom of the steps for hours was creepy. I was not going to bring that up. It wasn't worth discussing, especially since Gina seemed to be willing to talk about this like a puzzle to solve instead of a death that had occurred in her home.

"Dad told me it was about eleven at night." Jeremy stole from Max to make a four of a kind and had my man groaning. Poor Max only had one more set of tiles in front of him, a set of twos. He had every right to groan. If he didn't start making some moves, he was going to be dead last.

No pun intended.

"Eleven means that the woman circling in the car could have been here at exactly that time. And you all didn't see anyone out on the street when you left at ten?" Gina asked.

I did not want to admit that Max and I had been so caught up in each other as we crossed the street that I didn't even think to look both ways before I stepped into possible oncoming traffic. I just shook my head and Max did the same. Good thing.

"You didn't happen to be out, Jeremy, did you?" Gina pulled a tile from in front of him and he groaned. He was doing almost as badly as Max.

"No, I was sitting on my back porch, enjoying the moonlight."

Nicely done and a good visual. Gina gave a little sigh. I knew she liked living above her shop, but we'd talked frequently about wanting a yard and a porch and backyard stuff. She wanted that as much as I did. I might get it someday, but unless she wanted to rent this place out or got married to someone who already owned a house, that might never be in the cards for her.

"I'm still waiting to hear from Monty, but I don't know what he has, if anything." I filled in the two guys about the conversation with the florist, making them swear that they wouldn't tell anyone else because I did not want it to get around town that Monty had a security camera. Maybe some people already knew, but I hadn't and that said something.

"I feel like I'm at a dead end." I pulled another tile from Gina, one from Max, and a whole set from

Jeremy. I laid down the last of the tiles on my rack and called out "rummy."

"I don't like playing with you," Gina said.

Jeremy agreed.

"I do," Max said, and got his arm smacked by Gina.

"We do not need to hear that kind of thing."

But it broke us all out in laughter, which was good. Murder had happened in this house, and the more we could laugh and eradicate the feelings left in here, the better. Now, if I could just figure out who'd done it so that Gina could rest easy.

Max and I left and Jeremy stayed. I had no idea if he'd be going home tonight. Quite frankly, it was none of my business. I promised myself that I would not look out the window to see when his car left the street. And I didn't. Max kept me too busy. We talked and laughed and snuggled. This was the stuff a real relationship was made of. I had not the slightest clue what I was missing when I'd been with Waldo for all those years. It was never too late to learn, though, and I was a most apt pupil.

After a good night's sleep, I was up and raring to go. I had clues to follow and people to sniff out and a woman in the hospital to visit. I was fully aware Burton didn't want me within shouting distance of Brenna. For that matter, he probably didn't want me within driving distance of her. But he was out of luck.

I stopped at Monty's to grab a get-well bouquet and ask if he'd found anything.

"Not really. A couple of teenagers smoking out back and someone who tried all the doors, then walked away. I'll be reporting that. But nothing else out of the ordinary. I didn't even see the car driving around three times. Maybe she took a different route."

Dead end. But that was okay because I was hoping to get some real info from the woman who had survived the attacker.

The hospital was on this side of the river, but still ten minutes and two towns away.

I parked in the lot to the side and got my flowers out of the car. I had a story all prepared. I really was concerned about her welfare, so it wasn't that big of a stretch that I'd come visit her.

Matt had called me this morning to tell me Brenna couldn't remember anything. While that was disappointing, I was not going to miss out on the opportunity to ask my own questions. I might jar something loose that had stayed walled up when talking to the cops.

I rode the elevator to the fourth floor, very happy that I had not seen one glimpse of Burton. He should have other things to do and other places to do them. This murder might be the biggest thing going on right now, but that didn't mean the other, smaller stuff had stopped happening.

I made it all the way to her door, smoothed down my hair, ran over my lines one more time, and knocked.

"You might as well come in, Tallie," I heard a masculine voice call out. Burton. Of course.

"Hello!" I made sure to go cheerfully into the hospital room. No use in showing Burton that I was miffed he was here.

"Oh, Tallie, they're beautiful." Brenna rested in the hospital bed, her brown hair a slight mess, but not looking any worse for wear after her ordeal. I had been happy to hear that she wasn't really pregnant and even happier to hear that she hadn't suffered any long-term effects from the poison since her doctor had been able to get it out of her system before it did damage.

"Thank Monty if you ever get to that side of town."

"I will. I go there all the time. He has the best se-lection." She took the bouquet of yellow and white daisies mixed with yellow roses and shoved her nose into them. "They smell lovely. Thank you again. You didn't have to stop by though, you barely know me."

"Oh, she would have stopped by anyway, even if she hadn't known your name."

Glaring at Burton would do me no good, so I ig-nored him. "I just wanted to make sure you were okay. I was the one who found you, and I was so scared. I'm happy to see you sitting here and breathing."

"I'm happy to be here and breathing."

Now how to ask the questions that were burning my tongue without getting into trouble? Then again, Burton had told me to do my thing and bring him any info I found if it happened to fall into my lap. I guess this was me more plucking it out of the tree than waiting for the fruit to fall on its own, but it was all the same in my book.

"So now that you're recovered, do you remember anything?"

Burton twitched in his seat. I caught it out of the corner of my eye but did not turn to look at him.

"Not really. I wish I could because then the police could catch whoever tried to do this to me, but I really don't know. I remember a woman from your staff came in looking for more tissues, and I didn't want to be in the way. I got up to leave, but she told me it was fine and offered me more tea."

"Wait. Are you sure it was a woman who came in for tissues?" The answer would either help or put me into a tailspin.

Chapter Thirteen

I knew everyone on staff. I was normally the tissue getter. And I was the only woman working the memorial that day. We had others, part-time workers who answered the phones, made copies or ran invoices, but none of them had been working that day. Who was this mysterious person and was she the one who had poisoned Brenna?

Max had come looking for tissues after my father had pulled me out of the kitchen to take me to task, but there had been no one else that I knew of. I had indicated the tissues weren't in the kitchen as we stood outside the closed door. I distinctly remembered telling him they were in the closet down the hall.

"Yes, a woman," Brenna answered, cutting into my thoughts. "She excused herself and looked flustered to find me in there. I was quick to move out of her way because I didn't want to cause trouble."

"What did she look like?"

"Is she going to get into trouble? She wasn't mean or anything. Actually she was very nice. She helped me get some sugar for my tea and let me sit back down at the table. I appreciated that flowery stuff you gave me, but the sugar really helped."

"Ah, I always appreciate our staff being helpful, and it should be fine. I'll just send her your thanks." I willed Burton to keep his mouth shut as he sat on the edge of his chair.

"She had blond hair, piled on top of her head. I was surprised. With how tidy the rest of you were, she looked out of place. But she was so nice that I didn't want to judge. I thought maybe she was someone who worked behind the scenes. I don't know a whole lot about funerals and the places they happen."

She wouldn't have been completely wrong. We did have people who worked behind the scenes sometimes, but even they had to be pressed and spit-polished per my father. When working with the public you could be called upon at any moment and you had to look like you knew what you were doing even if you didn't.

"Oh, I'll make sure to tell her thanks for the sugar."

"I appreciate it." She fidgeted with her fingers in her lap. "After she doctored my tea for me, we laughed as she called me a sweet fiend because I kept telling her more sugar would be fine. She even apologized that she only had powdered creamer instead of the real stuff. I asked her if she could show me where the after-memorial party was going to be. I wanted to experience the whole thing, no matter how mad I was. She told me to take my tea with me. She showed me into the room and told me I had ten minutes before I had to be gone, and then she left me there. I wandered around and then I don't remember anything else."

"I'm sorry it happened to you at the funeral parlor."

"I'm just happy I'm okay. Thank you for being so quick to help."

"Of course," I said absently. My mind was whirling with questions and puzzle pieces clicking along. I had to get out of there and start looking for this woman who had access to the funeral parlor. "I should get going. I'm glad you like the flowers and I'll let Monty know." I rose from the side of the bed and patted Brenna's hand.

Burton rose with me. "I'll be back. I just have to talk to Tallie for a minute."

He opened the door and waited for me to go through into the hallway. I was prepared to be yelled at, though he'd have to keep his voice down. I found myself very okay with that.

"Say your piece. I shouldn't have come here. I shouldn't be asking questions. It's none of my business and I should keep my nose out of it. Does that about cover everything? Did I leave any scolding out?"

He shook his head at me and hooked his fingers into his belt loops. "You continue to amaze me. Not always in the best of ways, mind you, but amaze me anyway."

I stared at him, waiting for the other shoe to drop. I mean, it had to. It always did. That almost sounded like praise, and there was no way he was going to leave it at that when he had the chance to take me to the mat and tell me in his own terms to butt out.

"Okay." I dragged the word out when he didn't say anything else, just kept shaking his head as if he was dumbfounded. That made two of us.

"It really is okay. I'll tell you what, Tallie. I'm almost

tempted to hire you just to see what you could do if you actually had the authority to meddle in this kind of stuff. But you have your own jobs, and I really don't think we'd want to have to deal with each other on a daily basis. Not to mention I can't imagine you being okay with me being your boss. So I'm just going to say good job. She didn't say a word about anyone coming into the kitchen with her, and she didn't mention the sugar at all to me. Only that she had been alone in the room and the door had been unlocked."

Well, score one for me. No scolding and a job offer and praise. I had to change that number, though. Make that score three but minus one, to come out with two, since he wanted to hire me, but apparently could not handle the fact that he'd have to deal with me. Still, two out of three wasn't bad in my book.

"Really? She didn't say anything? I guess it wouldn't have occurred to her since the employee should have been ours. Do you think she used the poison when she put sugar in the tea? I can't think of another time she'd have access. And Brenna was clear that the woman wanted her to carry the tea with her, not leave it behind." Hmm. Who on my suspect list would have been in there and had blond hair? I was trying to run through the list but Burton interrupted me.

"Now, don't go getting all high and mighty on me. I still don't need your interference. What I do need to do is call the station and see if they picked up a teacup from the carpet. I'll be sending Matt around to pick it up if not. And he'll take the sugar, too, just in case."

"I'll make sure they're available." I even gave him a little salute, which made him grimace. Well, we couldn't have a great encounter without something going awry, or we just wouldn't be the frenemies we very obviously were.

I called my mom on the way back to the funeral home. I had a house to clean in thirty minutes, but May Davenport wouldn't mind if I was ten minutes late. She was a sweet mother of four and had a dentist for a husband. They lived in a nicer neighborhood, though not on the hill. I liked her enough to usually sit down and have a cup of tea with her to give her some real live adult interaction since all her four were under five years old.

"Mom, are you in the kitchen?"

"That's an odd question to ask before saying hello and asking me how I am."

Good Lord. Everyone was a critic and no one understood the kind of pressure I was under. "Hi, how are you? Are you in the kitchen?"

"I'm fine, and no, I'm not in the kitchen. I'm making sure everything is cleaned up in the downstairs. Why do you want to know? The kitchen is next."

"Because Matt is coming over and needs something from the kitchen." I didn't want to go into the whole thing because she would start fretting.

"Well, tell him to hurry because I'm cleaning out the cabinets next. Daddy decided he wants everything scrubbed down after the incident the other day. I told him I already cleaned, but he wants cabinets emptied and new contact paper put in there. It's not even spring yet!"

"Don't touch anything!"

"Why on earth not? Daddy wants it clean and I'm

going to clean it. It's the last room and I want to be finished. I want some time with my friends at the book club. I always seem to be the one cleaning up when I don't even make the messes." She harrumphed and I knew a tangent was coming about feeling under-appreciated and overused. It was a common occurrence.

Before she could get going, I cut in. "Please just don't touch anything. Matt will be there soon. There might be evidence in the kitchen they missed."

"Oh my goodness! Evidence? That's horrible! Daddy is going to be livid!"

"Mom, please. I need you to focus. Just keep away from the kitchen and don't touch anything else."

"Well, fine then."

I heard the huff of indignation and decided to ignore it. "I'm right around the corner. If Dad has an issue, tell him he can take it up with me and with Burton."

I pulled through the gates, down the tunnel, and around the back a minute later. My dad met me at the door.

"You know how we run things around here, Tallie. Your mother does not need to be talked to in such a way that she's upset when I walk into the kitchen."

"I'm aware of that and yet there was nothing else I could do. The woman who was poisoned here might have been poisoned right in our kitchen."

He took a step back. "What?"

"I don't know if it's in the sugar or if the person added something when they put the sugar in Brenna's cup, but I need everything. Burton is currently asking if the cup Brenna drank out of is at the station. Matt is coming for the items and I need them now."

"Of course. Of course." He strode to the counter. "Wait! Gloves!"

He halted with his hand hovering over the sugar shaker. "Uh, yes, right." He pulled a set out of his breast pocket. The man was rarely without them, just in case, he said. And this was a just-in-case kind of moment. Retrieving the shaker, he grabbed a plastic baggie from a drawer and gingerly placed it in there. "That should keep any contaminants out."

I only hoped that this would bring us one step closer to finding the killer. Fingerprints would be nice at this moment.

I met Matt at the front door with the sealed bag. He eyed it, then eyed me and shook his head. "It's always something with you."

"Just do your job and go away. Oh, and have your sister call me, or I'm going to call your mom."

He trotted back to his car while flipping me a wave. That might not work to get Deandra to call, but I wanted to give her one more chance before I called in the big guns.

I'd checked with Jeremy and Max to make sure neither of them had touched the sugar. Fortunately, they hadn't. Max demanded to know what was going on. I took the time to tell him and then told him to enjoy his batting cage time with Jeremy, and I'd see him later.

"Do you need me to help you clean?" he asked.

"Only if you want me to be done sooner."

"I do. I was wondering if you might accompany me to dinner tonight. I still need to make up for the one we never got to go to the other night."

"Fancy dress?"

"The fanciest you have."

"You're on. Meet me at the house and we'll get this done." I gave him the address for May's and told him I'd see him soon.

This might actually work out better. I could get all the cleaning done while I stuck him with talking to May. I really liked the woman and usually enjoyed our time, but I wanted to be out of there quickly this time, not an hour over tea talking about mundane stuff. I'd make it up to her next time. Max and I could head out in record time. Where was he taking me? Fancy meant what? Were we going to talk about serious things? Or did he just want to see if I cleaned up nice first?

I had never really wished that I'd kept anything from my days as Mrs. Walden Phillips the Third, but right now I found myself wishing for my closet and that I had at least one dress that I'd had custom tailored for all those parties Waldo had made me throw.

I'd find something, though, or I'd ask Gina if I could raid her closet.

True to his word, Max was already at the house and sitting in his car when I got there. He hadn't gone inside yet, and I appreciated that. This was my job, and I didn't want him to scare the client by showing up at her front door unannounced and telling her he was the cleaning crew, expecting her to let him in.

"You ready for this?" I asked as he climbed out of his SUV and kissed me on the lips.

"As I'll ever be. What are we doing with this one? Deep cleaning? Spiffing up?"

"Well, you're going to be talking while I'm going to be cleaning. Oh, and there are four kids here."

"Ah." It came out a little strangled, but he'd manage.

Two hours and ten minutes later—I timed it by the amount of times Max had mouthed "hurry" at me—we were back on the road to my apartment.

When we arrived, my mom was all aflutter.

"What on earth is going on?" I asked.

"Oh, Tallie, it's the worst thing. The cup tested positive for the poison and now Burton wants to talk to everyone again to see who was working that day and what they might remember."

"Is he in there now?" Visions of my night out with Max faded into nothing.

"He is, and he's not happy."

Of course he wasn't happy. He almost never was. Just for a brief moment this afternoon, maybe, but other than that, not so much.

"Let's get this over with."

Since there had only been my family and Max working that day, we were the only ones who had to be interviewed again. Max went before me, and I was last. No one had seen anything or had anything to add. I knew it hadn't been one of us. Burton was wasting time when I could have been trying to find out who had come in and poisoned a memorial-goer, or which memorial attendee had known enough to come into the kitchen and act like one of us.

I shared my theory with Burton.

"We're looking into that, Tallie, but I have to go through the proper channels. I can't wing it like you seem to like to do."

"And here you were just offering me a job based on my 'winging it' not three hours ago."

"You will not work for the police department," my mother cried.

"Now see what you did?" Burton said. "You've upset your mother for nothing since I also told you that I would never hire you."

"Oh, thank you, Burton. I always knew you were a smart one." Mom patted her hair. "I couldn't ever understand why Marilyn didn't see that and married Bud's brother Sherman instead. Not that we don't love Sherman, but he can be a pill."

Was that the reason Burton and Sherman didn't get along after all this time? I'd always wondered. But Aunt Marilyn had been gone for years, deciding that beach life was far more to her liking than dreary Pennsylvania. Last I'd heard, she had taken herself to the Florida Keys, where apparently, she was living with some fisher and gutting his catch every day. Not what I thought I would ever hear about my aunt, with her perfect manicure and hair styled to within an inch of its life. But she'd send pictures every once in awhile, overalls and top knot bun and a huge smile on her unmade face. One that I'd never seen when she had lived here with Sherman before they'd divorced.

Burton scowled. "We need to get back to business. While I have no intention of employing you, young lady, I do need you to go do something for me."

I met him stare for stare. Now he wanted something. Wasn't that typical?

"What could you possibly want? I have plans tonight."

"Well, perhaps you could take a moment out of your busy schedule and run on over to the Johnson house to get Michelle some clothes. She has no money to buy any more and is refusing to allow Drake to buy her any. She wants her own. Since she's not allowed in the house, she suggested you, and I was just crazy enough to agree to the idea."

Hold the presses! Michelle wanted me to look around for clothes in the house that hadn't been touched since the day Lily had tried to invade? I could also very possibly find so many other things that I had wanted to look for when we cleaned but couldn't with her hanging around.

I glanced at Max because this would put our dinner back.

He shrugged and I took that as a yes. Any restaurant worth its salt was still open at ten at night and we could easily be there at eight if I was fast and furious in my search.

"Of course I'll help. I'm always ready to do what needs to be done to keep people happy and clothed."

Maybe I'd poured it on a little too thick, because Burton narrowed his eyes at me. I jumped up and waved to everyone in the room before Burton could warn me not to touch anything that wasn't clothes. If he didn't say it, then I didn't have to follow it.

Max caught up with me at the back door. "I'd like to go with you. I'd feel better if you weren't alone. I have a bad vibe about this for some reason."

"Sure. Do you want to take my car or yours?" Two sets of eyes and hands would help immensely and maybe we could be at dinner at seven. I wanted that dinner and whatever it entailed.

"Let's take mine," he said. "In case you find anything that you think might be helpful *beyond* clothes."

Ah, he knew me well. I found that I liked that immensely.

* * *

First, we stopped at Drake's to get the keys. Michelle greeted us at the door, looking very at home even if she was in the same clothes I'd seen her in when she'd been sitting in jail.

Drake stood behind her with his hand hovering at the small of her back. Not quite touching but definitely there in case she needed him.

"I've made up a list for you, Tallie." Michelle handed over a sheet of paper. "It also has where you'll find the clothes. Some toiletries would be nice, too, if you think you have time." Her voice was not the coo she'd used when speaking with Craig, or the wheedling she'd done with Burton, nor the anger she'd displayed with Matt. It was even and strong, if a little sad. I had to keep reminding myself that she'd just lost her husband, and no matter if he'd been unfaithful in deed or just word, it still had to hurt to know you were never first on someone's list of priorities.

"I'll get it all and bring it back within the hour."

"Thanks. I'd really like to change."

"And I told you time and again that I could afford to provide for you, Michelle. Why are you being so stubborn?" Drake stepped into her line of vision but she turned her head away from him.

"Because I want to be independent, and I already have clothes. I don't need new. I want my own. Until this mess is sorted out I want to be me. Not someone else, not a shadow of myself, not an extension of anyone. Just me. And if you can't understand that, then I don't know what to tell you." She stormed off into the house leaving Drake standing at the door looking baffled.

I'd been thinking hard about her situation and

tried to offer Drake some insight. "I think she's struggling with having given so many years to a husband who might not have even been hers, and putting up with years of being shunted to the side only to find out that everything she thought they were working toward is no longer hers." I didn't know if it helped him or not, but I'd been wondering how I would have felt if some other wife had shown up out of the blue when Waldo and I were married. I would have probably been relieved to hand him off to whomever the woman was, but Michelle had loved her husband, flaws and all. And the blow of Lily waltzing into the memorial party was probably not the easiest thing Michelle had ever endured.

Wait. If Lily had sat in the café until the timing was right to announce her marriage, then had she been there the whole time? Or had she been at the memorial?

I was willing to risk Burton's wrath to ask Lily some pointed questions. If she had heard Brenna wailing about the child, not knowing that it wasn't true, then we had a player who might have had far more to lose and a whole lot to gain by getting rid of the woman and her supposed child.

We said our good-byes and got back into Max's car. Heading to the Johnson house, I ran over the list of things I wanted access to.

"I would love to be able to get into Craig's computer. I want to at least peek into his closet again. He struck me as the kind of person who would have kept track of his conquests. There has to be a list somewhere. And I want to check on the sleeping situation. Is there another bedroom that looks lived in, or were Craig and Michelle really close and she did totally ignore his infidelity?"

Max nodded. "I'm sure we can do all that, but we might have a problem with the police who appear to be surrounding the house right now."

I had been so lost in my musings that I hadn't realized we'd crossed the river and were now parked in front of Craig's house. Along with about ten police cruisers and a fire truck.

The house was not currently on fire, but it was definitely not in good shape. The roof was smoking and smoke belched out of the windows. Firemen were working on the outside of the house, and every once in a while one would go in dressed in full gear.

Because the house should have been locked up tight, I hoped that no one was in there for them to save.

"Well, I guess we're not getting any clothes out of that, or anything else for that matter," I said, slumping in my seat.

From what I could see through busted windows, it looked like the whole inside was charred black. What had happened? How had the fire started? Had someone set it? Was it deliberate? To hide something? Or to take something away from someone else?

Since this investigation would be led by law enforcement in this town, I had no hope of getting any info unless I could prevail upon Burton to ask for me. I didn't know if they would share information with him, but it was worth trying. I'd put it on my list of things to do after I went back to Drake's and let Michelle know that there was nothing to salvage, and her house was not only going to need cleaning this time but all-out gutting. If it even remained her house.

We stood there for another hour, just watching the men work and talking quietly about how it could have happened. I heard a few mentions of arson. That wouldn't have surprised me in the midst of all this chaos surrounding Craig's death. But who would have torched the place?

It couldn't have been Michelle; she was at Drake's.

And I doubted it was Lily, since she thought she was inheriting the house. Why would she ruin her own things? Unless she thought she'd get more out of the insurance money than she would from owning a house where her husband and his woman had lived for all these years. Maybe the reminders were too much for her. But when a fire happened like this, it wasn't like they just handed you a check. They wanted to know why and how before they'd sign anything.

The fire trucks rolled away and the police left after combing through things. Max and I had returned to his car, but I wasn't ready to leave yet.

Who would clean this mess? And was that something that maybe I should think about offering? I had a brief thought of expanding my company from just me and Letty to fire cleanup or even disaster cleanup, and then pushed the thought aside. I was busy enough as it was.

Once everyone had gone, I got back out of the car to get a clearer view of what had happened.

I had zero experience with fires, though, so I probably looked foolish just standing there. Hopefully, no one would think I was admiring my own handiwork and call the cops back.

Lost in that thought, I missed the woman waving to me from the house next door. The sun was lowering in the sky. Maybe Max and I would have to do dinner another night.

The woman was on the second floor with what looked like a towel wrapped around her body.

"Yoohoo! Yes, you!" she said when I finally turned to her.

"Um, yes. Hi." I had no idea who she was, but perhaps asking a few questions wouldn't hurt.

"Come on over. I'm coming down right now."

I hoped she would get dressed before she did.

All six feet of her answered the door. Her beautiful, rich, dark skin gleamed with droplets of water and her smile was like sunshine.

"Oh, thank you for coming over. Do you mind coming in? It's not chilly today, but I don't want to stand in the doorway in a towel." Her laugh was deep and infectious. It invited you in just as her hand was pulling me into the house. I grabbed behind me for Max because I was not doing this by myself. I was very happy that he had decided to join me this time.

Jade-green walls were accented with beautiful paintings of exotic locales. The hardwood floors beneath my feet shone so brightly I thought I should probably take my shoes off. But she didn't give me time to do much more than glance around before she continued to drag me along by my wrist, up the stairs and into a spacious bathroom. I'd tried to pull away several times from both her and Max on the way up the narrow staircase, but her grip tightened and Max would not let me go either.

"We're in this together," he whispered. "Where you go, I go." Wasn't that sweet? Although I was not exactly happy that he was in a strange woman's bathroom, with or without me.

Chapter Fourteen

As much as I wasn't happy about being in the woman's bathroom, I was floored when said strange woman dropped her towel and stepped back into her full bathtub. At least there were strategically placed bubbles to hide the most important pieces of her statuesque body. I wished I looked even a quarter like that.

"So, um." I cleared my throat once she'd settled in and was waving bubbles around like a mermaid in some kind of side show.

"Yes, hello. I'm Rose. Sorry I didn't introduce myself earlier, but I wanted to get back to my lavender bath before it cooled. You understand. Your skin is lovely. You must care for it like I do mine."

Well, no, not entirely. I used facecloths from the grocery store to wipe down every morning and evening, but that was about the extent of my beauty regime. Still, I thanked her because I wanted to get out of the fragrant bathroom with its naked lady. I truly hoped she had some information that would make it worth having come in here, because at the moment I seriously doubted the wisdom of not running as soon as she opened the door in a towel.

"Thank you." I looked anywhere but at her lounging in the bath. Max had better be doing the same thing. "You, uh, said you had information?"

"Yes, I did, and I'd like to share it with you. Those men were too busy putting the fire out, and I want this information in someone's hands before they come back around for me. I don't like the police at all. An incident from my past, if you must know, and I won't be answering the door for them, so I expect you to be my mouthpiece."

I didn't know if that would actually work. Even if I shared whatever information she had, they would still have to talk with her to collaborate. They wouldn't take secondhand information if they were any kind of smart.

"Of course," I agreed anyway. The logistics would be dealt with later. I did wonder briefly why she wanted to tell me anything, but I wasn't going to miss out on information from a next-door neighbor if I could help it. "What would you like me to tell them?"

She had beautiful small squares of tile inlaid into the wall in a mosaic of a mermaid swimming with a turtle. I counted every one of those tiles while I waited for her to answer.

"There was a person there at the house last night. I like to keep my eye on the neighbors just in case anything untoward happens, and so I use my binoculars if I have to in order to get a good idea of what's happening."

How many times had she watched any number of people doing things they shouldn't, or even things they should, thinking that no one was watching and they could be themselves?

It gave me the creeps and made me even happier that I lived in one of the tallest buildings in town. Other than Gina, I had no neighbors who could see into my living space.

"And what did you see, Miss Rose?" Max asked when I'd stayed quiet too long thinking about the many things she could have witnessed.

"Well, see now, not much ever goes on over at that house." She scooped bubbles and blew them toward her red toenails. "But last night someone was there, going from door to window to door to see if they could get in."

"Did you get a good look at the person?" I had a list of suspects a mile long, and if I could narrow it down, then we might start making some progress toward figuring this whole thing out.

"The person was dressed all in black. I couldn't really tell if it was a man or a woman because only wisps of blond hair stuck out under the ridiculous beanie he or she had on." She blew another handful of bubbles. This time toward Max. I stepped in between, taking them square in the gut. She laughed and winked at me. "Must've been hot in the night with all those clothes on, too. I think it was a woman, from the silhouette. But she also seemed to know where the cameras were. Mrs. Johnson installed those once she figured out how many nights she was sleeping in that house alone down the hall from where she thought her husband was snoozing away."

So, Michelle had installed the cameras, and she and Craig had not been sleeping in the same room. Was this whole "pushing me to run to her house" a ruse? Was this her big mistake? Did she want me to find the house on fire while she had a solid alibi?

I wouldn't put it past her. She was hot and cold, and her hot was like lava. I could see her burning down her own house to make sure Lily got nothing out of it. And without anywhere to go and possibly no money, would she torch it only to get caught and put in jail where she'd get three squares a day and not have to deal with life after Craig in a town that knew everything he'd done?

I doubted that last one, but it did bear thinking about.

"Let me make sure I understand. You saw someone checking things out and didn't call the cops?" I asked.

"Told you, I don't like the cops. I told you, now you go tell them." She swirled the bubbles so that they played peek-a-boo with her more rounded parts.

I figured that was our invitation to exit.

"Okay, well, thanks. We'll just see ourselves out. Do you want us to lock the door on the way out?"

"Of course. I'm a woman alone and don't want anyone to come in while I'm unaware. Thanks, sugar." She sighed. "And make sure you keep an eye on that big handsome man of yours, or someone else might snatch him up. Just sayin'." She laughed. I laughed haltingly with her, pulling Max out of the bathroom behind me.

We made it out the door and onto the street without any other incident.

"Did you find that weird, too, or was that just me?" I asked as we trekked to his SUV.

"Uh, no." He tugged at the collar of his shirt.

"No, you didn't find it weird, or no, that wasn't just me?"

"It wasn't just you. Did you get a look at the picture on the opposite wall with the squid and the woman?"

I'd totally missed that. "No, what was so special about it?"

"Nothing. Nothing at all." He gulped. "I don't always understand art. I hope that isn't a point against me when you think about the future."

I tugged on his arm and brought him down for a kiss. "Absolutely not. Now, let's go tell Michelle everything she owns is gone and see what her reaction is. Maybe she and Drake are still in this together. She might not want him to touch her, and she might not think he'd be good for her, but I wouldn't be completely surprised if she'd used his love to get what she wanted in the end, only to have had her rug burned out from beneath her."

"I can't disagree with that."

Back at Drake's, the scene was much different than when we showed up last time. Drake stood in the picture window with one hand on his hip and the other waving through the air like he was directing an orchestra, or maybe showing a plane how to land.

Michelle paced back and forth, gesticulating wildly, her hair a mess and her movements jerky. Were they fighting? Had the partnership finally broken down, and now they didn't know what to do with each other?

I was extremely tempted to just see if I could open the door but didn't want to be arrested for breaking and entering if Drake decided to press charges.

In the end, I knocked. There was a half-minute of silence before the front door was yanked open by a disheveled Drake.

"What took you so long? She wanted clothes and it's been almost three hours."

"Get out of the way, Drake. I'm going to my mother's once I have my clothes." Michelle stalked to the door and wedged in front of Drake. "You can take your precious business and shove it."

"So, um, there was a slight problem with the clothes." I explained the scene we'd come upon and Michelle's mouth went from slightly open to a complete jaw drop, then her lips pressed together and quivered. She was going to cry, and I didn't do well with crying. Neither did Max, but he stayed with me even though I could feel him trying to step back.

"Maybe we should leave," he whispered into my ear.

"No, I think this is the perfect time to be here. Let's ask questions while they're riled." I whispered it back, but Drake must have had the hearing of a bat.

"We're not riled up."

Michelle scoffed. "You might not be, but I certainly am. Drake just told me that he and Craig had words the afternoon he died and then he followed Craig around to see if he could talk him into keeping his shares of the company. The man was an idiot and was going to make us destitute. What did I ever see in him?"

I didn't know what to say to that question. I certainly wasn't going to try to answer it. I turned to Drake. "Did you follow him when he went to drop those flowers off to Gina?"

"Yes!" he yelled, frustration shouting from his every gesture. "Yes, I did. I went to convince him that

Gina would never forgive him. He thought that she was just putting on a show in the coffeehouse. He was absolutely and stupidly convinced they were really meant to be together. In his mind, he was going to leave Michelle for Gina, thinking they could run the coffee shop together since he'd never really wanted to remodel houses in the first place. His idea was to have me buy him out, but I didn't have the kind of money he was looking for." By the end, he had stopped shouting and just seemed defeated.

Wow, there was so much wrong with that, I didn't even know where to start. "And did you see how he got into Gina's place?"

Drake sighed and rubbed his chin. "He had a key. I don't know if he had it made, or if she gave it to him before they broke up, but he had a key and he used it. I followed him up the stairs and we fought in whispers at the landing. He wanted to knock, and I kept telling him to think this all the way through. Think about what he was throwing away and come back another day, after he'd divorced Michelle and was a free man, if that was what he really wanted. But Craig was always impulsive and had to have what he wanted at that very moment. I never quite understood how he had the patience to do the kind of work we did when he was so quick with split-second decisions in every other area of his life."

Were we standing in the presence of the killer? My heart about stopped. Was he going to confess all and then kill every person in the room? Although he was outnumbered three to one and so far he'd only used poison.

"And did you push him down the stairs?" I asked.

I knew that I was taking a chance here, but I had to know.

"God, no! I wasn't going to convince him, and I was done trying. He was a waste of breath, but I did not kill him. He wasn't worth it."

I glanced at Michelle and saw her expression go from a frown to rolling her eyes. Was something Drake said making her disbelieve how naive he was? And why wasn't she scared? Did she believe him? Was she the killer? My poor brain was overloaded with questions and suspicions.

Then again, seeing Drake right now, and watching Michelle's reaction, I had a very hard time believing either of them had done the deed. And neither of them was my blond woman.

"What do you have to offer to that, Michelle?" Maybe she'd confess to something I had been wondering about for a little while now.

"Only that Craig didn't have patience. My God, he didn't even like to wait for real coffee in the morning. He wasn't the one working with you." She sneered at Drake. "That was me. He would bring home the ideas the clients had, would take pictures of the layout of the house, or the room that they wanted remodeled, and I would sketch up a variety of ways things could be done. Since most of the work seemed to be for women, I was able to take what they wanted and make it so much better. Craig took the credit, acting like he was in touch with women, but in fact it was me giving them their dreams."

Bingo! Got it in one. The way his house was set up screamed lazy man, and that could have just been the way he chose to live to get away from what he did at work. But for the house to not have a single feminine touch, and with the changes Michelle had talked about while I was there to help her clean things out, it all made sense now that I knew who the real mind behind Craig was. According to Monty, the man hadn't even been able to pick out complimentary colors with regard to flowers. There was no way he had been able to decorate on his own.

While I was congratulating myself on a job well done, Drake was apparently having a crisis.

"Are you kidding me? All these years that we'd been paying Craig and had to deal with him expensing all those flowers and almost running us into the ground financially—and it was you all along?" While I thought he would be relieved because it meant business could go on as usual, and he would have his true partner so maybe things would even turn out okay for them, he looked pissed. Like royally pissed that he'd been lied to all these years. I guess I could understand that. Because it didn't directly affect me, I was looking at the big picture while he was focusing on the smaller pieces that made it up, like the mosaic in Rose's bathroom.

Which reminded me to tell them about the person sneaking around the house.

"The, um, possible arson isn't the only thing," I started. They both turned weary eyes to me. Maybe I should keep this to myself for just a little while longer.

"Go on, Tallie," Michelle said. "I'm about done, but I want all the info, and if this is someone's doing, then I want them punished. I might not have loved that house, but I had plans for it, and my new life, if I even have anything left after this is all over."

I had seen a picture once of an old couple turned

away from each other, obviously angry with each other in the rain, sitting on a bench, but he still held an umbrella over her head. It had some pithy wording on it about still caring even if you're mad. Drake showed that now, as he took Michelle's hand and cradled it in his own. He might be pissed, he might feel betrayed, but under all that he still cared for her and probably always would. I hoped one day she'd see that and appreciate it.

"Well, it seems there was someone skulking around the place last night before it caught on fire."

"We'll get the feed. . . ." Michelle trailed off. "No, I guess we won't since it would have burned up in the fire."

"Not necessarily." Drake patted her hand and glanced up at us. "Craig kept that going in the office, too, and had remote access from his desktop. We might be able to see who was there. He told me once that it backs itself up."

"The camera burned, though," Michelle said, taking out her phone.

"And the neighbor said that the person kept out of the line of the cameras."

Michelle giggled and the sound was almost unnatural in the tense mood of the room. But she laughed harder when we all stared at her.

"Did Rose just happen to be in the bath when she called you over, with all her bubbles and her art depicting various sea creatures?"

"Um, yes."

"She's a character but she's also watched out for me over the years. We've shared more wine than I can calculate on the nights Craig never came home. And she knows where all the cameras are placed, too—

well, most of them, since I had a few installed that only I can access. I didn't think of that because I was thinking about the fire."

Swiping her finger across the screen, she scrolled along and tapped the icon to make it bigger. The shot was grainy when I stood over her shoulder, but you could definitely see someone moving around and trying to keep to the shadows.

"Do you recognize her?" I was convinced it was a woman with the way the waist dipped in.

"No, she doesn't look familiar at all, but then I don't know everyone who would have been involved with Craig. I never knew any of them, except Gina."

And that would have been why she'd gone after the one person she thought she could reach out and slap. But then her husband had died and the real wife had come waltzing in. I still didn't know how Lily had known how to find him, but thought it would be best to ask Burton for his info.

Burton, who was waiting for me to report that I'd done his favor. Burton, who was not going to be happy that I'd seen the fire. Though, of course, it was his fault I was there in the first place.

"Can you send me that footage?" I'd hand it to Burton, who could then send it to the fire chief across the river.

"Yes."

I rattled off my e-mail address, then Max and I took our leave. There was nothing more to do here, and I still wanted to get to that dinner, though it was getting closer and closer to eight. If I wanted to look fancy, I was going to need time to actually shower and put some makeup on.

"Burton?" I asked Max, sitting in the seat next to me with the ignition running.

"I guess so, but we might need to do the dinner another night. I don't know if we'll have time."

"We'll make time. I'm sorry this is taking up so much of your vacation. I'm sure when you came up here you weren't expecting to be embroiled in another murder case."

With his foot still on the brake, he turned to me in the driveway. "I expected to spend time with you, and that's exactly what I'm doing. It doesn't have to be anything special; it doesn't have to be fantastic. I'd prefer it not be so mysterious sometimes, but it's time with you, and that's the important thing."

Be still my thundering heart. I leaned over the console in his SUV and kissed him hard. "Let's buzz by Burton's and then we, sir, have a dinner to attend."

"Yes, ma'am." He shoved the car into gear and hightailed it down the road and away from the two people I hoped might be able to get it right as long as neither of them had really killed Craig.

Burton only sighed when I told him about Drake and my feelings about his innocence. He was all set to go get the man for questioning anyway when I broke the news of the fire. He already knew about it, of course, but shook his head at me for being on the frontline once again. He did at least nod at me when I handed him the footage from Michelle's phone.

"I'd tell you 'good work' like I would a rookie, but I'm almost afraid it would inflate your ego to the point that I'd never get rid of you, even if you or your friends had nothing at stake in what was happening in the department or the borough."

Well, that wasn't exactly a thanks, but it wasn't a kick in the teeth, either. I'd take it.

"Oh, and I was able to look into that marriage certificate, and it seems that Lily is mistaken. Since she and Craig got married when she was underage, and she had no parental consent, the marriage is null and void."

"Holy crap."

"Yes, well, I was going to let Michelle know she could go back to her house, but I guess it doesn't matter now."

"Oh, I think it would matter to her. In fact, is there any way you'd let me tell her? Please. I want to deliver good news for once."

Burton sighed, but he fanned his hand to shoo me out with a nod.

I waved to him on the way out, letting him know I'd give him anything else I thought might help him actually solve this one himself. He growled, I laughed, and the world was back on track.

"Can we postpone dinner until tomorrow?" I asked Max. We walked out to the car hand in hand.

"I kind of figured you might ask, and it's fine. It's going to be ten before we even get back to your apartment. I'm tired, I'm sure you're tired, and I'd like to go on a day when we're not wrapped up in the middle of a murder case."

I listened for signs of irritation or anger and found none. Just my guy, tired but still sticking with me.

"I could ask Gina if she has anything left over from last night. We could heat it up on the stove and snuggle in for a movie?"

"That would work for me."

Me too. We got into the car, and I held his elbow as he drove. Life was what you made of it and I was just realizing that. Thankfully, I had Max to remind me if I forgot again.

To say Michelle was overjoyed when I told her about Lily and Craig's marriage being illegal was an understatement.

She even hugged Drake in front of us.

"What do you say to a different fifty/fifty split?" she asked him. "I promise to only expense the flowers I buy for my desk, and you and I can take the remodeling world by storm. We'll even give that other woman at Craig's funeral, Amanda, a run for her money. I've known her for years, and we'll be the place to go for deals and construction, too. I have some ideas that Craig always shot down that you might be interested in."

"Of course. Why don't you let me make you dinner, and we'll talk about it." He got a twinkle in his eye, one of respect and admiration, and I fully approved.

"Why don't we make dinner together while we lay out a plan. The first part is that you have to tell my brother to back off. He gets nothing and is not involved. I don't want him to have any part in this. Just you and me."

We left because the looks were getting intimate, and as much as I was rooting for them, I didn't need to see it happen to be happy for them.

Max and I made it back to my apartment with food from Gina in hand. Jeremy was at her place. I had no idea if that was still from the night before, and I really didn't need to know.

We settled into the couch after heating up our food and I really looked at Max. This could be my every night. No matter if we were here or in DC, this could be my every night, and I found myself very much drawn to that image. Now I'd just have to talk with him about it. But we could do that later. There was no rush when it was right. And this was very much all right. Now if I could just find a killer and nail him or her to the wall so that Max and I could enjoy the rest of his vacation without chasing people around.

The Bean was hopping with coffee and gossip the next day. I didn't normally hear stories about out-of-towners here, but this morning, the fire and voided marriage were hot topics. I didn't know how they'd all found out since I'd kept my mouth shut without even having to be told by Burton. But it was interesting to see the way everyone shared and then shared again.

Laura was so busy filling and refilling coffee that she looked like she might fall over at any moment.

I found Gina in the back, counting out pastries. "Hey, is Laura okay, or is the migraine back?"

"I'm not sure, but I did ask her if she wanted to go home. She said no, she needs the money."

"Do you think it might be time to hire someone else along with her?"

"Not yet. It hasn't become unmanageable, but I was hoping to put someone on staff who could actually help me run the place, not just work here. You know, in case I ever wanted to go away."

"But you never go away." I stole a chocolate chip

cookie and got a look for the trouble I went to be discreet.

"Well, I might want to every now and then, and while I'm fine with Mom watching the shop for a few hours here and there, I might want to be gone for longer than an afternoon sometimes."

"Did Jeremy ask you to go on vacation with him?" I don't know why that popped into my head, but it did. And the way his vacation was all of the sudden ruined and he was home without any explanation made me wonder.

"I'm going to plead the fifth."

"You're going to need to drink a fifth. Do you know how much he snores?"

Her laughter filled the back room. Laura ducked her head in and gave a weary nod. She looked exhausted, but was gone before I could ask her how she was doing.

"Are you sure she's all right?" I asked.

"It's just busy. I remember looking like that when I first started. You have to get your serving legs under you and then you're fine. She said she's okay and I'll take her at her word. Maybe she has a hangover, but I do appreciate her coming in. She's pleasant to all the customers, which is more than I can say for some of the people who applied for the job." Gina chose more pastries and laid them on a big, flat baking sheet. "Anyway, Jeremy and I are considering going on a vacation now, maybe just a weekend to find out if this is even a good idea. I don't want Mama Shirley here the whole time. If you know of anyone who might be interested and is qualified, send them my way."

"Will do. But remember, he does snore, and don't blame me if you don't get much sleep."

"Oh, Tallie, if I don't get much sleep I don't think it will have anything to do with him snoring."

"Touché." We laughed and laughed until Laura came back in and asked when the pastries would be done. They were running low.

"I'll send Tallie out with some in just a few minutes. Thanks for letting me know."

It occurred to me that perhaps I could offer my services for a weekend. Maybe if Max came up, we could handle it between ourselves for two days. I'd think about it. I wasn't the best at this, and the more I helped out here, the more it became apparent to me that maybe my dream to own a tea shop next door should remain a dream and not become a reality. I liked what I did. Cleaning wasn't for the faint of heart, or for the easily annoyed. But I was good at it, and it was good to me, especially since I ran my own company and could do what I wanted when I wanted.

Something to think about later. Gina handed me a plate of divine-smelling croissants and told me to put them in the display case. I walked carefully with the full tray, yet still managed to bobble it near the door. Something was in my way. I walked around it, thankful that I hadn't actually fallen, and placed the pastries as artfully as I could on the waiting tray. It wasn't a Gina-standards kind of job, but people asked for them as soon as they went into the case, so at least this time presentation didn't matter all that much.

I reentered the back to let Gina know to put a rush on the rest of the goodies when I saw what I had tripped over. Laura's purse lay on its side like a drunken floozy, spilling out its guts. I hurried to push everything back into the purse and picked it up to put it on the table so no one else tripped over it. I shoved lipstick and eye shadow, a flyer for one of those dating sites, and a magazine on perfect nails all into the bag. Was she also looking for Mr. Right? She might not find him in this town, but good luck to her.

"Here, Tallie, don't put it on the table. I keep telling Laura we have a set of lockers, but she never uses them." Gina took the bag and shoved it into one of the small squares. "I'll let her know where it is when she's done."

"Sounds good. I'm heading out then. Max and I are going to try this dinner thing again tonight."

"Have fun and take pictures. I want to see how you doll up in that dress I found at the back of my closet."

"Will do." I headed out and straight into the waiting arms of Max.

"Hey, I was just coming to get you to see if tonight is free."

"It is, and I hope you have reservations, because I plan on eating a lot, and laughing and talking even more."

"You're on. How long do you need?"

"I have one house to do, but it's a relatively easy, one-story spiff up. I'll meet you at the apartment in two hours."

"Until then." He kissed me and then walked into the Bean.

I watched him because I could, and because I enjoyed what I saw. I thought I would enjoy it even more in a pair of suit pants.

Chapter Fifteen

I was very much not disappointed by Max in a pair of dress pants. They were cut perfectly and outlined the physique that I had come to admire more and more each time we were together. His shirt was perfectly pressed and the bow tie at his throat made me smile.

"I look okay?" he asked.

"Absolutely. How about me?" I flared out the skirt of the deep-purple, knee-length dress as I spun around. I'd paired it with heels that put me right at Max's cheekbone. I left my shoulders bare with just spaghetti straps, the only thing keeping the empire-waisted bodice up.

We were pretty stunning if I did say so myself. And apparently, we were back on our way across the river to eat on top of an office building at a new restaurant that called itself Seven Crossings. The name was obvious when we got there because you could see all seven bridges that spanned the Susquehanna from the floor-to-ceiling windows.

It was beautiful, the atmosphere subdued and yet

glamorous. I was so thankful I had gone with this dress and that it fit.

We were welcomed in by a maître d' who bowed to us and then showed us to a table right up against the windows. Max held my chair and laid his hands on my shoulders, kissing the side of my neck where I'd clipped my hair up. I let the shiver run through me and enjoyed every second of it.

Water appeared on the table, along with a bottle of wine. We talked and chose items from the menu, waiting for someone to come take our orders. We didn't have long to wait.

I could have sworn I knew the woman who dropped off our food about thirty minutes later, but I didn't get a good look at her until after she had gone. When I asked our server her name, all I got was a shrug. It didn't really matter, but I was a sucker for not being able to place people, especially if they were in an establishment where I didn't expect to see them.

"So, dinner is fabulous, and so are you." I forked a bite of lobster into my mouth and savored it. I had appreciated and still appreciated the simpler life I was now living without Waldo. Many things had been great back then, with parties and no budget and careless times doing whatever I wanted, but I loved being responsible for myself and making my own money. I didn't miss the politics and the social niceties. I did, however, realize how much I missed really good food. I was either going to have to get Gina to cook for me more, or expand the line on my budget sheet for food expenditures and learn to cook the good stuff for myself.

"Thanks. I'm glad you liked it. I wanted to try to pick somewhere you'd probably never been before."

"Perfect choice."

"Good." We clinked glasses, and he winked at me.

"You know, if you ever wanted to be up here a little more often, I certainly wouldn't mind having you closer, or here more than a few days every couple of weeks."

"Is that right?" He sipped his drink.

I had maybe expected a little bit more than that, but he winked at me again, so I figured he was just messing with me.

I saw the girl deliver food to the table next to ours and she really looked familiar, but I couldn't place her.

"Hey, do you recognize her?" I asked Max, but by the time he'd turned around, she was gone again.

"Man, that is going to bother me all night. I hate not being able to place people."

"It'll pop into your head in the middle of the night. You'll probably wake me up to tell me."

He wasn't wrong, so I laughed. "Yes, I'm sure I will."

Sure enough, that night at about three o'clock I sat up in bed and nudged him. "Laura . . . That looked just like Laura, but she told Gina the Bean was her only job because she was going to school. I thought I recognized her, but something threw me off, and it was the hair."

I bolted out of bed while Max sat up, rubbing the top of his head. Probably still half asleep, but I was all the way awake and all pistons were firing now. I tried hard to remember the site that was on the flyer in Laura's purse. She'd had the opportunity to poison someone at both places. She would have been able to

slip something into Craig's cup when she'd given
him the complimentary cup from someone else. She
was only across the street when the memorial was
happening and often wore a black skirt and a solid-
colored shirt like the funeral parlor dress attire re-
quired by my father. I only lacked a motive. She was
far younger than Craig, but maybe she liked them
older.

I wracked my brain for the name of the dating site,
and finally it came to me. SeekingFrogs.com.

I wasn't entirely surprised when I typed in Craig's
name. He was on there, and Laura had liked his page
and also sent him a small pair of lips and a heart in
the comments. Had she been one of the women he'd
thrown away?

She'd come to work for Gina shortly after Gina
and Craig had started dating, so the timeline
wouldn't have been far off, and it all fit together
perfectly. Was she just out for revenge? Didn't like
getting dumped—so she killed him?

But then why would she have hurt Brenna? That
part didn't make a ton of sense, but that was the least
of my worries. Had Laura burned down the house,
too? I needed to warn Gina that she might have hired
a psycho. Glancing across the street, I saw that her
light was on. I took a chance that she'd have her
phone on her.

She did not sound happy when I called her. "Tallie,
I have things to do, and not a lot of time to do them in."

"What do you know about Laura?"

She paused. "Enough to have hired her. Her background check came out fine, and her references were
glowing. Why?"

"Did you know she's also working in a restaurant across the river?"

"No, but she's a free agent. I don't pay her much. I'm sure she needs more money than I can give her for part-time."

"Oh." Doubt crept in. Maybe I just wanted this solved so badly that I was jumping at any shadow, anything out of the norm, and thinking that it had to be someone, so why not her?

"What are you on about? You think Laura killed Craig?"

"No. Well . . . maybe?" It had all made sense at first, when I was still in partial dreamland, but now that I was awake it seemed ridiculous. "Probably not."

"Yeah, I don't think so. She has a boyfriend in State College that she goes to see at least once a month, and I can't imagine her being interested in Craig. Plus, why would she have killed him? She didn't strike me as crazy, and there were plenty of other women he dumped, not to mention you have two solid suspects who both thought they were married to him. My money is still on Lily."

"I found Laura on the dating Web site and she'd had her eye on him. I just thought it all fit together perfectly. Does she drive to work or walk?" The room she rented on Marble Street was only four blocks away and parking could be brutal downtown.

"She must have a car to go to State College, but I've never seen it so I can't tell you if it has your over-sized tires."

"I could go look."

"I really think you're grasping at the wrong person, Tallie. She had nothing at stake."

"Okay. Sorry to disturb you."

"No problem. I was up anyway, and ready to head downstairs." I heard snoring in the background and giggled to myself quietly.

"I hope you got at least some sleep last night."

"Plenty," she said with an edge to her tone. "Now go back to cuddling with Max and look at it fresh tomorrow. See if Burton will tell you where Lily is and talk to her. I bet you she slips up and says something that will absolutely nail her for the murder."

"Okay. Sorry. Have a good day."

"Well, my morning started out peachy, so I can only go up from here, right?"

I had to wait a few hours to call Burton so that I didn't get in trouble for waking him up before his beauty sleep was complete. Max and I talked the whole thing through and used my newly constructed spreadsheet to go over each of the women who could have committed the crimes, and we kept coming back to Lily.

"I think Gina is right," Max said. "She just *happened* to be there the day of the memorial; she had access to the kitchen at the funeral home if she was in the crowd seated in the room and slipped out. She would have heard the woman crying about the baby and seen you take her out. She was quick to try to take over the house, and I think she didn't want anything standing in her way of inheriting everything Craig had owned for leaving her all those years ago. Maybe when she realized that Burton was looking into her marriage and she knew it was fake, she burned down the house because if she couldn't have it, then no one could."

It made sense. It really did, but something in my gut was telling me that it was all too pat. Yet, I also didn't have anything else. I still wanted to clear Gina's name completely. She might have been snippy with me this morning because I was barking up her employee's tree, or she could have been snippy because she wanted this over. Either way Burton had not officially told me that he thought it was anyone else, and he wasn't actively pursuing anyone else, so the pressure was still on.

Right at eight, I called and spoke with Suzy at the front desk. Burton wasn't in yet, and I wasn't willing to use his cell phone number before he ingested his first cup of morning Joe from the station.

"You don't happen to know where Lily is staying, do you? I wanted to give her something Gina found at the Bean. She must have dropped it at the memorial and it had her name on it."

"She's at the B and B on Main Street. Just ask at the front desk. Or you could even leave it at the front desk. Mallorie would be happy to deliver it for you. She's a wonderful lady."

"And so are you, Suzy, thanks!" I hung up before anything more could be said. I wouldn't tell Burton where I got the information if I was asked with a hot poker at my eye.

A trip to the bed and breakfast down the way was next on my list, then. Warman House had been standing for years and had originally been a residence. The house next door to it was an exact replica but built in the opposite direction. They were called Mirror Houses. The front doors faced each other on the corner and then everything flowed out behind with the same plans, just opposite. I had no idea why they'd done that, but the history of the town said that it had been two brothers who had built the houses for their wives.

I pulled into the driveway around back with nothing to hand over to Mallorie since there never had been anything with Lily's name on it. But I could still fake my way into getting her information and getting to see her.

"Mallorie, hi! How are you?"

"Oh, Tallie, it's good to see you. We missed you around here when you were gone."

I had really only been up the hill, but I had never interacted with anyone down here in town except those I needed something from. And I hadn't needed Mallorie and her bed and breakfast for anything. I was ashamed of the snob I'd been and still trying to make it up. Maybe I'd buy a package for my parents to stay here for their upcoming fortieth anniversary.

"I missed you, too. Hey, I was wondering if Lily was here. I wanted to see if she might want to go have some breakfast at Meiner's."

"Oh, she stepped out just a minute ago. I hope she stays in the area when the estate is settled. What a nice lady, and so gracious. Did you know she used to be in the movies? She got tired of all the politicking and so left the screen before she made it big, but she had a commercial for shampoo that she did before she called it quits."

An actress—that was interesting. Apparently not a good one if she only had one shampoo commercial, but maybe she'd never been cast in the right role, like grieving widow. She hadn't played that role well, either, so I could understand that she probably never got those parts because she wasn't good at what she did.

"Did she say where she was going?"

"For a walk. I pointed her in the direction of the park across the railroad tracks. Beautiful day for it. I might try to get out there once I get my cleaning done. Sometimes I wish I could hire you to do the dirty stuff." She laughed.

I handed her a business card, anyway. "Anything you need, big or small, and I'd be happy to help. Just give me a shout. I'll give you a discount."

"Oh, well, thank you. My goodness. I'll certainly call." She tucked the card into her pocket. "Now, she just left a few minutes ago. You shouldn't have a hard time catching up with her."

"Thanks, Mallorie. Talk to you later."

"Sure thing."

I briefly wished I had told Max where I was going, but I had left him in the shower. I could handle this on my own. I thought it would be better woman to woman, anyway, rather than having Max standing behind me looking over my shoulder.

I walked to the park, coming up with how I was going to approach her. I had no intention of taking her down myself. I just needed her to tell me something, anything, that could be used against her. I would gladly hand the capture over to Burton after that. I just wanted my friend off the hook, not the dubious glory of catching another killer.

I walked the trail that wound around the park and didn't see anyone. It was too early for children to be out playing on the playground equipment, and as much as some tennis players were early risers, I didn't see anyone this morning.

The high school football field sat at the back of the park because there hadn't been enough room to build it at the school itself. It was only half a mile from the school, so convenient but different from most places where the football field was part of the school property. The trail followed along the perimeter of the football field, and I remembered doing some very interesting things under those bleachers. Feeling myself blush, I got back to my task.

I almost fell over my own feet when I saw a car with big tires parked in the parking lot. Big, honking tires that didn't seem to fit the car they were attached to. I dug through my memory for the car that had been parked in front of Michelle's house when Lily had tried to take the house over, but this wasn't the same car. Had Lily driven here instead of walking? Was this her car? If not, then was she meeting whoever did own it? Was I close to finally finding out what had happened?

Before I could get close enough to the car to jot down the license plate number, I heard yelling to my left and hustled through the trees toward the train tracks.

"I want you gone! I don't know what you hope to accomplish, but I've already done everything I'm going to do."

I kept back in the trees, watching as Lily flung her arms around and yelled at whomever was standing just out of sight. I tried to look around the tree, but was afraid it would expose me too much. I didn't want to give my position away if I could watch them duke it out and get confirmation of Lily's guilt without ever having to speak with her.

The other person laughed. I knew I'd heard it

before, but I couldn't quite place it. "You messed it all up. It was supposed to be simple and then you had to complicate it all."

There were two of them? A team of killers? But who had actually killed Craig? And that voice. *Holy crap.* It was definitely Laura. Gina and I had both been right. That did not make me happy.

"I did not want some child to be able to claim anything," Lily said. "It's bad enough that I have to split everything with you—and that there might not be as much as I had originally thought. Who knew he was spending all that money on flowers and gifts for women?"

"I did when I went out with him that one time."

"I still can't believe you let him wine and dine you. Didn't that feel disgusting, going on a date with your own father?"

Father? Oh my God. Laura was his child? And Lily thought she was his wife. How had these two gotten together in the first place?

"It was the only time I'd ever gotten to talk with him, and I used temporary dye on my hair so he wouldn't realize who I was after I started working for Gina. That woman is a piece of work."

I would keep that part to myself because Gina would not be happy about the comment. She was already going to be pissed that she'd hired a killer and had told me I was full of crap for thinking that.

"She was the last in a long line of floozies."

Yeah, I'd keep that one to myself, too.

"And yet he never got anyone else pregnant."

"Not that we know of," Lily said with an edge in her voice. "Are you sure you don't have any other brothers and sisters? Maybe you'll have to split your half with them."

Laura growled. "There aren't any more of us. I checked the records and from what I understand he's never slept with anyone except Michelle, my mother, and you. I've worked in bars where the women he took out would come when he dropped them for the next, and that was a common complaint. He never came in with them, just dropped and ran."

"They should count themselves lucky; he wasn't that good in bed anyway. And now he couldn't even be decent enough to leave us anything to split."

"And now we don't even have the possibility of insurance because you never told me you weren't actually married to the guy," Laura said.

"What were you thinking? I was still trying to work out how to make my marriage look valid and you messed that up, too."

"I was thinking I wanted things moved along and I didn't want you to decide to move in and not sell the house. That way there would be no question that you'd double-cross me about the property."

I technically didn't have enough to have Burton come in on them like a sledgehammer since it was all hearsay at this point, but I had enough that the police might be able to get them to turn on each other. If he could get them into interrogation rooms and tell them that the other had turned on them, then maybe that could work. But first I had to get back to Burton. I crept backward two steps when I heard Max shouting my name and the train whistle follow shortly after. "Tallie!" There he went again, and I had nowhere to go. I had been creeping backward but now I turned tail and ran. Unfortunately, I was no longer in my early twenties and, though cleaning was hard work, it didn't exactly make me a fast runner.

Laura had me by the hair and Lily clamped her hand over my mouth when I opened it to scream for Max.

"Oh, I don't think you're going to want to do that," Lily said into my ear. "We took out Craig, we can certainly take you out, too."

Holy crap, so they had actually killed him. Both of them. My mind snapped back to that cup of coffee that Laura had delivered to Craig on that first day. Had Lily been the one to send him the coffee already doctored and Laura was the one who had delivered it? How had Craig not recognized Lily? Although it had been years and he had been so enamored with being admired that he might just have seen another pretty face.

I wanted to ask those questions, but Lily moved her hand so it was over my mouth *and* my nose while Laura clamped my arms behind me. They walked me out to the tracks, the whistle shrilling from just down the way. Was I about to be killed by a train? Oh my God. My mother would have a heart attack and my dad would have to figure out how to put me back together before putting me in a coffin.

I bucked and kicked, but they both stayed out of my reach. Where on earth was Max? Not that I could blame him. If he'd been calling from the park, then he wouldn't be able to see me for the trees. I should have let him come along. He'd probably gone to Mallorie at the inn and found out I was looking for Lily. I had been stupid and that stupid was going to cost me my life.

I still kicked and tried to make as much noise as I could with shifting my feet through the gravel at the side of the tracks. Anything could alert him and I just needed him here.

"Stop moving around. This isn't the freaking dance floor." Laura shoved me closer to the tracks and I saw how my death would happen. I did not want to die.

Spots began dancing in front of my eyes from holding my breath.

"Let go of her nose, Lily, or she's going to die by your hand, and she'll have your prints all over her."

Lily let go of just my nose, but moved her hand down to more fully cover my mouth. I only had long enough to squeak before she applied massive amounts of pressure with her strong hand. My teeth ground together and my cheeks clenched around them.

"The train is coming," Laura continued. "We'll just throw her in front of it at the last moment and then run."

Except that the engineer would see them.

This apparently also occurred to Lily. "We can't take the chance that the guy driving the train will see two women throw her onto the tracks. We should tie her down."

Like those old cartoons my mother used to have me watch with the damsel in distress? I didn't like them then, and I certainly didn't want to replay them now.

I jerked left and right while they talked and finally managed to break Laura's hold as I slammed a knee into her leg. After that, I punched Lily in the throat and made a run for it.

I ran like my life depended on it because it did. If I could just make it to the football field I might be able to escape them permanently and keep them in the spotlight at the same time.

I had run this place in high school, working the

lights and the microphones and the scoreboard, all at different times. I just needed to get to the booth and then lock it behind me, hoping they didn't hurt Max if they found him before he found them.

I scrambled under the bleachers. Please let me still fit between the foot tread and the seats. It wasn't an easy squeeze but few things in life were. Someone grabbed my ankle as I broke free on the other side and I kicked out, not caring who it was.

And then I was up and running. I pounded up the bleachers like I was Rocky on the steps of the Philadelphia Museum of Art. But my footsteps weren't the only ones, and I had very little time to get into the booth.

I was lucky that the door was unlocked, but since it was Tuesday I figured it would be. The grounds-keeper was manicuring the turf with his headphones on, but he'd turned the floodlights on to make sure they worked and that there were no lightbulbs that had to be replaced before the big summer festival they held on the last weekend of July every year.

I shot into the booth like I'd come from a cannon and locked the door behind me.

Running to the other side, I locked that door, too, just as Lily showed up at the window. I was safe as long as neither of them knew how to pick a lock.

Laura began working on the door handle, and I flipped on the mic along with the radio station that played the games. "Burton, if you can hear me, get down here. I need help and you're going to want to bring some handcuffs."

That froze both of them in their tracks, but it was too late. The groundskeeper had taken off his headphones and moved to the bottom of the steps.

My brother Dylan had hands of steel and the physique to match them. Unless either of the women wanted to take the chance of jumping off the bleachers and hoping they didn't break anything, they were stuck. Especially when Max also arrived at the bottom of the stairs.

Sirens wailed and Lily and Laura both turned to me to scream obscenities. They were more than welcome to do that. I was in a comfy chair, on the airwaves, and there was nothing they could do about it.

"Tallie Graver, what on earth am I going to do with you?" Burton had me and Max in his office. "And why can't you control your woman?"

"Tallie is not mine to control, sir. I'm just along for the ride if she ever decides to let me in on what she's doing."

Ouch. We were going to have to have a talk about that later. He'd told me that he'd followed my trail to the B and B and then came looking for me at the park. I should have called him. I should have asked him to come along. I should have trusted him.

I had thought I had it handled. Ultimately, I did save myself, but saying that out loud was not going to make either male in the room happy.

"I'll be more careful next time," I said instead.

"Hopefully there won't be a next time. And if there is, then you're out," Burton responded.

"But both of the women are in jail cells right now. Isn't that worth something?"

"It is, and the public thanks you, but it wouldn't have been worth your life. That's the part you don't seem to understand. They could have killed you."

"But they didn't."

"And I'm grateful for that, at least at the moment, until I have you underfoot again. Let's just all hope that nothing happens around this town again that makes you go all vigilante. I do appreciate everything you brought me, but I also had to let your mother yell at me for putting you in danger, and that was not pleasant."

Ohh. My mother could be sweet and docile, but once you got her rolling it was hard to turn her off.

"Yeah, sorry about that."

"I'd be happier if you'd be sorry about doing this all yourself instead of bringing it to my attention like I asked you to."

"I was going to, but then Max started yelling, and they caught me and it all went out of control."

"Which seems to be the norm with you."

"Well then, you're welcome for my out-of-control."

He sighed. "I don't want to see you again for quite some time. In fact, if you want to speed, I'm not going to even pull you over. Got it?"

"Fine." Fat lot of thanks this was getting me. I solved the whole thing and he was treating me like a pariah. "We're gone. And you're welcome."

I sashayed out of the office with Max at my side. We waved to Suzy, then exited the police station. I really hoped I would not have to see this place except in passing for a very long time.

"You know, he does have a point."

Max held onto my hand when I tried to pull away.

"Keep an open mind," he continued. "I was never so scared as when I saw you up in that booth."

"I wasn't exactly having a grand old time myself."

"I get it. But maybe from now on you could be a little more careful."

I stepped into his arms on the side of the street in front of anyone who happened to pass by. "I'll be careful, and I honestly don't expect to ever be involved in anything like this again." I pulled him in closer so we touched from chest to knee. "And maybe you could keep me out of trouble better if you lived in the area instead of three hours away."

"Let's get some lunch and talk about it. I still have a couple days left of vacation and I have some ideas."

I was totally onboard with that. And maybe if I told my mom we were moving forward with our relationship, she wouldn't yell at me so much about putting myself in danger. My dad was not going to be nice about me solving the case, but I didn't expect him to be. And it would blow over once someone else decided to do something stupid, like streak down the street, or a new scandal happened. It was like clockwork, and I was hanging up my magnifying glass.

At least for now.

We headed back to my apartment and managed to get upstairs without running into my mom or my dad. I texted Gina when I got upstairs and settled in. She called right away.

"What were you thinking?" she yelled into the phone. "And your brother is not happy either."

"What is up with everyone being ungrateful? I did what you wanted me to do. I cleared your name and got you off the hook, and now you want to yell at me?"

"No," she laughed. "I want to treat you to dinner and thank you by paying for whatever you want. Thank you, Tallie."

That was more like it. I smirked at Max, who could hear Gina from my phone, and he kissed me. Looked like I was going to have a fabulous night after the harrowing experience of the train tracks and a double whammy of killers.

A good day's work in my book.

Keep an eye out for
Tallie's next adventure,

DECEASED AND DESIST.

Coming soon from
Misty Simon
and
Kensington Books!

Connect with